RUNNING FROM DESPAIR TO DESPAIR

Fayed sped off after every stop. He knew the longer they stayed, the bigger the gamble that an American jet might drop a missile targeting Daesh but also killing anyone in its wake. Although the American missiles were sometimes considered more precise in comparison to the Russian and Syrian militaries' indiscriminate bombs, they were still known to kill many innocent families too. Truth is, bombs may hit their specific targets, but for an innocent life standing nearby, its so-called precision is meaningless.

Tareq, Fayed and Susan finally made it to Raqqa before the sun had set. Tareq's father encouraged his son and daughter to try to take a nap even though they were not far from his brother's home. He didn't want his children to accidentally see anything he would find difficult to explain. He had heard too many stories and seen too many clips on YouTube of Daesh's rule in Raqqa and beyond.

And as they pulled into one of the main roundabouts, his fears were substantiated. Tareq was grateful his sister was still under her blanket playing with her doll, pretending it was a tent, unaware of the sight that made their father gasp and had Tareq choking on the bile in his throat.

The sticks were buried firmly in the ground, as the human heads were planted on top of the spikes.

OTHER BOOKS YOU MAY ENJOY

A LAND
OF
PERMANENT
GOODBYES

A

LAND

OF

PERMANENT

GOOOBYES

ATIA
ABAWI

PENGUIN BOOKS

PENGUIN BOOKS
An imprint of Penguin Random House LLC
375 Hudson Street
New York, NY 10014

First published in the United States of America by Philomel Books,
an imprint of Penguin Random House LLC, 2018
Published by Penguin Books, an imprint of Penguin Random House LLC, 2019

THE LIBRARY OF CONGRESS HAS CATALOGED THE PHILOMEL BOOKS EDITION AS FOLLOWS:
Names: Abawi, Atia, author.
Title: A land of permanent goodbyes / Atia Abawi.
Description: New York, NY : Philomel Books, [2018]
Summary: After their home in Syria is bombed, Tareq, his father, and his
younger sister seek refuge, first with extended family in Raqqa, a stronghold for
the militant group Daesh, and then abroad.
Identifiers: LCCN 2017021847 | ISBN 9780399546839 (hardback) |
ISBN 9780399546846 (e-book)
Subjects: | CYAC: Refugees–Fiction. | Bombings–Fiction. | Muslims–Fiction. |
IS (Organization)–Fiction. | Family life–Syria–Fiction. | Syria–Fiction.
Classification: LCC PZ7.A136 Lan 2018 | DDC [Fic]–dc23
LC record available at https://lccn.loc.gov/2017021847

Penguin Books ISBN 9780399546853

Printed in the United States of America.

Edited by Jill Santopolo.
Design by Ellice M. Lee.
Text set in Marathon LT Book.

5 7 9 10 8 6 4

For Arian

may you always choose
empathy over fear,
love over hate,
and knowledge over apathy

When I was a boy and I would see scary things in the news, my mother would say to me, "Look for the helpers. You will always find people who are helping." To this day, especially in times of "disaster," I remember my mother's words and I am always comforted by realizing that there are still so many helpers—so many caring people in this world.

—*Fred Rogers*

You were born to die. In that I have no say.

But *when* that happens is not up to me. It's up to humanity and—all too often—the lack of it.

The human heart is the most complicated creation I've ever encountered. The formation of the cosmos was easier to understand.

Yours is a group that is easy to read, yet difficult to comprehend.

You chiseled a wheel and transformed it from stone to wood to rubber. You have turned mountains into threads that control machines, computers and phones. You've even learned to fly without having your own wings.

All of this happened within a blink of the universe's eye.

Your greatest achievements came from your brain. Your heart is a whole different system. An intensely more complicated one. It's a place that can hold an incredible amount of love or an incredible amount of hate—sometimes both at the same time. And although there has been ample growth in the capability of your minds, not a lot has changed in the nature of your species.

A mother's affection thousands of years ago holds the same warmth it does today, covering her child with a blanket sewn of her soul even long after she is gone. A gentle kiss still sends shivers through the bodies of young lovers, and the memory of that embrace lives on as their bones wither and hair fades to gray. Decades later, you still feel the cold emptiness of losing someone you held dear.

But it is the growing divide between the mind and heart that I find so dangerous for your kind. Your new innovations don't help you to feel love as often as they contribute to spreading hate.

Your chest is a vault for your jealousy, prejudices and regrets—emotions that you once released through sharp tongues and bare hands. Until your tongues and hands were replaced with swords and poisons—and now bullets and bombs. The streams of blood turned to rivers and then to oceans.

I am the one often blamed for your actions.

Philosophers describe me as "the predetermined course of events." I am sometimes confused with Fate or Predestination.

I consider myself simply the end of a sequence of events that you and your kind actively shape.

I don't like to be held liable for the evils in the world. But often I am, through no error of my own. My work is to finalize the deeds of those who have paved their way toward me. I meet you at the end of the paths you walk on. Sometimes when I truly don't expect to.

I am not the reason why hearts can be so dark. I can't even take credit for the ones who do good. I am just the end result of your choices.

We will always meet, time and again. Sometimes you realize

I am there. Other times you ignore me. It's okay; I'm used to it. But even when you stop believing in me or you start despising me, I will never abandon you. I see most of you as old friends. I enjoy when we encounter each other on happy occasions. I weep when the moments are harsh.

One thing I ask—please stop condemning me or giving me credit for how, when and where we meet. That is not up to me; it has never been up to me. I just show up when it is time—and that moment will always arrive.

So yes, you *were* born to die. But in between, you are meant to live. If we run into each other prematurely, it's not because of my negligence. And often not because of yours.

Your world controls me; I do not control you.

I am Destiny.

PART I

CHAPTER 1

I like Tareq. I always have. The night the fair-haired boy came into the world, I swear I saw the moon smile.

From his very first gulp of air, he was a good boy. The kind every parent dreams of having. He didn't shriek like most newborns; he just let out soft whimpers as if not to disturb, but to let everyone know he was okay.

He was born during the crisp days when fall bled into winter, a generous gift to his mother, saving her from nursing a newborn in the sticky summer months. There was a celebration filled with music, food and family for the birth of not just a child but a son. His parents ordered an expensive cake with a little blue bear frosted onto it from the best bakery in the city, the one the wealthier folks went to. A modest selection for the store's usual clientele, but a luxury item for a young couple who were busy spending their finances on necessities rather than grandeur.

Tareq loved his parents and never dreamed of disobeying them. As he grew, he believed his parents were second only to God, fulfilling every request his mother made of him—from picking up tomatoes and eggs at the store to changing the diapers of his little brothers and sisters.

And his parents, Nour and Fayed, knew how lucky they were, often telling friends over cups of tea steeped in sugar, "The first child tricks you into having more!" *It's true*

This is a statement I have heard many parents say through the generations and continents, but in their case it was true. Because as Nour and Fayed's family grew, so did the lively and rambunctious energy in their crowded household, which included Tareq's paternal grandmother.

Tareq was excited each time his mother gave birth to a new sibling. Salim came two years after him, a wild and uncontrollable spirit. His light hair and sharp nose matched Tareq's, but the similarities stopped there. Farrah arrived several years later. Sweet and charming, she had her father wrapped around her finger from the moment he held her and stared into her dark doe eyes. Then came Susan, a pink-faced, curly-haired version of Salim, but with blue eyes and a sweeter edge. And then the twins, Ameer and Sameer—a mix of Tareq's and Salim's temperaments (with Farrah's coloring).

The family's small apartment never seemed to have much, but it was bursting at the seams with love. The affection of a gentle couple, tenderness of kind parents, zest of spirited children and the unselfishness and devotion of a family who felt deeply for one another.

I truly cared for these people. They did everything right.

They were making all the decisions that would lead them to the happy ending you all dream of.

But unfortunately, it was the decisions made by those in their country—and those outside Syria—that brought them to this night . . . where I had to meet them again, on a hot summer evening in 2015, not in happiness but in sorrow. This is their story.

★ The suspense built up from this moment of Syria changing their lives ★

CHAPTER 2

"Mama!" Tareq screamed, ignoring the burning in his throat. Even if his mother had shouted back, he wouldn't have been able to hear her. The ringing in his ears yo-yoed up and down. All other sounds were muffled and lost.

His blacked-out vision slowly transitioned to a blurry haze of grayish mist. He watched as black snowflakes floated down from the sky.

Too scared to move, all he could do was scream again, hoping someone—anyone—would hear him. His vibrating body was camouflaged in the rubble; the dust from the bombed-out apartment building had formed a thick layer on his skin, except for the paths down his cheeks washed clean by his tears. His shouting turned to silent sobs as he tried, with trembling hands, to lift the slab of concrete from his stomach. He grabbed hold of the kitchen wall that had pinned him to the floor, but he couldn't muster the strength to push it off.

Terror ripped through his body, burning his insides. Any ripples of strength he had left were used for his wails. But even those had weakened. Tareq had never cried like this before. He'd only seen these types of tears in the movies or on television newscasts—and in his worst nightmares.

"Mama. Baba . . ." His frail voice trembled before fading out completely.

Waking up in his bed, Tareq wondered now if it was all just another nightmare. He ripped off the thick blanket soaked in sweat and stumbled to the dresser, pulling out a mirror to examine his reflection. He couldn't see any scratches or bruises and didn't feel any soreness except for a little twisting pain in his stomach. Surely, he believed, it was from the trauma in his sleep. He studied the beads of sweat on his forehead and the dark patches underneath his blue eyes. He finally took in a steady breath, relieved that it was just another bad dream. He'd been having a lot of them lately.

Still feeling a twinge in the pit of his stomach, he slid a shirt over his head, then slowly opened the bedroom door, pressing down the cool handle. He could hear the television blaring from the living room. He walked toward the sound and saw Farrah and Susan on the couch, staring at the screen, the latter holding on to her doll as she sucked her thumb. *Tom and Jerry* had them in a television trance.

The five-month-old twins were lying on a white cotton blanket with pacifiers in their mouths, orange for Sameer and green for Ameer, their dark curls in sharp contrast with the throw. The boys kicked their chunky legs in the air as they tried to grab each other, letting out muffled squeals. Both had only their bottom teeth, which appeared in the last week, making their smiles even sweeter than before. *My little can openers are okay,* Tareq thought.

He decided to follow the delicious aroma of garlic and onions coming from the kitchen. When he saw the back of her head, hair in a bun and a mole on the side of the neck, he ran to his mother.

"Mama!" he grabbed her from behind and pulled her body in for a tight embrace.

"*Rohi!* Be careful!" She laughed, holding a stainless-steel paring knife in one hand and a zucchini in the other.

But Tareq didn't let go. He just kissed her shoulders before pressing his face against her bony spine once more, breathing in her scent of perfumed flowers and spiced cooking.

"Nothing for me?" his grandmother asked. Tareq turned and saw his *teyta* drinking her usual black tea. He ran over to his graying grandmother, bent down and laid his head in her lap. He felt her withered hand stroking his hair.

"What has got into you, *ayuni*? I love the attention, but I want to make sure you're feeling well." His mother was still smiling as she continued to scrape out the inside of the zucchini. "You don't have a fever, do you?"

"No, Mama, I'm just . . . just so happy to see you!" he muttered as the rubble from his dream flashed in his mind. He could again taste the fear of being separated from her. He walked over and pecked her cheek, thankful she was here and that he could still breathe her in. Nour kissed him back, seemingly grateful for the exuberant onslaught of affection from her teenage son.

"Youth." His grandmother picked up her steaming glass from the rim and slurped her tea. "We should all be lazy and take long afternoon naps so we can also be crazy." Tareq's *teyta* knew her curmudgeonly attitude was one that the family found endearing, so she kept playing the part. Everyone recognized that her dry sense of humor disguised her true adoration of the family she helped create and build. They all heard her prayers thanking God five times a day for the blessings bestowed on her.

"Is Baba home yet?" Tareq asked his mother.

His father worked with his uncle at the family shop a few blocks away. The mini market did well enough to feed their large family. But since the war began, business had been very slow. Many people were leaving, and the rest didn't have the money to purchase the few items in stock. And Tareq's father, Fayed, didn't have the heart to let his customers leave with empty hands and stomachs. So, much of the time he gave food away for next to nothing, and sometimes for exactly that—nothing.

But the biggest worry hadn't been business. It was the bombs that indiscriminately fell from the sky. Every morning, after Fayed closed the front door behind him, the family counted the minutes until his return. Tareq used to help out at the store, but with the continued air strikes in their city, his father had asked him to stay home and take care of the family. *God forbid, but if something should go wrong, I want you to be the man of the house.*

"No, Baba is not home yet, but do you mind finding Salim before he gets too far?" Nour asked her eldest.

"Yes, of course!" He welcomed the request. Any other day he would accept but be weary at the thought of reining in his younger brother. But on this day, he was just pleased he had his family nearby and alive—unlike so many people from his city. The task reminded him of how grateful he was.

"And make sure your sisters have an eye on the babies, not just on that silly cat and mouse!" he heard his mother call as he sprinted out of the kitchen. With a quick glance, he noticed Susan was now on the blanket with the babies, using her doll to kiss Sameer's cheek as he squawked with delight. Satisfied, Tareq continued out the door.

"Salim!" he yelled at a group of boys playing on the dusty side street. His brother's hair seemed lighter than usual due to the dirt and grit that had layered onto it.

"We're not done!" Salim hollered back.

As Tareq took in the view of his neighborhood, his breath caught in his throat. He still wasn't used to the mountain of broken concrete and twisted iron sticking out of the walls that used to make up the apartment block across the road. The building's skeletal remains gave a glimpse into the apartments of neighbors who no longer lived there and some who no longer lived at all. That air strike killed twenty-six people, including two of his classmates—a brother and sister who used to bicker all the time but would quickly fight anyone who bothered the other. Tareq shook his head in an attempt to scatter those memories, hoping they would fall out of his ears like crumbs—but it never worked.

"*Yallah*, Salim! Come on! Mama said it's time to wash up!"

"*Uuf!*" Salim got ahold of the soccer ball and kicked it toward the busy road that divided their building from the destroyed structure. If he couldn't play anymore, he wanted to make sure the fun was over for everyone. *I can relate*

"Salim!" the boys roared in frustration. They now had to decide who would go after the ball in the middle of traffic. They would never admit it out loud, but the boys were more afraid of the ghostly ruins on the other side of the road than the cars that whizzed by, superstitiously believing that by going into the rubble they would jinx their own families.

A group of girls parked comfortably on the steps of the building giggled as they watched what was unfolding. Tareq never grasped why these girls all seemed to embolden his way-ward brother. But the encouragement went both ways. Salim glanced at them with a crooked smile and winked, which made them titter even more.

As he ran by, Salim made sure to slap his older brother on the butt. "*Yallah!*" he now ordered Tareq to follow, as he bolted toward the door. "*Yaaallaaaaaaah!*"

Salim rushed to the bathroom to wash the grime off his body, still giddy about how he'd left his friends. Farrah ran after, beg-ging him to let her play with his old toy cars that were collecting dust on the wooden shelf. She was the little tomboy of the family. When Farrah was a baby, she saw her two older brothers as her heroes, wanting to be exactly like them. Especially Salim. Whenever someone asked her who her favorite brother was, she would get shy and say she didn't have one, not wanting to hurt anyone's feelings, but everyone knew by the sparkles in her eyes when she looked at Salim what the real answer was.

The extra attention didn't bother Salim the way it would many older brothers. He loved both of his little sisters and saw himself as their protector. He didn't like the way some of his friends would shoo their sisters away and treat them with disdain. Those boys would often commiserate about how annoying their sisters were. Salim felt that said a lot more about the brothers than it did their sisters.

One blazing hot afternoon when he was out with the boys from their apartment building, Salim's friend Azad decided to bulldoze through a group of little girls playing with their jump ropes, including Farrah. Azad thought it was hilarious to hear the girls screech. But Salim did not laugh. Instead, he saw the tear that was welling up in his sister's left eye. As his own lips quivered, he could feel the heat from the scorching sun permeate his body, setting it ablaze. Salim bolted toward his friend like a bull toward a matador's cape, still aware enough to leap over a little girl in the way, feeling the wind on his face before landing on Azad. With his fists balled up, Salim started pounding on the squishy flesh beneath him. No amount of "Stop!" or "Get off!" was going to stop him. It was only when Azad started to cry that Salim thought the debt was paid. The punishment Salim received from his parents later meant little to him compared to the hug and kiss he got from Farrah.

Salim's affection for his sisters was something that he was always conscious of, but he didn't know how much that love would change his family's world time and again.

A The family is so close and kind. They have good morales.

Tareq set the table as his grandmother flicked her prayer beads with the news blaring in the background. Susan was fast asleep on their grandmother's lap, hugging her doll.

"The barrel bombs struck a residential area, killing dozens of people, including many children," the television report echoed.

Tareq's nightmare came flashing back. He licked his lip and could taste the grimy dust again. The sirens from the newscast shook his brain as he smelled the smoke.

"Can anyone hear me?" he heard one of the rescue workers holler from the television set.

Tareq's hands singed, causing him to drop the spoons and forks. As he went to pick them up, his vision blurred and he fell to his knees. Charred fumes burned his nostrils. He glanced up and saw the darkness ooze from the kitchen.

Like he's in the moment

"Are you alive?"

The room spun as he strained to move, but he couldn't seem to pick himself up. The smoldering air enveloped his lungs and his eyes stung and burned.

"Yallah! *Over here, I think he's alive!"* A beam of light blinded Tareq as a storm of dust hovered, permeating the air. The glow spilled from the helmet of a man staring at him.

"You're going to be okay." The man's voice had an air of authority.

"Where's my mama?" Tareq gasped, confused and feeling alone again.

"Calm down and breathe," the man in the white helmet said to the terrified teenager. He had been pulling bodies out of the rubble all night. He didn't know if this boy's mother was dead or alive. But he knew the chances weren't good. He didn't want to tell him that, though, not when he needed his help in saving him.

"Where is my family?" The teen became more frantic, blinking away the tears in his eyes, coming to the realization that his nightmare wasn't a dream at all. The real hallucination was the one of his family peacefully at home.

"We are helping them as well. I just need you to be calm."

"Don't help me! Help them!"

The man in the helmet ignored Tareq's demand. "What's your name, *habibi*?"

Tareq couldn't answer him; his words were stuck in his throat, along with his emotions. He felt like he was choking on a clump of scalding charcoal.

"It's going to be okay. I just need you to calm down. Wouldn't your mother want you to be calm right now?"

Tareq knew the man in the white helmet was right. His mother would want him to be strong and collected. She'd want him to get out of the rubble and help locate his siblings.

"Tareq. My name is Tareq," he mustered enough strength to say.

"Tareq, good. I'm going to lift this piece of concrete up and I am going to need you to move toward me. Do you think you can do that?"

"Yes. I will try."

"Okay, good, on the count of three. One . . . two . . . three!" The man with the helmet grunted loudly. "*Yallah*, come toward me!"

Tareq could feel the pressure slowly lifting off his stomach, immediately sensing a surge of relief as he slid out, escaping the wall of his home that once held a golden-beaded hanging of the ninety-nine names of God—it was supposed to protect his family. Tareq hoped it still might.

The man in the helmet waited until he could see that the boy's whole body was safely away from the wall before dropping it back down, sending a dust cloud up into his own mouth. Coughing, he bent to pick the boy up. Instinctively, Tareq wrapped his arms around the man's neck, feeling the soot layered on top of sweat.

"Please, I need to find my family," he begged.

"I know, *habibi*. I'm going to help you." The kindness in his voice convinced Tareq that this man was telling the truth.

And he would help find them, but he couldn't promise that they would all be alive.

CHAPTER 3

Hours passed at the site of their bombed-out apartment building.
Most of the survivors could do nothing but watch and weep as
the corpses were lined up on the ground—bodies that included
Tareq's grandmother and mother.

The moon shone bright as he lay between his mama and
teyta. Holding their lifeless hands, Tareq tried breathing in his
mother's scent one last time, but all he could smell was smoke
and dust.

He squeezed her palm, ignoring the sirens that engulfed
his neighborhood. Although limp, it was still the same hand
that he had held as a timid child when stepping into crowded
souks in search of spices and clothes. He stroked the elegant
fingers that had caressed him gently, making him feel warm
and safe. "I will be okay, Mama, please don't worry. I will take
care of my little brothers and sisters just like you took care of
us." He looked at her closed eyes with those perfectly arched
brows and took in her beauty. Even dead, his mother looked
peaceful and gracious. Tareq brought her delicate hand to his

mouth, pressing it to his lips ever so gently. A kiss goodbye. A finality he didn't want to accept; no child ever does, no matter their age. *It's true for me*

When he looked up, he was brought back into the current chaos, listening to the sounds of wails and the sirens. The man in the white helmet wasn't alone: There were many wearing the same uniform—they all had the same tan vests and tired eyes. Some helmets were brighter, others stained with the gloom of war, a thick layer of death and broken souls.

Tareq spotted the man who had pulled him out—Ahmed—marching forward, carrying something. His headlamp beamed in front of him, making it hard to see what was in his arms. It was when he got closer that Tareq recognized the long dark brown hair bouncing with Ahmed's every step.

"I'm sorry, *habibi*."

He handed Farrah's wilted body over to her big brother, who rocked the young girl in his arms as he kissed her round cheek. The tears falling from his face cleaned the dust from hers.

"I found her in the room next to where I found you." Ahmed quickly turned and walked away, unable to take the grief. His only way to cope was to keep working and continue digging. He promised this boy he'd help find his family, and right now that's all he could do for the kid.

Tareq went to lay his sister down next to their mother when he spotted the red car still clutched in her hand, Salim's toy that was passed down from Tareq. A Matchbox sedan that would live in Tareq's dreams and memories forever, connecting him to his days here and a life that no longer existed.

He examined the small toy and couldn't find a dent on it. "How did you survive this and they didn't? How?!" With a rage he had never felt before, he threw the car toward the rubble. "How are you whole and not them?" He fell to his knees, crying again.

After more time passed, Ahmed returned to say that he couldn't find any additional survivors. "You should go to the hospital. Before we pulled you out, there were others who were sent there. You will likely get more information if you go there."

Creases surrounded his rescuer's light brown eyes. They were the eyes of an elderly man who had seen too much, the eyes of an old spirit coming toward the end of life. Not the eyes of a twenty-five-year-old who, a few years ago, was studying to be a doctor.

Once the war broke out, Ahmed's plans for his future came to an end. No longer able to study, he decided the only way to help his fellow Syrians was by joining the Syrian Civil Defense—an organization full of men and women who rushed toward the fire while everyone else ran away from it. His mother begged him to stop his work, as they too were now targets, but he told her, "If I can't help my people, I am already dead."

Ahmed convinced one of the men watching what was going on to take Tareq to the hospital and helped him into the small blue hatchback. "I'll take care of your family here," he assured the boy. "Good luck, *habibi. Massalame, Allah ieshfeek.*" With a wave, he closed the door on the kid that he knew he would likely never see again—this was what Syria had become, a land of permanent goodbyes.

...

As the car drove down the street, Tareq surveyed the destroyed and dilapidated buildings along the way. What was once considered strong, indestructible construction now looked like a city made of the thinnest cardboard, crumbled by the hands of the devil himself. Tareq shut his eyes and leaned his forehead on the cool glass, unaware of the blood that dripped down his scalp. The physical pain was numbed by the enormous emptiness in his soul.

The middle-aged driver didn't know how to console the teen, so he too stayed silent. When they pulled up to the hospital, Tareq stepped out of the car, strengthened only by the hope of finding someone, anyone from his family who was still alive.

"*Yislamu,*" he muttered to the stranger who had brought him there, thanking him, before shutting the car door.

The tears and screams inside the emergency room echoed the sounds from his bombed-out home, but now were contained in what felt like a powder keg of emotions waiting to explode and tear the hospital apart. The stench was more concentrated. The tang of blood and death was everywhere. There was no escaping the sour odor inside the hospital doors.

A doctor ran over to Tareq, eyeing the blood that trailed down the side of his face. "Come with me!" she demanded, grabbing an arm and pulling him to a room full of other patients, none of whom were critical. Pushing him down onto a plastic chair, she pulled over a tray on wheels. As she dabbed liquids from her bottles and searched his head, her panic steadied. "You're going to be fine." She took a breath. "I just need to bandage up your head and you can rejoin your family." She instantly regretted her words as the young man's eyes began to well.

"I'm here to find my family," he whispered. The compassion in the woman's face made it hard for him to keep his emotions at bay. Evading her tender gaze made it easier. She began to wrap a bandage around his head. "My youngest sister and brothers, they may have been brought here." His lips quivered and voice trembled while he fixated his eyes on the blue wall. "We couldn't find them. Al Defa'a al Madani told me to come here."

"Can you describe what they look like?" she asked, using surgical scissors to cut the gauze.

"Salim is thirteen, Susan is four and the twins are almost six months. Here, I have pictures." He pulled out the old cell phone his father had given him last year. It wasn't as fancy as the ones some of his friends owned, but it had all the features he wanted, including a camera. The doctor continued to wrap, tuck and bandage as Tareq scanned his photos. He felt guilt and pain as he swiped past the lively, smiling faces of his mother, grandmother and Farrah.

He quickly found a family picture of everyone together, longing for the day it was taken. An afternoon when they'd wanted to go to the park but thought it was too dangerous to leave the apartment. Instead, they had settled for a barbecue on the balcony and laid out a blanket on the living room floor.

Eating off the plates set on the ground, with the TV off, just enjoying their time together.

"I haven't seen him"—the doctor pointed at Salim—"but I have seen her and them." She looked at Tareq, who was unable to read her expression.

"Can you take me to them?" he asked, excited to see his siblings. All he wanted at that moment was to kiss and hug them. They needed one another more than ever.

"She's being treated right now, but she will be fine, I promise."

His eyes widened, elated by those words. Susan was going to be okay. Suddenly the emptiness he had been feeling started to fill.

"I will take you to your brothers," the doctor said, this time not sharing any more information.

Tareq followed her down a busy corridor that got quieter as they continued to the end, abandoning the mayhem. The stillness sent a chill up his spine. He suddenly longed to hear the wails of a baby. A sound he spent so many hours of his life rocking and cuddling to stop. They paused outside a light blue door. She put her hand on his back and said, "I'm very sorry," before walking away.

He is so compassionate with his family

Tareq stared at the bodies of his baby brothers. His eyes were as lifeless as their small bodies, which lay on a shared hospital trolley. Ameer wore the white booties their grandmother had knitted for him, and Sameer the yellow. Their pacifiers were still attached to their striped blue-and-white onesies—orange for Sameer and green for Ameer.

Tareq continued to look intently at his brothers, hoping to see their tummies move up and down, like they used to when they would sleep peacefully. He stayed motionless, listening to the clicks of the clock above, losing track of how long he had stood there staring. He didn't know what else to do. His job was to protect them. He was their big brother. He was the one who'd changed their diapers every morning when they woke up. He was the one who'd given them their bottles. He was the one who would dress them, attach their bibs and clip on their pacifiers—orange for Sameer and green for Ameer.

Tareq finally found the courage to move closer. He glided his fingers through Sameer's dark wavy hair and grabbed ahold of Ameer's pudgy hand. It was then that he noticed a spot of blood inside Ameer's nostril. The doctors must have missed it when wiping his sweet face. That one tiny stain was the proof that Tareq did not want to see. His brothers were dead. That blood made it feel instantly real.

"I'm so sorry! Please forgive me!" He began to sob, pressing his face into the unmoving bodies of his little baby brothers. "I'm so sorry!" He struggled to breathe through his wails.

He begged for the forgiveness of his youngest siblings, who wouldn't have been able to answer him even if they were alive. He begged for the forgiveness of his mother, grandmother, and sister Farrah, whose bodies were still lying on the ground, cold and alone. He begged for the forgiveness of God, believing he must have done something to deserve this suffering, to deserve this emptiness.

Tareq felt a hand on his shoulder, jolting him back into the dark and desolate hospital room. He turned to find his father, who immediately held him tight.

"Baba, I'm sorry, I couldn't save them!" Tareq continued to cry.

"Shhhh . . ." Fayed said, choking back tears as he firmly held his eldest son while staring at his youngest.

Sometimes, not talking is the best way to cope in these times

CHAPTER 4

That's a sad reality most have

They didn't find Salim's body. That often happens in war.
Families are forced to suffer not only loss, but also the bleak
existence of living with dark hope. These are the people I meet
with broken souls, tired hearts and lost minds, clinging to the
fantasy that their loved one is living in a dreamed existence.
They know, at least deep down, that this is not the truth, but
they dream it anyway, because to fool the mind helps fool the
heart. And to fool the heart is what they think they need to
survive. In reality, it's more like being addicted to a drug that
controls your every breath and thought. It doesn't allow them
the freedom to be happy, because no matter what, the darkness
will always shadow the dream.

This black cloud positioned itself in the back of Tareq's
mind as, days later, they sped down the highway. His thoughts
raced. *What if Salim was able to get out? The chaos would have
made it easy for him to go unnoticed. Maybe he was too dazed.
Maybe he has amnesia like they do in the movies when someone has head trauma.*

"Baba, we need to go back and find Salim!" he blurted out.

"*Ibni.*" Fayed's shoulders dropped even lower than they had been. "You must stop. Please." His voice was weak and his words soft. "Do it for your sister. She can't keep hearing this—it will only hurt her more."

Tareq shifted his gaze toward Susan, who was fast asleep with her mouth open and head pressed on the red-haired plush lovey. The doll survived the bombardment that killed more than two dozen men, women and children. He found it in the rubble during the days he was searching for the body of his little brother. Susan's first smile after the air strike came when he handed her the doll, and she hadn't let go of it since. It's a connection to a life she will barely remember as the years pass, but the feelings of tenderness and love will forever be encapsulated in that ragged and tattered little doll.

Tareq didn't respond to his father, and he knew to stop asking. Not just for Susan, but also for the man behind the steering wheel, the only parent he had left—their shattered caregiver who lost his wife, mother, daughter and three sons while he was at the shop. The man who just left his own brother behind in that destroyed city in order to give his remaining children a chance, not knowing what that prospect would be.

Instead, Tareq vacantly stared out the back window, watching the arid landscape that whizzed past. In recent years, the once-lush greenery that held beautiful loquat and citrus trees had disintegrated into dusty brown cracked earth. He thought of the news stories he'd read in social media posts since the war started, pieces trying to reason why his country had fallen

It is human to want to blame something [handwritten]

into a bloody abyss. The parched ground seemed to advocate the article that accused climate change and the region's drought. *Did global warming kill my family?* Tareq wondered. More than ever before, he wanted someone or something to blame for his loss.

The article Tareq thought of was one shared primarily by friends and family who supported the government. It claimed that the loss of fertile land sparked the anti-government revolt in 2011, beginning in an area where farmers were feeling more than a pinch in their wallets because of the decade-long dry-up. The protests started in the southwestern city of Daraa, where some audacious teenagers sprayed graffiti opposing President Bashar al-Assad's government for not doing enough to help the croppers. *There's always multiple reasons* [handwritten]

That online piece, and many articles for that matter, made a lot of claims about what may have ignited the war. In reality, there were many sparks that started the inferno that burned a great civilization into the ashes—there always are.

Fayed steadied the vehicle as he saw another checkpoint ahead, the third since leaving their home city. And not the last before they would reach their destination.

After the strike that killed his family, Fayed decided that he needed to get his two surviving children out of his homeland, a decision he would regret putting off for the rest of his life, as the ghosts of his other children and wife constrict his every breath.

But before leaving Syria, he needed financial support for the journey. And his older brother had promised to lend him the cash as long as he could come pick it up. Fayed didn't want

Protests do like our independent lead to war [handwritten margin note]

That's hard to live with the rest of your life [handwritten margin note]

to go to Raqqa—deeper into the belly of the beast—to take his children there, but that was where his eldest brother lived.

The city had become the de facto capital for Daesh, al-Dawla al-Islamiya al-Iraq al-Sham—or, as the world started to call it, ISIS. Since forcefully taking the city, the fundamentalist organization had created their own laws, calling them religious but not caring whether they contradicted Islam and humanity.

As Fayed let up on the accelerator, the crumbling of dirt, glass and broken concrete pressed deeper into the rubber tires, waking Susan. She stretched her arms and let out a loud yawn. "Baba, are we here?"

"No, *albi*, just another checkpoint. Nothing to worry about, go back to sleep." Susan nodded in approval and let her lids drop again before leaning back on the car door.

"Baba, who are they?" asked Tareq. The knots in his stomach returned, as they had at every checkpoint.

"Don't worry, we will be fine." Fayed scratched the beard he'd started growing in preparation for heading into Daesh-controlled land, part of their strict uniform. He stopped his car behind a halted bus. There was a group of about ten men standing outside the coach, drinking water out of thin plastic bottles and smoking.

Inside the car, both father's and son's palms began to sweat as a young disheveled man approached their vehicle. He was not with the gaggle ahead. His green camouflage uniform identified him as a fighter for the government army.

"*Merhaba.*" The soldier scanned the car as he offered a lackluster greeting.

"Hello." Fayed forced a smile.

"Where are you headed?"

He told the truth. "We are going to Raqqa to visit family."

The young soldier shook his head. Fayed couldn't decipher if it was out of concern or judgment.

"I have a brother there, and we need to see him," Fayed continued.

"Yes, I understand." The university-aged man put a hand up. He'd heard enough. "That bus is headed there too." He flicked a finger in the direction of the group. With a longer, more attentive glance, both father and son now noticed an aging woman among the riders ahead. "They came from Beirut. Our people are scattered everywhere." He clucked his tongue. "But we need you to wait here for a while; there is fighting ahead and it's too dangerous. We will let you know when it's clear."

Fayed bobbed his head in agreement. He wouldn't argue.

Dark circles surrounded the young soldier's sunken brown eyes. "But I don't recommend you go at all." He looked no older than twenty. His uniform was ragged, matching his unkempt hair and the dirt on his face. He examined Fayed's face to see if that statement had changed the older man's intention. When he saw that it had no effect, he gave up. It's all the effort he could muster. What's another life lost in a land where the devil roamed free? "Fine. It's your death wish. I need to see your identification."

Fayed handed him the few papers and IDs he had found when searching the rubble, withholding the passports to keep them safe. The young soldier took the papers over to an older man with salt-and-pepper bushy eyebrows and a mustache to match. A cigarette hung limply from his lips as the smoke billowed up. He was the commander of the youth that surrounded him, fighters for the Assad regime. The officer didn't know it, but he was the only one in his group who still believed in their mission—the frail conviction of a man who trusted no other option.

There were non-Syrians in fatigues as well, including a couple of Afghan refugees and Iranians—sent by government ally Iran—and some Lebanese Hezbollah fighters. But it was the men dressed in black that they could see in the distance that sent a shiver down Tareq's spine: the *shabiha*, the pro-Assad civilian militia who invoked terror for the government. He remembered the story of a university student in his town three years ago, walking back from her lectures. She was abducted by two *shabiha* men. Her body was later found raped and murdered. One man was captured by the rebels; the other escaped. When asked why he did it, the prisoner said, plain and simple, "Because I could. I was given the power and I took it."

The young soldier brought the papers back. "Your last name." The boy tsked. "It's on our list. We are going to have to arrest you."

"What?" Fayed said, suddenly frantic.

"Baba!" Tareq, on the edge of tears, bellowed.

"Shh . . ." The soldier put a finger to his mouth as Susan fidgeted in her sleep. "You will wake your sister," he added sarcastically as he tilted his head. "So cute, she is." He turned back to Fayed. "There is something you can do if you don't want to be arrested."

"What is it?" Fayed trembled. He knew what heading to a state prison would mean. He would be better off shot here than forced to endure the excruciating torture of incarceration.

"A payment of sixty thousand pounds can secure your release." The soldier sniffed comfortably, used to these negotiations.

"I . . . I don't have that much." Fayed's heart sank as he met his son's gaze in the rearview mirror.

"How much do you have, then?" he spat back.

"Only twenty thousand." His name was never on any list. He was sure of it. Yet he had no choice but to cooperate. Powerless, once again.

"Okay, that should do. Give it here." The boy snapped his fingers as Fayed reached into the glove compartment and grabbed an envelope holding the cash. The most he was able to pull out of the store's register, leaving some behind for his brother. The little he had would now be gone, along with the token of belief that he could protect his remaining children.

"Can I give you ten thousand, please? I need this for my children," Fayed begged.

The soldier grabbed the small package, his hands grimy and fingernails crusted with dirt, before handing back their papers. He was not interested in another sob story or compromise. Fayed smelled the body of an adolescent man who hadn't met a shower in days, possibly weeks. The hygiene of war and corruption. "Wait here. We will let you know when you can leave." He turned and dragged himself back to where his commander was standing.

It's a scary time and they're showing the emotions of anyone in this situation

Father and son stayed quiet as their racing hearts steadied.

Fayed, feeling broken, eventually cracked open his car door. "Tareq, I'm going to step outside and have a cigarette. You stay with your sister."

"But, Baba, my legs are getting cramped. Can I please get out?" he asked, afraid of staying and enduring the silence. He needed to breathe.

Tareq's father didn't fight him. He nodded. "I will just smoke right out here. You go and stretch your legs. I'll watch your sister and keep an eye on you. Don't go too far."

"*Aa rasi*, Baba," he thanked his father.

Tareq avoided the soldiers and militiamen as he stretched out his hamstrings and calves. He could hear passengers chatting near the bus. He wasn't trying to eavesdrop, but it was impossible not to listen in.

"You have to change your pants," said one man as he took a drag from his cigarette, the orange tip reflecting off his black plastic sunglass lenses. He tugged on his flowing white button-up that draped over his loose-fitting charcoal pants.

Tareq scanned the small crowd. All the men were bearded; most of the beards were longer than the one his father was trying to grow out and much manlier than his own kitten whiskers.

"What's wrong with my pants?" replied the younger man wearing a black T-shirt and tight-fitting denim jeans.

"They're too tight, *wallahi*! Believe me! You look like a party boy from Beirut. They won't let you into the city."

"Come on, it's pants! I'm covering my body, and I'm not a woman. They have to let me in."

Other men started to chime in.

"*Inte ghabi!* You really are an idiot if you don't know how much Daesh hates jeans," said another college-aged passenger as he puffed out a cloud of smoke. "They symbolize the West to them. They don't want a dark-haired Justin Bieber coming into the city—they want young Osama bin Ladens to join." He let out an uncomfortable snicker. A laugh that had become common in Syria as the jokes got darker and light humor slowly disappeared while the war intensified.

"I've done this trip several times, and at least twice I've seen Daesh fighters at checkpoints pull a man off the bus for wearing tight-fitting pants and tell him to walk the two hundred twenty kilometers back to Aleppo," said a middle-aged father in the group. "*Wallahi*, I'm not lying." He put a hand on his heart. "And that's the best-case scenario."

"Fine. I will see what I have in my bag." The boy gave in and headed back onto the dingy bus, knowing that the last thing he wanted or needed was to be singled out by fundamentalist thugs or any group at that point.

"And, you guys, those cigarettes will have to be thrown out before we get to the first Daesh checkpoint."

"Yes, yes. We know, *ammo*," said the man in sunglasses as he threw his cigarette to the ground. Digging the disintegrating butt into the dust with the tip of his shoe, he reached into his chest pocket, pulling out a fresh roll. "But in the meantime, we get our fill!" The men all chuckled.

"Laugh it up! And while you're at it, pull out your prayer beads." He raised his own. "And if you don't have any, you better see if anyone has extras."

As Tareq turned to go back to the car, he caught the eye of the only woman there, dressed in black from head to toe. Her eyes were sad but warm. For one brief moment he thought it was his *teyta*, until reality sank in. This rattled his heart and retied the knot that had been slowly loosening in his stomach. The old woman smiled at him as she fiddled with her own wooden prayer beads.

Tareq will never know that for a moment she saw her grandson in him, a teenager who died in this relentless war. A boy who was forced to fight for something he didn't believe in. A soul I met far earlier than either of us would have liked or expected.

After an hour passed, the regime fighters got a call that the fighting had ceased for now and the roads should be clear. The bus and the few cars that had piled up were told they could leave.

Tareq's father sighed in relief. He wanted to get to Raqqa before it got dark and the onslaught of air strikes began. He threw away his anger as he took a final look at the young man who had stolen his money, choosing not to see a thief, deciding instead to see him as a young man who, too, was a victim of this war.

The drained soldier caught his eye before quickly turning away, not wanting to remember the faces of the man and children who left with another chip of his soul. He had enough to haunt his dreams.

. . .

The scenery of the drive was much the same. Arid land and run-down buildings with bullet holes throughout. A far cry from the lush greenery speckled with vibrant wildflowers and cotton fields that he remembered.

"*Ibni*, help your sister cover her head. We are nearing another checkpoint," instructed Fayed. Beads of nervous sweat began to form on his forehead, the sixth time for the sixth stop.

Both knew that the checkpoints from then on were under the control of Daesh; an extra chill blew through their hearts at the thought. They'd been used to the wicked dealings of the others, who guarded the regime- and rebel-held territories. But they hadn't yet dealt with Daesh, and they were unaware of who and what would meet them at the next stop. They feared them as much as they did the *shabiha*. Especially because they had no money now for bribes.

Tareq's family always considered themselves good Muslims. They said their prayers, not always five times a day, but they believed in a forgiving and merciful God. That was the Islam they knew and loved. His mother wore a headscarf in mosques and in areas where she deemed it necessary, but never thought of it as a requirement. His father disliked the hijab and all those who thought themselves better Muslims than he or his family—he believed a true Muslim would know not to judge, "because God is the only and final judge," he would tell his children. Tareq's *teyta* had worn the hijab and prayed five times a day, but she had never judged those who didn't because, like her son, she'd believed the only judge should be the Almighty.

For that reason, Tareq had not been back to visit his uncle since before Daesh took over. His family had refused out of fear; Daesh was unforgiving and ruthless in their atrocities and horrors. They were not alone in their evil actions, but still the risk did not outweigh the reward to see family.

Like many before them and many that will come in the centuries ahead, Daesh is a group of thugs who latched onto a religion in order to spread their darkness. Not unlike the shabiha. I have seen it throughout time and in recent history with groups like the Nazis, Al Qaeda, the Ku Klux Klan and the Taliban, among so many more. Some believe in their cause because they know nothing else, but most join because it gives them a sense of importance. But when I finally meet them at the end of their deeds, their path has never led them to the place they imagined. Minds like theirs are brainwashed and delusional. Even at the end of their journey, they are surprised at the nightmarish destination their path led them to. As much as I hate going there to meet someone, I feel a sense of relief that they will finally pay for their atrocities. Because it is their actions that have me meeting decent people in situations that they did not deserve—that no one deserves.

Out of habit, Tareq's father reached for his packet of cigarettes and pulled one out, placing it between his lips. It's what he did when his blood pressure began to rise and heart raced.

"Baba, you have to hide those!" Tareq said, frightened.

"Ya Allah!" Fayed remembered. He rolled down his

window and threw all the cigarettes out. He fumbled to open the glove compartment and found a lemon spray his wife had put in his car to help it smell fresh. For once, he didn't have time to reminisce and quickly pushed the nozzle down over and over to spritz a citrus mask over any lingering smell of tobacco his car's old fabric interior may have absorbed.

Tareq wrapped Susan's head in a blue scarf, stuffing every last curly strand of dark blond hair into the bulky fabric made for an older woman. Susan's wide-eyed confusion broke yet another piece of her big brother's heart. He grabbed her doll and put it back into her lap. "*Habibti*, don't worry. Everything will be fine. You just play with her."

"Farrah," Susan said to her brother.

"What?" Tareq asked, feeling the recently formed chasm in his heart crack further.

"Farrah—her name is now Farrah. She's my sister. I can talk to her and watch *Tom and Jerry* with her." Susan picked up her doll and gave it a kiss.

Tareq swallowed a painful serrated gulp of emotions. "She is pretty like Farrah was." He forced a smile.

"Different pretty, but yes." Susan examined the barrel-bomb-stained toy in her hands. The teardrop in the corner of her eye didn't go unnoticed by her big brother. He kissed her bubble cheek and enveloped her warm little hand in his before blotting the tear away with the fabric hanging on her head.

"Okay, we are pulling up. Just let me do the talking," Fayed said, eyeing his children in the rearview mirror.

He slowed the car down upon reaching a group of men.

forced to join?

But as they got closer, Tareq noticed that they weren't actually adults, nor did they resemble the seasoned fighters he'd seen on the Internet. Some looked younger than him, sporting flimsy whiskers like his own.

"*Salaam alaykum,*" his father said, giving the proper religious greeting as one of the teens approached the car.

"*Walaykum asalaam,*" responded the fighter. Tareq immediately noticed the weapon hanging off his lanky shoulder. "Where are you headed?"

"Raqqa, to visit my family," his father said, handing him his identification.

"Why is your beard so short?" The fighter spat on the ground. "You are an old man, it should be this long." He pointed to his chest.

"I haven't been blessed with beautiful hair." His father cracked a joke in hopes of easing the tension.

It didn't work.

"You are a *kafer*, shame on you!" The other boys came closer to the car, holding their weapons tight. The brown-haired boy leaned his head closer, gazing through the window. "And look at your trousers! Have you no shame? The law of God is to wear them ten centimeters above your ankle." His voice cracked.

"I'm sorry." Fayed wanted to tell them that the Quran doesn't use a metric system and that they were being foolish little boys. But instead, he put his head down, unable to argue through the indignity of his circumstances. They had the power in this situation.

"And your daughter," the kid added. "What is that on her

head? Put a blanket on her. A proper man would not expose his female kin this way. You disgusting *kafer*! God is always watching." He pointed to the sky.

"We didn't have the proper shops where we came from." Fayed made an excuse, ignoring Susan's whimpers. "*Shukran.* We appreciate you sharing your vast knowledge," he said nervously as Tareq looked down, holding in the hatred boiling up inside him.

The sweet words hit the belligerent boy's teeth as he shared a sadistic smile with his soft-skinned comrades.

"*Massalame.*" He waved them off with drunken power. "Go!"

"Peace be with you too," Fayed said. He quickly pressed his foot on the accelerator, not wanting the aggressive teen to change his mind.

They suffered through two more groups of brainwashed Syrian children who'd begun manning these stops as the experienced fighters were sent to the front lines. Tareq felt shock and outrage with each encounter. He wanted to defend his father but knew that one misstep or wrong word could cost them greatly.

Their mobile phones were checked at the second. Thankfully, Tareq had known to delete their music and photos, taking away further ammunition to be called heretics. Although he'd saved the pictures online, it felt like a betrayal of his dead loved ones as one by one he erased their images from his phone—the one object that never left his side.

Fayed sped off after every stop. He knew the longer they stayed, the bigger the gamble that an American jet might drop a missile targeting Daesh but also killing anyone in its wake.

Although the American missiles were sometimes considered more precise in comparison to the Russian and Syrian militaries' indiscriminate bombs, they were still known to kill many innocent families too. Truth is, bombs may hit their specific targets, but for an innocent life standing nearby, its so-called precision is meaningless.

We aren't completely good guys like we want to believe

Tareq, Fayed and Susan finally made it to Raqqa before the sun had set. Tareq's father encouraged his son and daughter to try to take a nap even though they were not far from his brother's home. He didn't want his children to accidentally see anything he would find difficult to explain. He had heard too many stories and seen too many clips on YouTube of Daesh's rule in Raqqa and beyond.

And as they pulled into one of the main roundabouts, his fears were substantiated. Tareq was grateful his sister was still under her blanket playing with her doll, pretending it was a tent, unaware of the sight that made their father gasp and had Tareq choking on the bile in his throat.

The sticks were buried firmly in the ground, as the human heads were planted on top of the spikes.

It's a difficult journey but it must be done for their survival

CHAPTER 5

"*Baba . . .*" Tareq said.

"*Habibi*, turn your head," Fayed ordered his son. "Keep an eye on your sister." But Tareq couldn't move. His eyes were glued to the image of the three human heads on metal spikes, bloated from the sun, eyes still open but lifeless.

"What's happening?" Susan asked, popping out of her covering.

"Nothing!" both Tareq and Fayed blurted out.

Fayed pushed his foot on the accelerator—just enough to speed past the roundabout without garnering unwanted attention from outside elements. Susan's small voice was the jolt that Tareq needed to detach from the barbaric display and focus on protecting her from witnessing what he would never unsee.

"What were you saying to Farrah?" Tareq asked.

"I was telling her that we're leaving Syria." Susan looked at her doll. "And she's coming with us. Everyone's coming. Because they're all here," she said, tapping her chest in the exact spot her father had told her their family would forever remain.

"But I'm telling her that we must say bye to Ammo, Khale and Musa first."

"Yes, but remember, we tell everyone else who we meet that we are not leaving our country. And that's technically not a lie because we'll be back." *She doesn't understand*

"Then why can't we say it?" Susan raised her right eyebrow, perplexed. Yet another feature she shared with their mother. *Leads to problems later*

"Because not everyone will understand." Tareq's words sounded as tired as his sunken eyes looked.

"Why? We go. We come back. It's easy to understand." Susan rolled her eyes, making her brother crack a half smile.

"You're right. But for me, will you just keep this information between us?"

"*Uff* . . . okay," she puffed. Tareq kissed his baby sister on the forehead, releasing a spate of giggles from her tiny mouth. She pushed him off and started to whisper in her doll's ear using the made-up language she had shared with her older sister.

Tareq reverted his attention to a city he no longer recognized. The streets looked lifeless compared to what he remembered from his last trip to visit his uncle. He saw two men and noticed their long beards and the Kalashnikov rifles hanging off their shoulders. Members of Daesh, the reason the streets were void of color and life. *They don't look Syrian,* he thought.

Growing up, he used to come to Raqqa a few times a year. He loved visiting his family there. Taking trips to the river with barbecues by the water, baking in the hot sun and jumping into the Euphrates to cool off. He closed his eyes, trying to remember the pebbles and rocks beneath his feet and the green water lined with trees; he could still feel the sun on his chest when he concentrated hard enough.

Tareq remembered a simple city that was full of energy. But now he saw the same signs of damage that befell his hometown. Bombed-out buildings and the smell of war. It's an odor that has changed little through the ages—a recipe of dust, death, destruction and despair. It's a stench that sticks in the noses of those who've inhaled the vile concoction, and it never leaves—always finding a way to return in a dream, a memory or even in a time of joy, when it manages to slip forward and harass you, a painful reminder of the moments—the parts of your soul—that were stolen and replaced with anguish.

The sun continued to set as they pulled into the street where Tareq's uncle's house was, tinting parts of the sky into a deceivingly peaceful pink hue. Uncle Waleed ran out to greet them before telling them to quickly move their car inside the property, at every instant looking around to see if anyone was watching.

He opened the rusting metal gate and rapidly waved them in as his eyes swept the road. When the car was in, he slammed the gate behind them.

CHAPTER 6

"Did you sleep well?" Aunt Nada asked the next morning. Her eyes were warm and her presence comforting.

"Yes, *shukran*." Tareq forced a smile out of politeness, but the action felt unnatural. He knew his mother would want him to put on a brave face for their family, especially for his aunt. He wanted to tell her about his vivid nightmares and why the dark circles around his eyes wouldn't disappear. It's difficult to rest when every night you are stuck in the rubble again, but this time it's not your body trapped under the kitchen wall, it's that of your younger brother. Your dead brother Salim.

Instead, he quietly watched his aunt pour water into a metal saucepan. She added coffee grounds and stirred it over the stovetop, waiting for a full boil. When the bubbles raced, she moved the small handheld pot off and on the flames, three times, letting the foam build up and then die down before pouring the hot coffee into tiny ceramic cups.

"Here you go, *ibni*." She handed him a mug. The smell of cardamom and coffee started to relax Tareq's mind, which still

The glory of 3rd person omniscient

couldn't shake the image of the severed heads from the round-about—an image that would forever be tattooed on his brain.

Flashback

She pulled a chair next to him. "You know I loved your mother so much." Nada had been waiting to speak with Tareq alone.

"She loved you too," he said. His mother had truly cared for his aunt. They were brought together by marriage, not by blood, but they were as close as true sisters. They even called her *khale* instead of *mart'ammo*, which was expected for an uncle's wife. The sound of the laughter between the two was one that he could still hear in his head. Squeals that would stop people in the street, curious to see what was going on. Sometimes the strangers would give them raised eyebrows and disapproving glances. Which would only set them off again.

A sandstorm of more memories began flying around Tareq's mind, clouding his aunt's words. Memories that would fade in time but for the moment were ever present. His favorites occurred in the yard outside. Tareq and his cousin, Musa, would kick the soccer ball around, pretending they were playing in the World Cup. The laundry basket made the perfect goal. There would always be a baby or a toddler nearby. His mother and aunt would drink coffee and shriek with laughter in the background. After the boys built up a sweat, the mothers would replenish them with lemonade, *halawe' tahine* sandwiches and an over-whelming amount of kisses.

The image lunged at Tareq's heart. He would give anything to hear his mama's chuckles again, the music of her laughter. He felt guilty for even thinking about why his mother was gone but

Musa still had his—but it was there, with all the other thoughts he tried to shake out of his head.

"Are you okay?" his aunt asked, breaking through his trance. That's when he noticed he was actually jiggling his head again. Trying, like he had before, to get the bad thoughts out.

"Yes, sorry, I'm fine." His cheeks flushed.

"You will always be like a son to me too," she carried on. "God only gave me the ability to have one child, and I will always be grateful for that gift. But you and your brothers and sisters—I felt you were my other children." Her voice cracked. "Children I wasn't able to have, but my sister did."

"*Shukran,*" he thanked her.

"She was my sister. And you are my son."

"Yes, *shukran.*" He tried to smile but couldn't. He had no doubt that his aunt meant well. But he also knew that no one could take the place of a mother. His aunt recognized this too and couldn't help but feel for Tareq. He was only a year younger than her own son. She saw him grow from a baby to a young man. And now he seemed like the small boy again who would ask for a gentle kiss when he skinned his knee.

In my experience through the millennia, every man, no matter the age, becomes a boy again when his mother dies. He can have gray hair and withering bones, but his heart will always be of that child who longs for the caress and touch only a mother can give.

Musa slammed into the room with his wild energy. The short and stout boy had grown to be a tall and skinny man in the few years since he and Tareq had last seen each other. Tareq realized his aunt looked thinner too—her cheeks gaunt and nose pointy. The last several years of war had visibly affected them as it had affected all of Syria. Food was scarce, and the supplies you could find in the markets had drastically risen in price—even in places like Raqqa, once considered one of the breadbaskets of the country.

"Man, this house feels better with you in it." Musa hit his cousin on the back. "I feel like we're cut off from the whole world, and now a piece of it has returned. At least for a little while."

"The world has more than forgotten us, Musa," Tareq muttered.

Musa furrowed his brows, holding back his usual jokes, aware his cousin was hurting. Instead, he grabbed the hot cup of coffee his mother had just poured for him.

"*Ibni*, if you are going out for a shop today, can you get me some hair color?" Tareq's aunt looked at her son. She instinctively pointed to her roots, which had white lines sprouting through like weeds.

"Yes, of course, Mama. Usual color, or can we get a bright red one this time?" Musa smirked.

"*Uuf!* This boy! My regular color!" She pretended to be annoyed as she went to grab some biscuits from the cabinet.

"Tareq, you want to come with?" Musa asked. "I can show you how much this place has changed. It's really depressing."

"What's not these days?" Tareq's uncle came into the room with Fayed, immediately eyeing the pot on the table. "Ah, coffee! Perfect timing!"

The country is unstable so everyone must

"Musa, please don't drive around too much," Tareq's aunt pleaded. "It's too dangerous."

"I agree with my brother's wife." Tareq's father greeted his sister-in-law with a gracious nod before putting a hand on Tareq's shoulder. "How did you sleep, *omri*?"

"Fine," Tareq lied. "You?"

"Same," said Fayed. The dark circles around his eyes showed Tareq that he was being untruthful as well. "Your uncle and I are working on a few things today to help with our trip out. Will you be okay here?"

"Actually, Ammo, I was hoping that Tareq could go for a shop with me. If that's okay?" asked Musa.

"I don't think I feel comfortable with that," Fayed responded.

"Let him go!" Tareq's uncle chimed in. "He'll be fine. With the proper clothes, no one will bother him. Besides, the boy is invincible, Fayed. A building fell on him, and he barely has a scratch to show for it."

"Waleed!" his aunt yelled as the rest of the room stared, horrified by his uncle's brash statement.

"What?" Uncle Waleed looked around. "Are we going to just pretend nothing happened and ignore it all?"

"No, but . . ." Aunt Nada stopped herself. She looked as broken and lost as Tareq felt. The pity in her eyes upset him even more. He knew he couldn't stay in the house and deal with those sympathetic stares all day. It would drive him crazy.

"It's fine. Uncle Waleed is right. The worst has happened to me." Tareq avoided everyone's glances, afraid the compassion would burst his emotions into a puddle of tears. "I want to go

They're just trying to protect him but help him through this tough time

out with Musa. As long as Aunt Nada is okay with taking care of Susan."

"Yes, of course." His aunt gave in. She couldn't say no to Tareq right now; her heart wouldn't let her.

"Okay, great, that settles it." Tareq looked at his father, ignoring his rightfully concerned frown.

Something bigs coming

CHAPTER 7

"I'm glad you came," Musa said. His hands gripped the steering wheel. "Truth is, I don't like leaving the house by myself. As much as I hate being stuck in that place all day."

"Do you get scared when you leave?" Tareq asked.

"It's not that." Musa nudged the accelerator, making the car speed up slightly. "I just feel like I have more freedom inside than I do out here. Everyone's watching us now."

"It's so different. It all looks dead." Tareq scanned his desolate surroundings. Abandoned homes. Closed shops. An absence of women. "It's like an alternate universe."

"It is dead. This is the city of the walking dead. Even in the areas that still have people in them—they're not living, they're just surviving," Musa said. He scratched his scruffy face. "It feels like our whole country is living in an alternate reality. You've got Russia, Assad and even America in the air, and Daesh, the Free Syrian Army and militias on the ground."

"Syria is gone," Tareq said with glazed eyes.

"Well, it's not the same Syria, that's for sure. Welcome to

the caliphate." Musa turned the steering wheel. "The people who run this place are not Syrians. This land no longer belongs to our people." He glanced at the rearview mirror. "I wish my father would take us away too. But he believes the war will end soon; he's thought that for years." He rolled his eyes. "He's afraid if we leave, someone will take over our home."

"Would they do that?"

"I mean, when other families have left, they've spray-painted on the houses, claiming the Syrians who lived in them were American spies. So the homes become a free-for-all." Musa raised his right eyebrow. "Really, it's their way of stealing the best property. And if the family comes back . . ." He lifted a finger and slid it across his throat.

Tareq shifted in his seat. "Have you told your father that you want to leave?"

"No, because he never would. And I wouldn't go without him . . . Look." Musa tilted his chin toward a man walking on the side of the road. His thick black beard fell to the chest, and a rifle hung off his right shoulder. He was wearing white clothes with a black vest, skullcap and sandals. He looked just like the men Tareq had seen yesterday as they were driving in.

"Is he Daesh?" asked Tareq.

"Yes." Musa's eyes were pained as he glanced at his cousin. "They are absolutely horrible, Tareq. If they are soldiers of God, God is truly the devil."

"He doesn't look Syrian."

"Many of them aren't," said Musa. A car horn honked from a few streets away. "I mean, yes, there are Syrians among them. But this city has been taken over by the world. They come from France, Saudi Arabia, Tunisia, America, Kuwait, Britain, Libya—everywhere. I swear I hear them speaking more French and English than Arabic, *wallahi!*" Musa put his right hand on his heart, keeping the car steady with his left. "Although we prefer those, because they leave us alone. The ones who speak Arabic, especially the Iraqis, harass us the most. Always calling us *kafers.*"

"The Iraqis?" Tareq wondered why they were in his country when they have battles going on in their own.

"Yeah, they're mostly the leaders, because that's where Daesh was created." Musa slid his hands around the steering wheel. "But really, they're all bad. They come here to give false purpose to their lives while stealing the oxygen out of ours."

Tareq took a look around the grim surroundings as he tried to remember how it used to be, a small city that once held so much life.

"You remember those apartments?" Musa pointed to the posh-looking neighborhood they were driving through. The coral-colored apartments were wide with beautiful balconies. Some were walled complexes with large metal gates for entry. "Most of the businessmen and government officials are gone. Some were even executed, and foreign members of Daesh took them over. It's called the Thieves District now." Musa pointed at a woman covered in black with a matching niqab covering her entire face as she pushed a stroller. Her husband was next to her, sporting a beard, a weapon strapped behind his shoulder. "It's like two different worlds in this city now. Them and us."

They use religion as an excuse! It's not their actual purpose which is power

"How is this Islam?" Tareq asked rhetorically. This wasn't the religion he grew up with.

"These people don't know the first thing about Islam." Musa squinted as the sun's rays hit the windshield. "I guarantee most of them have never even read a Quran in their lives. They are criminals in their home countries. Literally criminals." Musa looked at Tareq, unblinking. "Do you know that they even found out some of the guys who came here from England had purchased a *Quran for Dummies* book instead of the actual Quran?" Musa gave off a frustrated laugh. "The Salafi cancer has spread."

Although Tareq grew up Muslim, he didn't know much about extremist Salafis. All he really was taught was that there were two main sects in Islam: Shia and Sunni. And although there were conflicts between the two, his parents shielded him from most of it. His mother always called it "a silly political feud, nothing to do with the religion." He always knew that the feud was an important one, but he never gave it much thought. All he knew was that he loved his neighbors and didn't care if they were Christian, Armenian, Alawite, Sunni or Druze.

"If they are Salafis, why aren't they all Saudi? Or from the Gulf? Isn't that where they all come from?" Tareq asked, feeling ashamed for not having read more about this instead of playing games on his computer.

"Oh, many of them are. But the Saudis have had the oil money to spread this deadly disease," Musa said. "Think about it. The world buys Saudi oil—they're so rich, they have golden toilet seats. They also have the money to print their own interpretation of the Holy Quran in every language you can think of and ship it out. They claim to have the purest form of Islam, when in reality they created it more than a thousand years after the Prophet Muhammad's death!" He took a deep breath to calm his nerves. It didn't work. "And then on the other side, you have President Assad, the Alawite, and his backing from Iran and the Shias. This is a proxy holy war being fought, and our lives—your family's lives—used as martyrs!"

There was quiet in the car. Tareq didn't want his cousin to get any more worked up, and he really didn't know much about the dynamics to contribute to the conversation. Musa regretted losing his cool. It was the first time he could talk to someone other than his parents about the situation, and he had underestimated how much it had built up inside him.

Sometimes, you have to let out this emotion

War has always fascinated me, as much as it has hurt to observe. The beginnings are so unpredictable, like a small spark. You're lucky if your eyes catch even a glimpse of the golden flicker. Oftentimes the faint fiery glint cannot even light the kindling in a fireplace. But at certain moments, that first flare can be what sets off a blazing inferno, burning everything in its path into ash. This war was no different. What some thought might bring about small changes and freedoms broke apart a country. And the paths of people like Tareq and Musa were forever changed. The saddest part was that different responses and choices to those initial sparks could have brought positive alterations, but people with different plans got in the way.

. . .

Musa broke the silence. "You see that?" He directed his eyes at what was once a white building. "That was the city's church before. They've painted it black, like their flag, and now it is used as a brainwashing preaching center for Daesh." He looked away. "God, I wish the uprising never happened."

"I'm hearing that a lot," Tareq said.

"Don't you?" Musa asked. "I mean, we all wanted it at first, but now look."

Tareq shrugged. It didn't matter to him anymore. He knew those thoughts wouldn't bring back the family he had already lost.

"All we wanted was freedom. Instead, we received a different type of oppression." Musa shook his head.

"Yeah, but the strike that killed my family was Assad's." Tareq looked out the window. "No matter who we turn to, they all want us dead. Even if the war is won by someone, they all have blood on their hands."

He stared at some young boys digging through a garbage bin. A sight he'd become familiar with at home. Behind them was an old poster advertising what looked like a clothing shop, but the models' faces had been covered with red paint. As they drove on, Tareq saw more people on the streets. He suddenly recognized the area. They were pulling up near the square where he had seen the severed heads. "What are we doing here?"

"This is where the shops are," Musa replied. "It's hard to find shops these days that sell things for women. The storekeepers

See: multiple groves

are tired of being harassed by the *Hisbah*." He referred to the group that enforced Daesh's laws and punishments in public.

"Can't we go somewhere else?"

"What's the matter?"

"We passed this area yesterday, and there were heads . . ." His words trickled off.

"You passed Naim Square," Musa said, unmoved. "That's where Daesh carries out a lot of its punishments. It's not the only place. It's horrible, but it is now our new normal. You can't avoid it." Musa found a spot to park his father's car. "Ironic that Naim means 'paradise,' but it has become our city's hell." He sighed before pulling the keys out of the ignition. "*Yallah*, let's go. Try not to talk too loudly. The *Hisbah* are always around and they have spies everywhere. I'm not in the mood for lashes." He winked.

Crazy how killing is the new normal

The boys walked into a shop. Musa asked the storekeeper for women's hair color. "Over there," the old man said, pointing to a shelf by the window, blocked off by a curtain. When they walked over, they saw boxes of hair dye, the faces of the models on the cartons blacked out with permanent marker.

"Do these boxes get lashes if they don't wear niqabs and cover up too?" Musa asked the man, ignoring his own order to not speak loudly.

The old man with graying hair and a matching scraggly beard looked up at him. "They will be fine. I will be the one on the receiving end of the lash."

Musa picked up a box and took it to the register to pay.

"My son," said the storekeeper, "be careful when making

Not like vs with speech

these jokes. You don't know who is an informant these days." He eyed Tareq, the unfamiliar face. "I have young children coming in here asking me questions. Daesh pays them to be their moles. We weren't free to talk under the regime and we're not free to talk now."

"You're right. I'm sorry," Musa said. "And don't worry, he's my cousin from out of town. He hasn't had enough time here to be recruited." He smiled at the old man.

The boys walked outside, their feet crunching on the dusty pavement. They were moving toward their car when they heard the loudspeakers nearby blaring orders. The vibrations sent chills up their bodies. The panic was palpable, a murky flavor of defeat and frailty. And that's when Tareq felt a sharp object hit his back. *Suspense!*

"*Yallah, yallah!*" he heard a man yell in accented Arabic.

He felt it again, the tip of a rifle digging into his spine, forcing him forward.

like his dream

Imagery is so real with how he feels hurt

CHAPTER 8

Is this a way to scare people?

Tareq could feel his temples pulsing as he and Musa were rushed forward. Through the pounding in his head, he could still hear the loudspeakers blare. This time he could make out some of the words. "Ii'dam!" They were announcing an execution.

This is it, this is how I die. The thought raced through Tareq's mind. *I can still die with dignity. Don't show fear and hold your head high. They may have my life in their hands, but they will never have my soul . . . at least I will see my mother again.*

Their togetherness is comforting

He shifted his eyes to his cousin, finding slight comfort in the fact that they would die together. Musa looked ahead, hiding his fear, but Tareq knew him better.

The broken Arabic by the rifle-wielding thugs behind them continued, but the boys didn't respond. They were ushered to a crowd of men in the square where Tareq had seen the severed heads.

"Ebqa huna!" The men with guns ordered them to stay in place. Another man with a long dark beard marched forward.

Tareq instinctively put his hands up, preparing to be struck. Instead, he watched the man slap the gunman behind him.

"You don't force them with guns." He pushed the rifle down before turning to Tareq. "These fools are new. My apologies, young brother." He grabbed the goons and dragged them deeper into the square.

Tareq waited until he knew they were far enough away and then mumbled to Musa, "What is going on?" The crowd continued to form around them.

"There is about to be an execution." Musa's petrified brown eyes didn't budge.

"It's not us?" asked Tareq. His body warmed with a relief that was immediately replaced by guilt. If he was not dying today, someone else was. He peered around. "But where are the heads? I saw the heads here yesterday."

"The ambulance probably took them away this morning—they will have new ones to replace them with today." Musa's face was still. "They keep them up for at least three days for the city to see, and no one is allowed to take them down but the ambulances."

"*Ya Allah.*" Tareq had heard the cruel stories about the various groups, including Daesh, but the reality was more frightening than he had imagined. It was a different type of fear than from bombs and air strikes.

This felt more intimate.

The idea of seeing your executioner face-to-face as you feel a blade run through your flesh made Tareq almost nauseatingly grateful for the quick deaths of his family members. "He said we can go. Let's—"

Foreshadowing Musa's death

"I'm not going." Musa's voice sounded detached, as if he was already preparing his body and mind for what was about to occur. "We are a small city. We know almost everyone. I need to know who they are killing." He handed Tareq the keys to his car. "But I understand if you can't stay." He gazed weakly at his cousin. Tareq knew that meant he wanted him near. Not wanting to witness this alone. Not again, not ever.

And truthfully, Tareq was curious.

These group of people show themes of togetherness

That is what's bemusing about humans—oftentimes curiosity drives you to do things that you know will haunt you, but you do them anyway. And you do them again and again. The worst of you take that curiosity to measures that are unfathomable to the best of you. But the curiosity is in you all.

"Just keep still and stay strong," Musa ordered gently. He was relieved his cousin hadn't abandoned him. "Pretend that you're watching a movie and that it's all fake. Like a show with props and Hollywood makeup. It makes it easier."

It is easy to bystand

A man wearing a thick black beard that masked most of his face started to talk; his eyes shone with darkness as he read his script. Tareq couldn't make out his words clearly and tried his best not to.

But some still seeped into his ears. "Insulting divinity . . ."

Tareq knew there were Daesh eyes monitoring the crowds. He felt them on him—waiting for a gasp, a flinch or disgust. Instead, he stared blankly ahead.

"Insulting the caliphate . . ." the black-bearded man continued.

Tareq took in what was unfolding in front of him. A young

man with disheveled brown locks was blindfolded and his hands were tied behind his back. He didn't look much older than twenty.

Not too far away was a woman hidden in her niqab, covered from head to toe in black, even wearing gloves. She held back tears that only those next to her could see, and only then if they tried hard enough. But nothing she could do stopped her body from trembling. The loose fabric couldn't hide her shudders. She was the boy's mother, forced to watch the execution of her youngest son. Her husband had his arms around her, feigning strength, his sunken eyes visible even from a distance. Tareq noticed that his gray hair was neatly combed and beard coifed, a sign of a man living on autopilot and disbelief. Both looked like people who had nearly had the life beaten out of them and were waiting for the final blow.

"This city was once famous for not praying, we saved it . . ." the sermon continued, prolonging the inevitable.

Tareq's attention darted back to the young man. He didn't move, as if he were already dead, peacefully awaiting his horrible fate.

There were others dressed in the same uniform as the man spouting off to the crowd. One man held up the black flag of Daesh, which read the shahada: There is no God but God, and Muhammad is the Messenger of God. They all carried their weapons. Two had pistols pointed at the blindfolded man.

As the tirade stretched on, Tareq suddenly heard the chant, "God is great!" A call that had been hijacked by the maniacs, along with his religion.

The cracks followed.

Tack, tack, tack, tack, tack.

A battery of bullets ripped through the young man, whose body convulsed. His mother collapsed; his father too shocked to try to lift her back up. The firing eventually came to a halt. But the horror didn't end.

The man who had been chanting made his way to the pock-marked corpse. He grabbed the limp head by its mane, lifting it from the puddle of blood it had rested in, and ran a sharp blade back and forth across the neck, slashing the flesh. The boy's father finally fell next to his wife, thumping to the ground.

A maroon pool formed from the faucet of blood.

Then three strikes. That's how many it took before his head ripped off and rolled like a ball in a play yard.

All the while, the chants continued.

Tareq felt like someone had punched him in the stomach and twisted their fist inside his gut. He kept his eyes on the executioner, remembering his face. He wanted to recall it for when Judgment Day arrived and he could be a witness against him. There was no way God would let such a monster into heaven, but Tareq wanted to make sure he emblazoned every detail in his brain—from the beady eyes to the mole on the man's right cheek to the wrinkles on his forehead—just on the off chance.

The crowd finally began dissipating. Most of the faces were pale and unable to mask the shock, despite seeing this time and again.

Musa and Tareq tried to follow and hide among the crowd. But unknown to them, they had been spotted long before they started walking.

CHAPTER 9

Nobody can stop them. Outside nations aren't knowledged.

The ride home was silent except for the motor's clunking. The boys couldn't muster the energy to talk, and even if they had been able to, they wouldn't have known what to say. So they rode quietly, with vacant expressions.

When a heart is clean but the eyes bear witness to such atrocities, the body falls into survival mode. Oftentimes there is numbness, followed by confusion and hopelessness. This is a feeling that has been shared by thousands of years of humanity in various parts of your world. It doesn't change. And it baffles me how it continues, with all the wars and bloodshed throughout the generations, how anyone can still kill. The words *never again* are uttered but not attained.

In this war, it's not just Daesh who have cold blood running through their veins. The shadow this war casts reaches beyond one country. It's a mushroom cloud, and Syria today is its ground zero. But like a nuclear explosion, the debris and emissions have widespread, long-term catastrophic effects.

"This one was particularly bad." Musa broke the deafening

quiet. "They're all bad. But I mean . . . I don't know." He stopped his failed attempt at trying to comfort his cousin.

"Did you know him?" Tareq asked.

"No. I don't think so. But I'm sure someone we know did." Musa took a deep breath before he wiped a tear from his eye. "His poor parents."

"What will happen now?"

Musa shrugged. "The usual, I guess. They will put a sign on his body that says something like, 'This man was an apostate. He was a *kafer*. And this is what will happen to you if you do the same.' It's about ruling us through fear." Musa rubbed his forehead, containing his emotions. "Daesh have started putting up screens on the main streets broadcasting their executions. It's put on repeat for everyone to watch."

Tareq shuddered. "How many executions have you seen?" He looked at his cousin, who took another calculated breath.

"I don't know." His eyes weakened. "I really don't know. They replay in my dreams at night. Like a Daesh screen in my mind." He tapped his head. "I went to school with a boy, he was a few years older than me. He came from a good family. He joined a group of citizen journalists, exposing the horrors of our lives for the world to see. He was caught." Musa's voice broke. "They stabbed him in the heart, shot him and cut his head off. Over and over, it played. What kinds of monsters do this?" Tareq watched as another tear formed in his cousin's right eye.

"*Allah yerhamo*," said Tareq.

"Yes, may God have mercy on all these innocent souls lost."

. . .

As Musa pulled into his neighborhood, he glanced at his rear-view mirror. "Dammit!" he barked.

"What's the matter?"

"Shit, shit, shit!" Musa continued. "I'm so stupid!"

"What? What's going on?" Tareq asked, now scared.

"I was so lost in my thoughts that I wasn't paying attention." He looked ahead. "Use the mirror," Musa instructed as he pointed a finger up, "and carefully look behind us."

Without moving his head, Tareq saw a white pickup truck behind them. The two men in the cab of the vehicle had their eyes on the cousins. "What's going on?" He recognized the man in the passenger seat. He had seen him at the square.

"They're following us." Musa turned onto another street, and the truck wheeled after them. "Shit!" He pulled into a spot by his home. "Look, we'll get out of the car and go into the house. Whatever you do, don't look at them as you walk." He grabbed the bags from the backseat and opened his door. Tareq kept his head down and followed his cousin's motions. Both boys closed their doors at the same time. Tareq shifted his gaze to the house. And they kept their eyes on the door as they walked.

Tareq could feel the men's glares burning his back as he approached the entrance to the courtyard. Musa creaked open the heavy metal door and quickly slammed it shut once they were in. No longer in view, they ran into the house.

"*Merhaba!*" Tareq's aunt greeted them before quickly registering the looks on their faces. "What's the matter?"

"Nothing, don't worry, Mama," said Musa.

"Musa . . . ?" She looked at her son with concern. "Waleed!" she called. Not long after, Tareq's uncle and father entered the room.

"Yes, my queen!" Tareq's uncle said. With one look at his wife's face, his mood changed. "What's going on?" He turned to his son. Musa tilted his head down and kneaded the back of his neck. "I said, what is going on?"

"There are some men outside," Musa finally responded. Chilling words, even before the war. "I think they followed us from Naim Square."

"You were where?" Tareq's father turned his eyes to his son, who shifted his head uncomfortably while nodding. He wasn't in the mood for chastisement, but neither was his father, who ran over and embraced the only son he had left.

"Baba?" Susan's small voice broke into the room. She was clutching her little doll.

"*Binti*, let's go watch some cartoons," Tareq's aunt said. She looked up at the men with distressed eyes. Her husband bobbed his head. A private language both husband and wife understood. Nada would keep Susan away from this, walking her to her own bedroom to watch television. "I bet there's a channel showing *Tom and Jerry*. Do you want to watch it from our bed?"

"Yes!" Susan screamed in delight. "Can Farrah watch too?" She lifted her doll as high as she could.

"Yes, of course, *habibti*." Aunt Nada kissed the top of her curls.

The men put on a smile and waited with feigned patience for them to leave. But as soon as they heard the door click shut, the conversation continued.

"I recognized one of them from the square," Tareq said.

"Shit!" Musa blurted out.

"Stop!" his father ordered. "We will deal with this, but no profanity. If they hear you, they can punish you with forty lashes."

Tareq's eyes widened at the thought. *Forty lashes for cursing?*

Before they could discuss any more, they heard the doorbell ring.

"You three stay here," Tareq's uncle said. "I will take care of this." The other three nodded in agreement.

Time went by slowly for the three men waiting.

"What do you think they're talking about?" Fayed asked Musa. Tareq could see the fear in his father's eyes.

"Truthfully? All I can think, Uncle, is the cubs of Daesh," Musa answered. The dread in Fayed's eyes built. "I mean, I think we're too old for it. But you never know with these guys."

"What's that?" Tareq asked. Both boys avoided looking at Fayed when they noticed the tears building in his eyes, giving him a semblance of privacy and dignity.

"Daesh has camps, training camps, for children," Musa said. "Indoctrinating them. Teaching them how to use weapons. But really it's a month or so of brainwashing. I've heard of some kids coming out and executing their own parents for not following their rules."

"Impossible!" Tareq said, horrified. *Terrible acts*

"*Wallahi*, it was in the news and our neighbor witnessed one," Musa continued. "They said the mother tried talking her son into escaping Raqqa together because she wanted to save him from the war. Instead, he turned her in and was the one who executed her in front of a crowd."

"*Ya Allah.*" Tareq dropped his gaze as they all fell silent again.

They heard the handle squeak and the door creak open. The men stopped breathing as Tareq's uncle stepped in. He was alone. They let out the air they had trapped in their lungs.

"Everything is fine for now," he said, rubbing the beads of sweat off his forehead. "But we need to be ahead of them." He was met with blank stares. Uncle Waleed shifted his attention to Tareq and Fayed. "You guys have to leave sooner than planned. The money we got out today will have to be enough. It should get you to Turkey." He then turned to his son and put a hand on his shoulder. "And you will go with them."

"No!" Musa yelled. "I'm not leaving you and Mama. I'm your only son, your only child. I can't leave you."

"*Hayati.*" Uncle Waleed's voice was soft and eyes were gentle. "There is no choice. When the war is over, you will come back. Or, if it comes to it, we will join you later. Either way, we will reunite." *They want the best for the family. These acts are done to make the story more intriguing and suspenseful.*

. . .

But they all knew that might not be possible. And the truth is, I know so many families who have said the same with only sadness to meet them when I did.

This family was no different.

They will sadly not make it out then !!

CHAPTER 10

Many decisions in life are not made by us (govt. (people in power) ⭐

The invisible lines in your world hold so much power.

Your eyes do not see them, but whether you live or die can depend on which side you stand on. The trajectory of your life is conditional.

On one side of the line, fighter jets rip through the sky, releasing cluster bombs, lighting up entire neighborhoods and painting the streets with the blood of limp corpses lying in *Can't* the rubble. Hearts shudder with fear at every breath, in every *control* minute of every day. Awake or asleep, you live with terror. *that*

On the other side, the only danger from the sky is the storm that rolls in, shooting lightning through the clouds, or from the birds that flap their wings, dropping their lunch on an unsuspecting street merchant. Children go to school kicking rocks while filling the air with the music of their laughter. There are still problems, but your chances of survival outweigh a premature demise.

Your borders were devised by man. A rain cloud or even a bird does not recognize the barriers created by the human mind. Neither does a gazelle or an ant. The tremors on your planet didn't cut up your land the way mankind has.

As desperate Syrians fled their homes and stepped over those artificial lines in search of light, they watched as others walked into the darkness, continuing to fuel the flames of disorder. Like in other war-torn countries, foreign elements destroyed their homes and their homeland even further.

There was initial relief when they first crossed those invisible lines. But the hardships did not end. Days turned to months, every moment a struggle filled with uncertainty. It included regret for leaving. And anguish for not departing sooner. There were days without food and months lacking proper shelter. Although it was a battle to survive in their new homes, I continued to see worse in the cities they'd left behind.

They are called the "lucky" ones. But in these situations, no one is truly lucky. Luck has abandoned them, sometimes never to return.

Neighboring countries like Turkey, Jordan and Lebanon have borne the brunt of the refugees who have left Syria. They've taken in the millions who flooded their borders, completely altering their populations. But it hasn't always been a generous welcome. Nor do those who arrive all want to stay. Most would like to eventually go back to their homes once things settle, like many refugees throughout history. They don't realize that they likely will never have a true home again. Doomed never to be a part of their new world and forever ripped from their old.

A once proud people, many Syrians have been forced

Auful how these peoples' lives had change without their control! Will no one else help?

to endure lives of squalor and indignity. Some forced into prostitution, others used as slave labor.

The tourist spots of Istanbul are now filled with children selling tissues to help feed their families. Old, frail women who should be sitting in their kitchens having tea, like Tareq's grandmother used to, now spend seventeen-hour days on the streets of Beirut begging for alms. And fathers can be found giving away their young daughters in marriage, far earlier than they should, at Jordan's Zaatari refugee camp, because it makes it easier to feed the rest of their family. Terrible lifestyles

There are the richer refugees who are able to afford their new lives in new places, able to start businesses and buy new houses. But they, too, don't feel as if they truly belong. They are in a new world.

When you are a refugee, everyone has lost, at least for the time being.

It's usually just the wicked who benefit from the misery of millions.

And the journey beyond those invisible lines can become just as heinous as living inside the fire.

CHAPTER 11

Destiny has once struck in gov

Taken just two days apart, the trip to leave Raqqa was as heart-pounding as the one to enter. But Tareq and his family were lucky. They left mere weeks before Daesh closed off the city, after which the only way to leave would have been through smugglers.

Musa's neighbors sent their two older daughters, Shams and Asil, with Fayed. Their parents were afraid that Daesh would try to marry the attractive sisters to fighters. To save them, they said goodbye. "We will meet again," their parents said through tears. Those words would become another broken promise.

Having the young women along worked well for Fayed and his family. Traveling with women made the checkpoints some-what easier—especially when the girls gave their brother's ID to Musa, making him their chaperone. Fewer questions, less harassment.

They decided the safest bet was to go through the Aleppo countryside. A trip that used to take two and a half hours would

Strict law to ensure their policy

now take them twenty-four, passing eight checkpoints along the way. Fayed left his car with his brother, and they instead shared a beat-up white minibus carrying other passengers.

"What happened there?" Asil asked the driver as they passed the charred skeleton of a similar vehicle.

"A mortar shell," he answered, unblinking and unfazed.

"Who was in it?" Her voice began to shake.

"People who were trying to go to the border." The driver looked at her through the rearview mirror. "Passengers like you, with a driver like me, and a talisman like this." He tapped his hand on the holy verses hanging from his mirror before pulling out a cigarette from his front pocket. "Most of them are dead." He shook his balding head. "They feared a death at home; instead, they died searching for life."

They would kill them rather than have them leave! Is that really God's work?

Following those words, one of the passengers decided to get off the bus at the next town and find his way back home. "If my fate is to die, I will die in my own house with my family," he said.

Their hearts raced at every checkpoint.

The government ones were the hardest for Fayed. Despite passing areas of conflict and shelling, his chest would thump the loudest when he thought about their money being taken again. It's all he had to take care of his children and Musa until he could find work.

Will they have enough to pass?

Little relief came when they reached the border. Hundreds of people were there, also trying to cross. Many had longer and more difficult journeys, spending nights in stables, in fields and inside dilapidated factories—wherever their smugglers would

Everyone wants to leave for new life and opportunity

take them. But they all arrived exhausted. And now it was a
waiting game to see if the Turks would let them in.

Syrians have cumulatively spent millions of hours at cross-
ings like these. Forced to endure the elements—the blazing sun,
relentless rain or blistering cold. Waiting, only to wait even more. If
it wasn't the weather, it was the fear of not being allowed through—
and the wrong customs agent could cost you your freedom and
possibly your life. Racial and religious profiling intensifies in wartime, and this war was no exception.

Tareq attempted to ignore the faces around him. They
upset him. Every face had a story, a family, a struggle. Instead, he
fixed his eyes on the landscape. Soaking in Syria one last time.
He whispered his goodbyes to the vegetation, the red dirt and
the olive groves that surrounded them.

Their wait was only three hours because they had their
passports. Far shorter than the days it could take the others
who'd left their IDs behind.

They just missed the bus to the Turkish side of the crossing, so they took the mile-long trek by foot. A silent walk with
other families carrying bags, belongings and regrets.

With each step, Tareq knew this was another permanent
goodbye. No matter how he tried to deny it. There was no coming
back. He thought of the country, the cities and the people he
was leaving as he walked between the fences that held signs
warning of land mines. He thought of his family, forever a part
of Syria's land where they were laid to rest. *What kind of person
abandons his family?* he thought as he looked at the wires
lining the top of the concrete walls. And as a droplet of sweat

trickled down his eyebrow and into his eye, he suddenly saw a misty vision of Salim standing beside him. The little brother he was abandoning.

"I don't want to leave you," Tareq said to his brother's visage, glancing around to see if anyone else could see him. But he knew he was alone. This was all in his head. *Exhaustion?*

"You have to. Think of Susan. You couldn't save us, but you have to try and save her . . . and Baba. They need you more than I do."

"But . . . I don't want to leave our family," Tareq whispered, not wanting to look crazy to those around him but also grateful for the hallucination.

"You mean our dead family? What can you do for the dead?" Salim raised his brow.

"I'd rather be near them." A tear fell from Tareq's eye. "I'd rather die near them."

"This isn't your time to die." Salim rolled his eyes. *"Always trying to take what I got."* He smirked before looking at his big brother. *"I will take care of them. But you take care of our father and sister. Promise me."*

"But . . ."

"Promise me." Salim's hazel eyes glistened through the hazy apparition.

"I promise."

It was a promise Tareq intended to keep. If the world allowed him to.

Salim's smiling mirage disappeared just as they approached another building, one bearing the pockmarks of AK-47 and

DShK fire. The duty-free stores lay abandoned with pictures of Syria's past luxuries for travelers—perfume, candy and alcohol. Nonessentials to today's traveler. All the shops contained now were shattered glass and a broken past.

Dozens of little boys ran toward them with wheelbarrows and pull carts. They were persistent and pushy, competing for two or three liras to take back to their starving families.

When they passed the third and final check, Tareq and his family took a deep breath despite the insolent treatment from the Turkish officers. Walking forward, they saw a line of yellow taxis ahead. Anxious families were waiting for their loved ones to arrive, some desperately approaching arrivals and asking if they'd seen their relative make it through customs. Syrian money changers chanted out offers of Turkish liras for the Syrian pound. Others offered Turkish SIM cards for their phones. And not far from where they were standing, they could see Turkish armored vehicles on patrol looking for Syrians trying to cross the border illegally.

They had made it. They were in Turkey. Legally. Tareq couldn't believe that the steps it took to make it past this crossing were all that was needed to escape warfare.

But relief was short-lived, and they had to say goodbye again. This time to each other.

CHAPTER 12

"Are you and Susan okay?" Tareq asked his father, his ear pressed against the telephone. It had been nearly four months since he saw them last.

"Yes, *ibni*, don't worry about us. It's my job to worry about you." Fayed sounded distant. Tareq hoped it was due to the connection. "How are you and Musa doing?"

"We're fine," Tareq lied. Before the war, he had never deceived his parents, and lately he felt that was all he was doing with the one he had left. "We have a nice place to stay and have made good friends." He tried to change the subject. "Have you heard from Shams and Asil?"

"Not since they found their aunt and uncle," Fayed said. "I'm sure they are fine. How about food, are you getting enough to eat?"

"Yes." Tareq's stomach pinched. He had no idea when he had last eaten. "Baba, I should go. Musa needs to call his parents." Another lie. "But please kiss Susan for me. I hope we can meet soon."

Suspense! Why have they been separated?

"We will, we will. Make sure you find a good jacket to stay warm," Fayed said before they hung up.

Tareq and Musa exchanged looks of consternation. Both boys had aged more than their years in the months since they'd left Tareq's father and sister in Gaziantep—not too far from the Syrian border—and arrived in Istanbul. Although they could have afforded four bus tickets to the transcontinental city, the men decided it was cheaper for Tareq's father and sister to stay in the border town while the young men saw whether Istanbul was livable.

The goal was to save money for the trip to Europe. The difficulty was making it. Turkey wouldn't grant them work permits; they'd heard the opportunities would be better for a new life in Europe.

But Tareq and Musa quickly discovered that finding work without permits in Istanbul was not as easy as they'd hoped it would be. They were alone in the crowded city of nearly fifteen million people, struggling to survive. When they'd first arrived, they found themselves sleeping in alleyways on some nights, under a bridge on another and in empty lots. They ate the scraps left over at tourist locations—their favorite was by the Galata Bridge, off the waters of the Bosphorus, where tourists often left behind half-eaten fried fish sandwiches, too lazy to take the extra few steps to throw them in the trash. That's not to say they hadn't dug through trash cans searching for edible items on certain occasions.

When he didn't find work, Tareq visited the Sultanahmet Mosque, or the Blue Mosque—as it was known to tourists. The

Does he not pray because of their struggles?

seventeenth-century structure with its six minarets and large courtyard was his escape. He wouldn't pray—at least not until he was guilted into it by a worshipper. He'd go to think and often to forget—a meditation of sorts. And to stay warm as the temperatures started to drop. Seated on the crimson carpet, staring at the blue and red tiles, Tareq dreamed of home, imagining he was in a mosque in Syria, not Turkey. The soothing trancelike tones of the prayers were the same; all he had to do was close his eyes and he was transported. Other times he'd listen to the kaleidoscope of languages that echoed in the large space, concentrating on the sightseers who donned borrowed blue head coverings and scattered about taking pictures. He'd wish he were in their position—on vacation in Istanbul, days away from going back home to their warless countries and living family members.

It is easy to take advantage of people in these tough times

Although, outside the walls of his sanctuary, there were days when Tareq almost felt grateful his mother was not there with them as he witnessed how poor Syrian women were being treated by men who exploited their desperation, poverty and beauty. Walking through the crowded streets of Taksim, across the water from the Blue Mosque, he often spotted the predators who lurked in the shadows, hovering over young female refugees. The men's eyes were soulless and could turn a body into ice with just a glare. Tareq always tried to warn the girls away, and he quite often paid the price with a fist to his gut. It was always worth the pain, though it didn't always work.

One thing was abundantly clear: He didn't want this for Susan.

Good man!

. . .

Tareq sat in a Syrian café sipping on some Turkish coffee. He heard the buzz of conversations around him, people talking about the war, sharing their foolproof plans on how it should end. The room smelled of books and coffee beans. On this occasion, he was able to afford to pay for the caffeine pick-me-up.

The longer Tareq stayed in Turkey, the more he longed for home. But he knew that home was now a myth, despite what other Syrians he met in Istanbul claimed. What they really craved was the past.

He was told about this café by different people he met in "Little Syria," the bustling neighborhood of Aksaray in Istanbul, but as he looked around, he felt out of place even among his own countrymen. Everyone at the bookstore café was also a refugee, but by their wrinkle-free pants and crisp-looking sweaters, he knew they were the elite.

Scanning the room, he spotted a young man around his age sitting in the corner, tuning a shiny gray guitar. He had on clean jeans and a black turtleneck. His hair was perfectly styled.

"I think they all have to be from Damascus," he whispered to Musa.

"Possibly?" Musa glanced around. "But why would they need to leave? Damascus is more than the capital of Syria, it's like the capital from *The Hunger Games*—untouched and safe. Protected by the evil president."

"Not everyone here is from Damascus." A man's voice came

from behind them. "And not everyone is from Syria either." He pushed his long salt-and-pepper hair back with a sweep of the hand. *"Ahlan wa sahlan!* My name is Rami. I am the owner of this establishment."

"Thank you." Tareq stumbled to answer the man's welcome as Musa choked on his coffee. "We didn't mean any—"

"Stop, stop. Everyone is welcome here with his or her thoughts. As long as those thoughts don't support Assad." He winked at them. Rami was a man in his mid-forties but dressed like a twenty-something bohemian. "But you are right, I am from Damascus. And I will go back when that filthy man is defeated."

"Syria is no more," Musa said with dim eyes. "It's not just Assad anymore—"

"It is just him!" Rami cut him off with burning eyes. "That family has destroyed the country from his father on down. I can find a way to live with Daesh but never with him."

Tareq thought he could choke on the air of arrogance that had just been spewed his way. *How can anyone think that a country under Daesh is livable?* he thought as his mind escaped back to Raqqa. He looked at the hurt in Musa's eyes, reflecting thoughts of his parents, who were still stuck there. But then Tareq remembered his own mother, grandmother, sister and brothers. It wasn't Daesh that killed them.

Rami was oblivious to the emotions in front of him. "You know, even my daughters, I believe they would be safer under Daesh than Assad."

"You would let your daughters live under Daesh?" Tareq

struggled with his hatred for all sides of the conflict as he remembered both his family's lifeless bodies lying on the cold ground and the execution that he witnessed in Naim Square.

Rami shrugged. "Well, eventually. I would go first, of course."

"How does your wife feel about that?" Tareq was genuinely curious to know.

Then Musa joined the conversation. "And would you say that to a Yazidi girl who watched all her male relatives executed and then was sent to be a sex slave for those monsters?"

"Assad is no better. You know his militias did similarly atrocious things." Rami slammed his hand on their table. "But Syria is home. This place is not home. Nowhere else is home. So for now, I make this shop a home for all."

Tareq took a gulp of his coffee and looked at Musa. "Well, I think it's time for us to leave."

"Nonsense!" Rami said, his energy shifting. "Stay! Tonight is open mic night. Listen, contribute, feel!" He made his hands into a ball and placed it on his heart.

"No, really, we should go."

"If you had someplace to be, you wouldn't be here right now." Rami's eyes softened. "How about I give you a slice of carrot cake and more coffee? You should stay. It will make you feel better."

Tareq wanted nothing more than to feel better. He hadn't felt whole since his home collapsed around him, taking most of his family with it. Every day since had been a struggle that seemed to get harder instead of easier.

When you lose someone or even something you love, you

never feel complete again. Time tends to help the moments between the pain last longer—but when it returns, if even for a second, it pricks at your heart with the same stabs and pangs.

"A slice each?" Musa asked with anxious eyes. Tareq could see the hunger in them. He was embarrassed that his cousin would ask about the extra slice; it sounded like they were beggars. But his empty stomach was grateful even so.

"Shayma, two carrot cakes and more coffee for my friends here." Rami snapped his fingers at the girl in a red hijab behind the counter. He turned his attention to the cousins. "You know, she wears only red scarves. Her hijab is art! It represents blood, the blood of our people. She wears her art every day," he proclaimed loudly, before whispering through the corner of his mouth, "although, I hate the hijab." He shuddered before walking away. *Trying to spread awareness*

"He could live with Daesh, but he hates the hijab?" Musa sighed.

Shayma came over with a tray carrying the slices of cake and two more cups of coffee. "He means well," she said. "He can be a bit much, but he tries. Most of the men in his family were murdered in the Hama massacre more than thirty years ago. He only survived because his mother smuggled him out. She was raped by Hafez al-Assad's men and left to die." *Sad and understandable now*

"That's horrible." Tareq felt guilty for judging the man.

"Now you know why he hates the regime so much. Like father, like son," she said as she clanked the small plates onto the round wooden table.

"Thank you," Musa said, smiling up at the pretty girl.

His hunger for the cake disappeared at the sight of her brown almond-shaped eyes outlined in black liquid eyeliner.

She smiled back. Everyone usually did. His smile was his secret weapon.

"Of course." Shayma cast her eyes down as her cheeks blossomed pink. "The open mic starts in a few minutes. If you want to join, the list is right there." She pointed at the wall behind where they were sitting.

Musa looked over. "I see you're on the list—unless there is another Shayma." He smiled at her again—a half smile this time, which was somehow even more charming. "What will you be doing?"

"I'll just be reading something I wrote." She finished placing the coffees on the table and slid the tray underneath her arm. "You'll see others with amazing talent. Our people are very talented."

"I look forward to your reading." Musa beamed. Shayma kept her eyes down and walked back to the counter.

"I can't believe you," Tareq said with envy. "Even during all this, you can still find time to flirt."

"What?" Musa shrugged. "She's cute! She could be my future wife."

"Really?" Tareq rolled his eyes. "A conversation about Daesh, Assad and Hama—and your mind is on love?"

"I mean, with life as unpredictable as it is right now, who knows? Maybe we will meet again when we all make it to Germany or back to Syria. You have to keep your options open." Musa winked at his cousin before digging a fork into the cake.

Rami made it to the microphone and started tapping for a sound check. *"Ahlan wa sahlan,"* he greeted the guests. "Welcome to Cover to Cover, my bookshop and café that welcomes all! Tonight is a night for us to come together and share our art and our heart." He flipped his hair and pursed his lips. "We have a great lineup and always have room for more. Please add your name to the list when you feel it in your heart . . ." He balled his hands on his chest again. "First, we will listen to the beautiful sounds of Jamil on the guitar."

The boy who had been tuning his instrument got up. His confidence seemed to slip with every step he took to the microphone. He sat down on a blue velvet chair and cleared his throat in the mic, sending off a loud shriek through the speakers, which made the crowd flinch. "This is an original piece I have been working on," he said, and his voice cracked. "I hope you like it." He positioned the microphone stand so that it pointed down and began to play.

He started off by slowly pulling on the strings of the acoustic guitar. Tareq was surprised at how good the music sounded and how it made him feel. It was like every strum and pluck sent vibrations through his soul. As Jamil played, he got lost in his own composition—which grew louder and faster. Soon the whole room was with him, entranced.

Tareq felt pride in the music that was being played. Even though it was not his, it was of a fellow Syrian's.

As more people took the mic and the night continued, Tareq felt completely whole and even more broken all at the same time. Despite the pain and anguish that their people were

Continue the culture elsewhere (love it)

going through, they were still the same sublime and unique individuals that they were before the war—just uprooted from the land they shared. The ones spilling blood weren't the real Syrians; the people here tonight were his countrymen.

Before too long it was Shayma's turn. The young woman took her seat on the velvet chair and pulled out a sheet of paper that she unfolded.

"My piece is called 'Goodbye, Syria.'" She took a deep breath before beginning. "*Goodbye, Syria, please forgive us.*"

The words tugged at Tareq's heart. She had immediately verbalized his feelings since crossing the border into Turkey. Praying for forgiveness from his country—and also from the family he left behind.

The graves he left behind. *It's good to express yourself*

> "*Goodbye, Home—never leave us.*
> *We didn't want to go . . .*"

Tareq's head was not the only one in the room that dropped. Grown men around him looked down in shame.

> "*We saw the people run, so we ran too.*
> *We saw our loved ones die; we didn't want to die too.*"

Tears pooled in Tareq's eyes. And again, he was not alone.

> "*The bombs kept dropping,*
> *And we kept falling,*

The guns kept firing,
And we kept falling."

Images of home flashed through the heads of everyone in the shop. From those wearing suits to the ones in ripped jeans. From the most tenacious to the most broken of hearts.

"Our rivers went from blue to red, drop by drop.
Our dirt from brown to black, drop by drop.
Our great nation fell, city by city, town by town,
So we left . . . following the trail of blood and tears."

At this moment, the room was no longer filled with individuals from different cities or different towns. They were not rich or poor. They were not male or female, Muslim or Christian, Sunni or Shia. They were united in the fact that they were all Syrian.

"Hello, Strange Land, please take care of us.
Hello, Strangers, please don't hate us.
We know this will never be home and
we will never be yours.
But please remember our hearts beat and
our blood flows.
And our pain, only a few people know."

Tareq peeked around the room and witnessed the pain that ran deep in his soul reflected in the eyes of the men and women around him. For the first time in a long time, he didn't feel alone. This excruciating journey was shared by those around him, by the people who died along the way and the ones who would join them tomorrow and in the days after.

It was the pain of a nation, not just an individual.

"Goodbye, Syria, please forgive us." Shayma cleared her throat. "Thank you." The room began its applause as some took a moment to dry their eyes, reemerging from their memories. Many of them longed to go back home. Others, like Tareq, knew that wasn't possible anymore. After war, home never holds the same warmth as it did before. To feel it, you have to close your eyes and hope that, in flashes, you can forget your reality and go back. When one learns eventually that home is not an object, comfort begins to return. But that knowledge takes time, and some never learn it at all.

Among the applause and the tears, Tareq noticed his phone buzzing. He'd received a message from a Syrian number he did not recognize:

Tareq? Is this you? I need to know if this is you.

More suspense!!!

CHAPTER 13

A week had gone by since Tareq had received the mysterious message. He'd responded but never heard back from the sender. He hadn't had much time to think about it either.

Blocked in by two bulky fishermen standing above, Tareq and Musa leaned their heads back on the window of the tram they were riding in. During afternoon rush hour in Istanbul, they were lucky to get seats, let alone two next to each other. The smell of the fishermen's unwashed, dirty buckets overpowered their nook, but both boys were too exhausted to even cover their noses like everyone else who was crammed in.

They'd spent their days and nights working odd jobs, marching from shop to shop in Little Syria and asking the owners if they required assistance. After frequent rejection—due to the competition of cheap labor from other refugees—they'd gone farther out. They were worn and drained.

Tareq had walked so much of the city in search of employment that his feet oozed with blisters.

Every so often someone would take pity on him and give

Refugees have it tough

him a job for the day. Even bohemian Rami employed him a few times a week to wash dishes and clean the bathrooms and floors.

Tareq learned the hard way to stick with the places that paid him daily rather than those who told him they would provide a weekly or monthly salary. Twice he had been cheated by nasty business owners who promised payment but, after he labored for days on end, failed to compensate him at all.

And that's why they were on the tram. Musa said he would try to help Tareq get his just payment from his last employer: money for a week of floor scrubbing and dish washing at a fairly new boutique restaurant catering to wealthier Turks and tourists who were visiting the sights near Taksim Square.

They finally spread their legs wider and breathed easier when the men with the grimy buckets departed from their tram car. Tareq imagined those buckets wouldn't even be a quarter full after several hours of fishing off the Galata Bridge. The fishermen crowded on that bridge, competing for fish, reminded him of the refugees flocking to Istanbul, competing for livable wages.

He tried to focus on the bustling Bosphorus instead, watching the ships and boats float on the deep blue waters. He wondered if the waters that connected Turkey to Greece would be as stunning as this strait that connected Asia to Europe.

As the buildings whizzed by, his eyes landed on the beautiful Dolmabahçe Palace and its mosque. His mind went back home, thinking of the historic charm that Syria once preserved—before everything was destroyed by the war. He tried to remember the Great Mosque of Aleppo, with its large marbled black-and-white courtyard, before the fighting between the government forces and the Free Syrian Army shattered it.

His thoughts were disrupted when the tram came to the final stop at Kabataş station.

The rest of the trip would have to be by foot; it was the only way he knew how to find the place. The gravel from the broken wet concrete crunched beneath their feet while the cool air nipped at their faces. But it was the sweet smell of corn boiling and roasted chestnuts that was making their mouths water. They kept walking, though. They couldn't afford the few liras it would take to satisfy their craving.

"And to think, people say Syrians are treated better here than in other countries." Musa broke Tareq's thoughts of hunger. "Every day is another story of people being swindled and taken advantage of." He shook his head. "This is why, no matter what, you have to make sure you get paid daily. If they don't pay, don't go back. Better you lose money for one day than for one month. You can't trust anyone."

"Trust me, I've learned my lesson." Tareq shivered in the chilly air as he eyed a Syrian woman with a stroller begging for cash. He peeked in and saw a baby in a pink knitted hat—no more than a month old, he guessed—sleeping through the chaos that surrounded her. He wondered what her future held if this is how her life had started.

The boys pushed their way through the crowds of Istiklal Street. The pedestrian thoroughfare was crammed with tourists, shops, vendors and restaurants. It also had its fair share of beggars and scammers. This is where Tareq had been walking when he was approached by a man who spoke Arabic, offering him work. *Heartless bastard,* Tareq thought as he remembered the man's face. He had known something wasn't right then, but he was desperate for cash, so he'd followed the guy. The memory alone made him despise his life here even more. He'd had enough; he couldn't live like this anymore.

"Do you think we have enough saved up to leave?" he asked Musa. "I mean, if we get this payment, with what we have saved. Do you think it's enough to get us to Europe?"

He wanted to make his way to Greece sooner rather than later. *Things have to be better there,* he thought.

"What? No. Are you crazy?" Musa asked.

"But I want to leave. I can't take this humiliation any longer. We can't stay here and go in circles. There'll never be a right time to go, so we should just go now."

"Have you talked to your father?" Musa avoided Tareq's eyes, instead watching the happy coffee drinkers at the restaurant they were passing. "There may never be a perfect time, but it's too soon."

"How is it too soon?" Tareq's eyebrows arched, trying but failing to catch his cousin's gaze. "We've been in Turkey for months. Nothing is changing. We live like dogs." At that moment Tareq saw an old Syrian woman wrapped in a long white headscarf sitting on the cold wet ground with her wrinkled, withered hands out, hoping someone would take pity on her. But her head was turned, and her attention was on a stray dog behind her. She watched silently as two strangers brought him a bowl of water and food. "I take that back—dogs live better than we do," he said. "At least in Europe we'll have opportunities that we aren't allowed here."

"How do you know that?" Musa's tone changed. "Have you not seen what the newspapers are writing about refugees going to Europe? They don't want us either. At least the Turks let us in. Many European countries are closing their borders. And using batons to bang our people out. For God's sake, Hungary's building a fence!"

"Turn here." Tareq pointed to an alley past a *simit* shop. He breathed in the aromas of freshly baked dough and sesame seeds as they walked by it, and for a second he remembered the flatbread he used to pick up from the bakery near his home in Syria. "There are more opportunities in Europe, especially in places like Germany and Sweden. Even the Netherlands. They grant asylum to refugees, they care about human rights—they have laws about it—and then, after some time, they will allow citizenship. We can work and build a life there." Tareq realized that he was trying to convince himself just as much as he was trying to persuade his cousin. "We don't have a future here. Turkey is also getting dangerous. There was just a suicide bombing last week. Here! On the street we were just walking on!"

"There are bombings in Europe too," argued Musa. "Nowhere in the world is safe anymore." He stopped. "Is that the place?"

"Yes." Tareq lowered his gaze, hoping not to be seen. From the outside the restaurant was beautiful, decorated with small golden lights lining the window. He couldn't understand how a place that glamorous would screw him on pay. "The second we try to go in from the back, they'll call the police."

"We're not going in from the back." Musa ran his fingers through his hair, brushing it back. "We're sitting down like real diners. Just follow my lead."

Tareq nervously followed his cousin through the glass door. *"Hoş geldiniz,"* the blond hostess greeted them.

"Hoş bulduk." Musa flashed his smile and began using his newly learned Turkish.

She smirked at his charm before seating them at a table for two, handing them each a menu. *"Buyrun."*

"Teşekkürler," Musa thanked her. "Is your manager here?" He then turned to Tareq. "What was his name?"

"Omer." Tareq fidgeted.

"Omer." Musa grinned at the hostess.

"Evet." She nodded. "I will get him for you."

"Thank you." Musa turned his attention to the menu.

Tareq waited until she walked away before speaking. "What are you doing? This place is crowded." He looked around and saw a Turkish couple sharing a bottle of wine and flirtatious smiles. There was a family of what looked like Gulf Arab tourists nearby, tackling the belt of the high chair for their baby. The father looked frustrated as he yanked on the fabric, and for a moment Tareq wondered what it was like to have a simple task like that as your biggest stress of the evening.

"This is why we are here now." Musa pushed the lit candle to the side of the table. "Pull out your phone and hold it up."

"What?" Tareq followed suit. "I don't under—"

"I think he's coming, just relax."

These people are something (handwritten)

"Yes, may I help you?" Omer approached the teenage boys. His half smile faded when he recognized Tareq. "Leave now, or I will call the police."

Tareq was about to push his chair back and do just that when he felt Musa's foot step on his. He knew not to move.

"*Hayır*," Musa said, rejecting the order. He stared at the man unblinking and continued in Turkish. The confidence in his cousin's face was something Tareq envied. He watched as a sixteen-year-old Syrian boy weakened this older Turkish man. The man pulled out his wallet and threw some cash on the table and mumbled something angrily while looking around the restaurant.

A good negotiator (handwritten)

"*Teşekkürler.*" Musa smiled, pulling his chair back, and stood up. He signaled for Tareq to do the same. "Bye-bye."

"What just happened?" Tareq whispered to his cousin as they walked out of the restaurant.

"Simple." Musa smirked. "I told him if he didn't pay right then and there, I would make a scene in front of all the guests, telling them how he takes advantage of Syrian refugees. I told him that he could call the police if he wanted, but they wouldn't be there before I finished what I wanted to say. And that you were filming everything right now and would be posting it on every website, including TripAdvisor," he said, pointing to a sign in the front asking customers to leave good reviews. "I told him this could be very damaging to a new business."

Good idea (handwritten)

"How did you know that would work?"

"I didn't." He shrugged. "These thieves pay us only a fraction of what they'd pay a Turk for the same work, and they're still stingy. He probably realized it wasn't worth the embarrassment, since your pay costs less than one of his overpriced meals."

"This is why we should go," Tareq said as they turned back to the crowded pedestrian avenue. "We don't belong here."

"We don't belong anywhere but Syria. At least this is close to home." Musa stopped at one of the chestnut vendors, purchasing two small bags with their newfound money. "Here, take this." He handed a bag to Tareq before walking to the kneeling old lady. This time they could see the dirty cardboard she was sitting on, barely protecting her from the cold, wet ground. Tareq watched as his cousin knelt down and handed the other bag to the woman. She cracked a smile and patted Musa's cheek in gratitude as her eyes welled up. Musa placed his hand on hers before getting up to walk back to his cousin. "I've been craving those nuts. I can't imagine how long that delicious aroma was stuck in her nose. I hope you don't mind. I gave her some of your payment as well."

"No, of course not." Tareq meant it. "My mother always told me, 'The more you give, the more you get back from God.'"

"My mom says the same thing." Musa shared a broken smile. "Look, all I'm saying is that by staying in Turkey, we are at least close to Syria. In the meantime, we live here, learn the language and customs. You need to do more to make this your home for now."

"But it's not my home." Tareq clenched his jaw. His agitation toward Musa had been building for weeks, upset at how well his cousin was adjusting to this new country. How he'd been able to learn the language. Talk to the locals. And get better-paying jobs than him. "We are not Turkish, and we will never be Turkish."

"And we will never be German or Swedish or Dutch either." Musa grabbed a nut from Tareq's bag. "This is how it is for now."

"You just wish you were Turkish!" Tareq knew how petulant he sounded but didn't care.

"I want to be Turkish?" Musa slowed his words and sharpened his gaze as he stopped in the middle of the street. "How about, I want to learn the language and customs of the country that let me stay after escaping the hell that our home has become," Musa spat out. "Maybe if you weren't so busy sulking every day, you wouldn't be so miserable. This is what we have right now. You're not even trying to fit in here."

"There's no fitting in. Why bother trying." Tareq turned his head. "I just want to leave."

"Look." Musa's voice softened. "I know this doesn't feel like home. But you are wrong if you think Europe will be better. Our home is gone. We have to work at making a new life. And I want to do that here. Not too far from my parents—who can't leave without giving up everything they've worked for."

What Musa didn't say was that he also didn't want to be too far from Shayma, whom he had started talking to, mostly through text messaging and visits to the café. He knew she wanted to stay and find a way to study medicine in Turkey, to become a doctor like her father. She made him happy in a way that no one else had since he'd left Syria. The ecstasy of falling in love often helps numb the soul from pain. But like the drug that has been named after the feeling of a trancelike bliss, the effects will eventually crash. But for now, he was high on it and didn't want it to end.

"Well, I want to go." Tareq stared at his cousin. "And I am sure my father wants to as well. We are exploited here. At least there is hope in Europe."

"Then you go." Musa grabbed his cousin's shoulder, his eyes intent. "I know you're not happy. And I know you don't want to leave me. But I will be fine. I just hope that the answer you are looking for is in Europe. Because I'm not sure it is."

will they separate?

CHAPTER 14

Tareq walked through the shops of Little Syria. The neighbor-
hood had transformed into a Syrian enclave in the last few years,
with Syrian stores and bakeries popping up everywhere. More
Arabic conversations could be heard than Turkish ones over
cups of tea and Syrian sweets at the bakery. The local grocery
store was packed with *molokhiyya*, sheep's milk butter and the
aromatic seven-spice mix. It was a home away from home for
the Syrians.

Through time this has happened in many countries and
continents. As people migrate, they bring with them their languages, foods and cultures. And as the years pass, they adapt
what they've brought to fit into their new lives and countries. This
is why the tastes, smells and feels of San Francisco's Chinatown
are slightly, and in some ways vastly, different from that in
Manila's Chinatown. The greatest of your nations, I've learned,
are those that embrace the cultures and customs of the people
who immigrate there—the best learning from the best.

It had been almost a month since Tareq made the decision

[handwritten margin notes: It is like an ethnic neighborhood (more like home) they shared]

Oh nevermind

that it was time to leave. He'd spent his days toiling and saving his cash. And now he was ready.

Walking off the main road, trudging through the damp, dirty snow, Tareq found the clothing store other refugees had told him about. It had a life vest displayed out front amid the clothing, usually a telltale sign that there was a smuggler in the back—or at least someone to point you in the right direction.

"*Merhaba,*" Tareq greeted the overweight, gray-haired man sitting on a chair behind the counter.

The man peered over his Turkish newspaper and gave Tareq a once-over, then nodded to the back of the shop before yelling, "Karim!" He rubbed his nose with the back of his hand and went back to his article.

A young man popped out, throwing the curtain back. He wiped a hand on his tight stonewashed jeans. His black turtleneck clung to his skinny body, the color matching his stiffly gelled hair. "*Merhaba,*" he said, waving Tareq back past the racks and sliding the curtain closed behind them before sitting down on a metal folding chair. He pointed to the one across from him in the small room. "*Yallah,* sit," Karim said, struggling to pull out a green lighter from his impervious pockets. He grabbed the pack of cigarettes off the flimsy plastic side table, colored by years of smoke and tar, while offering one up.

"*Lah, shukran,*" Tareq politely refused.

Karim pushed up his sleeves before shifting the electric heater so the blazing orange rods pointed at both of them, sharing the little heat it produced.

"So tell me, what brings you here?" The smuggler lit up

and took a drag, studying the teenage boy in front of him. He knew full well why Tareq was there—why all Syrians came into this shop looking for him.

"I want to go to Europe," said Tareq.

"Mmm-hmm." Karim took another puff before pulling a water bottle out from under his chair. He tapped the ashes into the grimy sludge swirling inside before sticking the cigarette back into his mouth, sucking till the tip turned dark crimson. "So is it just you?"

"No, it's my father and sister too." Tareq stared at the pink serrated scar that ran from Karim's hand to just past his elbow. This didn't go unnoticed.

"Small price of war." He lifted up his right arm. "At least I made it out alive. My sisters and father didn't." His eyes were still as he stared at Tareq. An action he had polished.

"I'm sor—" Tareq started.

"Okay, so most people will charge you forty-five hundred liras," Karim cut him off. "That's around seventeen hundred US dollars. The men I work for can charge you fifteen hundred dollars each. It will be a rubber boat; you will have to make your own way to Izmir, and I will connect you to my people there."

"We can't afford that. We only have one thousand dollars." Tareq's chest sank. "I was told that some people charge five hundred per person in the winter and that children ride for free because they don't take up a seat."

Choking on a drag, Karim chortled out clouds of smoke. "*Habibi*, I don't know who you have been talking to, but no one will give you that deal," he said, still laughing.

Poor Tareq

"There's nothing you can do to help us?" begged Tareq.

"I'm sorry," Karim said as he stood up and pulled the curtain back, gesturing for Tareq to leave.

Tareq could feel the curtain blow shut behind him as he stepped out. He stood there for a minute trying to regain some composure. His dream of Europe was crushed along with any semblance of hope. What made it worse was that it was done by his own countryman.

As Tareq walked toward the door of the store, the Turkish store owner peeked over his paper again. In broken English he said, "Go to Izmir. Better deals," before licking his finger to turn the page.

Why do you think Musa
is so okay w/ leaving
Tareq to go to Europe?

Why are countries
so opposed to helping
other countries in
a time of need?

PART II

CHAPTER 15

Invisible lines

There was someone that Tareq had yet to meet. She'd been waiting for him in Europe, as she worked on the shores of Greece. Neither knew how much a stranger would change both of their lives once the universe brought them together. I didn't know this either. They were from what some would call different worlds—but to me, you are all from the same world. You have the same hearts, needs, wants and desires. You come from the same beginning, and your earth will have the same end.

As Tareq's life came crashing down by a missile in Syria, Alexia's was changing as well.

She had come to Greece on vacation, dreaming of ouzo-filled nights on the island of Mykonos. But as she visited family in Athens, she caught a glimpse of the suffering and changed her ferry ticket to land on a different island where she could be of help.

Alexia watched the refugees as they slept on the sides of

roads, in front of the village school and on the very beaches they had landed on. They were elderly, infants, sick, healthy, wives, husbands, lovers, parents, sons and daughters. On any given day or night, thousands of courageous souls from various countries scattered like the pebbles that lined the shores. Most were grateful to be alive; others mourned the loved ones who didn't make it. And as more desperate people sailed across the turquoise waters in search of European hope, more lifeless bodies washed up on its coasts.

A person we need

Alexia's father was a Jewish refugee to the United States from Russia, and her mother a descendant of immigrants from Greece. And with every hand that she gripped and small baby she carried to safety, she felt increasingly connected to them and yet further from truly understanding what they'd been through.

treatment of refugees

The refugees arrived dehydrated, pregnant, ill and blistered. And as much as it meant for her to be there to help them, there was an emptiness inside her. One that only seemed to expand as she saw the arrivals multiply in number and their horrors continue with each border they crossed. The joy of saving one was always overpowered with the grief of not being able to save another. She was grateful that fate had given her family a fighting chance and wondered why it couldn't happen for everyone.

Every boat weighed heavy on her spirit—both those that didn't make it and those that did. The load made her body ache to do more. She wanted to go beyond just offering them help off the boat or a new pair of dry socks to wear. But she felt powerless in the face of their crisis.

One person can only do so much

So Alexia decided to defer a semester from her university and stay longer than the two weeks she had already given as she tried to figure it out. She knew if she went back to Connecticut, she wouldn't be able to concentrate on her studies as the images of the refugees continued to pop up in her Twitter feed. It was no longer just an urge to help; it felt like a calling. A repayment of sorts to those who had helped her family and ancestors in the United States.

"Are we really any different from them?" she said, trying to convince her parents through video chat not only to let her stay, but also to help pay for it. Although displeased with her missing school, Ilia and Maria understood, and deep down they were proud of their daughter. While other college kids were manipulating their parents into buying them new cars and gadgets, their child was doing it to pay for a rented room to help those in need.

The story of displacement and loss is woven into the fabric of human history. One day it's them, the next day it's you. But as generations pass, most forget that their people, too, have suffered. Some, though, still hold the empathy in their souls. But others choose not to; they choose to help themselves before helping others. Those are the souls who never find true happiness. Their hearts are never full.

Greece is one of the many countries in your world whose people know the story of displacement and have felt it in the last century, and the community in Lesvos had mixed reactions to the crisis that upturned their small island.

There were those who were upset about the onslaught of thousands of refugees. Greece's recent economic woes were hard enough on the community, which relied on tourism, but adding the worst refugee crisis to hit Europe since World War II . . . it was enough to break most cities. For the most part, though, they had compassion. Alexia noticed that village hearts were not as hard as the city ones she was used to.

Better than Turkey + Tarea's exp.

Sitting outside a coffee shop in Skala Sikamineas, Alexia watched as Annis pulled out her lighter with a picture of the Greek flag wrapped around it. Alexia still wasn't used to the smoking culture of the Greeks, or the refugees for that matter. "You likes it?" The older woman caught Alexia staring at her latest gas station purchase. "You can have it." She lifted the blue-and-white lighter toward Alexia.

No smoking. Kind-she's perfect

"No, thank you. I don't smoke." Alexia shook her head. "It would be a waste." Annis shrugged before igniting the device and touching it to her cigarette. "And it's actually 'You *like* it.'"

"Yes, of course. Thank you." Annis smiled appreciatively. She had asked Alexia to correct her mistakes in English.

Annis was fond of the young girl with brown hair and piercing blue eyes. She'd been here longer than the other foreign volunteers. "You're one of ours now," Annis had told her the last time they met. "Besides, you are Greek first, then American next."

Humans have always found ways to divide themselves, to identify themselves. Whether it be by families, tribes or

They should be one

Still happens today (we mention all this)

nations, it has always been your way to individualize. These identities define you before you are even born and follow you from one end of the earth to another. But what's puzzling is that what you hold so sacred can be forgotten after generations. Your great-grandchildren may learn to hate something you held precious, not knowing that that piece lives within them. Like when a man of Irish Catholic descent in America joins the Ku Klux Klan, unaware that generations before, his family was targeted by that very group. Or the opposite can happen, like when a Muslim marries a Christian—both unaware that they are descendants of ancestors who fought one another during the Crusades.

So true

Alexia and Annis first met on one of the many busy days in Molyvos. Annis had stopped to yell at a group of young volunteers who were taking pictures of refugees in the middle of the road as cars were trying to pass by. Alexia pulled over and took Annis's side, then offered one of the Afghan families a ride, something the locals were prevented from doing—told by the authorities that they'd be aiding in human trafficking if they helped. They were threatened with fines and jail time.

"How are things going?" Alexia asked, ripping open a packet of brown sugar and pouring it into her cappuccino. "Any better?"

"Eh." Annis took another puff and blew it toward the sky. She watched as Alexia clanked her spoon in the mug. "It's crazy out here. Every day I am like this." She stuck her hand out stiffly, exposing the protruding veins on the inside of her wrist.

"Tense?"

"Yes, tense!" She threw her hands up.

"The refugees?" Alexia asked.

"I do not have problem with the refugees." She tapped her cigarette into a clear glass tray, letting the ashes scatter. "It is the organizations and their workers. Most are too much arrogant to the locals. This is not good. If you do not respect the people in the place which you are visiting, how do you expect them to respect you? My problem, at least"—she gently hit her chest and shook her head—"is not with the refugees."

Many of the Greeks living on the island knew the pain of exodus better than most of their countrymen. They'd seen these tortured eyes before on the pained faces of their own loved ones. Their parents and grandparents had taken similar journeys after the population exchanges in the 1920s, when Anatolian Greeks were forced to leave Turkey and Muslim Greeks were pushed out of Greece—what is often referred to as the Asia Minor Catastrophe. Both sides suffered indignities and losses as they were involuntarily ripped from their homes and often violently chased out.

"Their fates are not so far from those of our parents," said Annis. "How can I hate them when I know my father and mother lived through the same pain?"

But it was difficult, no less.

Clothes still salty from the sea hung on community buildings, left to dry. There weren't enough facilities, including bathrooms, to handle the extra thousands who came every day. Men and boys could sometimes be seen abashedly trying to find any dark corner to relieve themselves in, feeling indignity and shame during the most human of actions.

Many of the locals had directed their anger about the upheaval toward the volunteers. It was easier than targeting the helpless refugees.

"These people," Annis sniped as she pointed to the foreign workers cackling while having lunch at a restaurant nearby. "Why they are really here? I tell you why, it's a money game. A big black game." She took a puff of her cigarette and stared into Alexia's eyes. Alexia knew she was referring to the town gossip that some of the nongovernmental organizations were profiting off the refugee crisis. "Some of you are good, don't misunderstand. But look around. These organizations make millions in donations but don't do much anything. Then they bring kids who too busy taking selfies with refugees behind them than to help them or us. This is war tourism!" She pushed her dark black hair out of her eyes. "And if they are really volunteer, how they afford to be here? Who pay for this? Money game!"

Alexia did not dare argue, even though she didn't necessarily agree. She was just grateful to get a perspective that only someone rooted here could share. The people from Lesvos had all witnessed their sleepy tourist island go from a virtually unknown dot on a map to the focus of TV screens and front pages throughout the world, in hundreds of different languages. That, on top of all the refugees arriving and the volunteers crowding onto the island, could not have been easy.

"Then they try to tell us we are not doing enough," Annis huffed, tilting her head to the side. "They are here to teach us?

We've been helping refugees for years. Decades!" She pointed her cigarette toward Alexia. "And we do it without posting our pictures on Facebook."

Alexia took a sip of her cappuccino. She knew this was one of the moments in life when it was better to listen than to talk. *They do give you 2 ears vs. 1 mouth*

"We were once famous for Lesbians." Annis coughed a smoke-filled laugh, referencing the story that the word "lesbian" stems from Lesvos.

It was Alexia's friend Stephanie's favorite story to share with new volunteers: "This island was the home of an ancient Greek female poet named Sappho, who wrote love poems about women. If you notice, the Greek letter for *v* looks like a *b*. So technically, we are surrounded by Lesbians. And I'm a double Lesbian here," she'd say, beaming. *That's a weird history*

"But now it is because these poor people keep dying. I miss the Lesbian reputation—it was less sad." Annis smiled ruefully and tapped out more ashes. "It's tough for them."

Alexia had seen firsthand the warmth that Annis and her neighbors held in their hearts. They had borne witness to the tragedy day after day, year after year. A righteous soul is not able to ignore the suffering it witnesses before its eyes, particularly on this scale.

Some families offered up rooms despite the threats from the government and xenophobic neighbors, sharing their meals, blankets and bathrooms. Local fishermen continued to go out every morning, but hardly to fish anymore. Instead, they searched for boats and tried to save lives. When they did fish, it was often *It's bad for overpopulation and the economy (possibly)*

Terrible True Abadym

to pull dead bodies from the water, images that would replay in their dreams until their own dying breath.

"My friend said he took his boat out last week. He see a dead baby floating in the water." Annis gesticulated, her hand moving as if it were floating on the sea. "He tried hard to retrieve it. But he could not; it get too far. When he looked up, he saw many bobbing before him, all dead." Annis cut her hands in the air. "They look like sleeping dolls, he said. His eyes were—like—empty. I know this is all he sees now."

"That's terrible."

"Yes, but you know, too, this is every day," Annis said, her face masked in defeat. "The stress on the heart and mind cannot handle being spectator, not when the suffering is literally washing up on our front yard. You are not human if you don't want to help."

"Well, now more people are paying attention," said Alexia. "It's finally making the news. Maybe that's why you are seeing so many more people. They want to be a drop in the bucket in the hope that, with enough drops, we can fill the pail with compassion." She knew she sounded naive but hoped she was right.

Alexia heard stories about people of all ages who wanted to help. Donations from young children oceans away sacrificing their new Lego set to help a refugee child. Or an old couple who gave up their vacation to the Caribbean to purchase tickets to Greece so they could make thousands of cheese sandwiches for the famished arrivals. And the doctor who used her vacation time wrapping patients in fluorescent space blankets to prevent hypothermia. *There are still so many kind hearted people while others watch*

"You are a sweet girl." Annis smiled at Alexia. "And I agree, most people's intentions are pure. But, my darling, please keep your eyes open. When I said 'black game' before, I mean it. Where there is suffering, there are people who want to exploit it. In ways that have nothing to do with humanity and everything to do with money. There are dark souls out there. Be very careful."

There are also these people who deserve worse

CHAPTER 16

Later that day, at the back of Saint Panteleimon cemetery, over-
looking Mytilini, Alexia's heart dropped to her stomach. She
scanned the plain dirt mounds with small white markers sitting
atop them. The graves of refugees who died trying to make it to
Greece, to Europe, to a better life. Sad but strong piece of writing

"They tell themselves it's better to die trying to come here
than to live where they came from." The caretaker spoke English
with a strong Greek accent as he walked up to Alexia. "And
that's what is happening too much now." The old man's skin
was soft, his face gentle. The thinning hair on his head was a
bright white, like freshly fallen snowflakes.

"What is that word? I see it a lot," she said, and pointed to
the writing squiggled by a black permanent marker onto a flat
white stone.

"*Ágnostos,*" he said without looking back up. "This means
'unknown.' And this one is 'unknown baby.'" He walked over
to the round bulge next to the small dirt bump. "This one is a
mother who died with her two babies," he continued, "and this is a

ten-month-old—he died when his mother could not save him. The water was too rough and she could not swim. Her husband was already in Germany, she take trip alone with their two children to meet him." He pointed to the small pile again. "She had to leave him behind here." The wrinkles around his eyes creased as he let out an exhausted sigh. "But her eyes were dead too. Believe me."

"I don't understand how this can keep happening." Alexia allowed a tear to escape.

"We ask ourselves that every time." The man pulled a tissue from his front pocket and offered it to Alexia. "It's easier when the whole family is together." He pointed to five graves side by side. "It hurts the heart this much less." He pinched his thumb and finger together and nodded, as if to convince himself. An obvious coping mechanism that Alexia could only imagine was necessary with his job.

"Is this part of the cemetery new?" Alexia asked, glancing past the mounds to the greener and grander section up front. The area that held gray-and-white marble tombs, family graves of the villagers, which were topped with flowers, religious icons and burning candles—tokens of remembrance and love.

"No, no. People dying in this sea for decades. Many Afghans buried here. For more than ten years they coming. The Syrians are more new. But it is multiplying. We are running out of room." He put his arm out, showcasing the cramped land.

"What will happen then?" Alexia asked.

"I don't know." He lifted his shoulders. "But we will need to figure out soon." He looked at her curiously but kindly. "So you are here just to look?"

"No, I . . ." Alexia started. "A body. I mean, a person." She stopped to take a breath. "I wanted to be here for one of the people who died, because he didn't have family. He was a teenage boy traveling alone. I spoke to a group who said they would hold a funeral for him this morning."

"Yes, local charity holds a ceremony for every migrant. They bring flowers and give respect." He pointed to a grave with fresh flowers on it. "But I am afraid you have missed them today."

"Dammit," Alexia blurted as tears raced down her face.

"You are here," he said to her, with kind eyes, lifting her hand that held the tissue. "You treat him with respect, this is good thing." He patted her on the back and walked away.

She still showed her respects

Alexia paid her respects to the teenage Afghan boy whose body had washed up on their beach yesterday. His passport was found in his jacket pocket, revealing his beaming eyes and age. Seventeen years old. It made her think of what she was doing the autumn she turned that age—in her last year of high school, playing for the field hockey team and having Frappuccinos at the outdoor mall. *How can a life end up so different, just because of where your mother gives birth?* she wondered.

Those invisible lines

Alexia walked through the plots, holding back tears as best she could. There were Christians, Yazidis and Muslims, babies and grandparents, individuals and families. One section held three generations—a grandmother, her daughter, her daughter's husband and their three children.

Looking around, she was reminded of something Annis had said to her: "I'm disappointed in the ten people in the world who has the control of the planet. They need to help fix this. But where are these leaders of the world? I feel helpless, unable to fix anything."

Alexia felt the same.

Invisible lines (what I said)

She left the cemetery, using the car some of the volunteers shared. As she was pulling up near the access point that led to the beach, she passed a man holding a long-range camera standing on top of the ridge, overlooking the water. It wasn't unusual to see people with cameras, especially with the onslaught of media that had flooded the island, but most of the journalists preferred to be by the water, and often in it, for that perfect shot.

They are capturing it for money (jobs)

She parked her car on the edge of the rocks before trekking down to the shore. Kicking up sand and pebbles along the path, she made it to her team, and sure enough, a group of photographers and reporters were knee-deep in the water as a dinghy pulled in. Alexia looked up, peering at the dark-haired man with the messy stubble as he snapped from afar. *Odd,* she thought. But she let the observation pass as she ran to the water, lending a hand.

The raft made it in smoothly, but there was panic on board as the passengers helped push a woman forward. There was a man behind her holding her weight, preventing her from falling back. As they stumbled through, her protruding pregnant belly became visible. It pushed her flowery cotton dress forward. Her face was creased with pain as she let out heavy breaths.

"My wife," the man yelled. "She is in labor. Please help!" The medics raced to retrieve the woman from her husband and phoned in for assistance.

"This baby is coming now," one of the doctors said, trying to stay calm. "We need volunteers to grab some blankets and form a barrier around her to give her privacy." Alexia immediately went to grab the donated gray wool blankets and ran them over. Several volunteers grabbed one each, lifting them up to box her in.

The pregnant Syrian began releasing bloodcurdling screams.

"Don't worry." A middle-aged woman next to Alexia grinned after witnessing the young American woman's bulging eyes. "That's childbirth."

"She was in labor before we left," the husband frantically explained to one of the medics. There was a seven-year-old boy attached to his leg. "We told them we couldn't go, but the smuggler pulled out a gun and stuck it on her forehead." He pointed two fingers to his own forehead, imitating the experience, just to make sure they understood what he was saying. "He said she must go or we will miss our chance and not get our money back. We had no choice. Please help her."

Another roar was heard from behind the blankets, followed by a high-pitched gurgling wail.

"It's a girl," the female doctor shouted out through laughter. "It's a girl!"

The husband fell to his knees, hugging his son. *"Alhamdulillah!"* the man thanked God while kissing his older child. The whole group joined his cheers.

"Mabrook!" people sang out, congratulating him.

"Shukran!" he thanked them all, joyfully crying. "Can I see my wife and baby?" he begged the doctor through the wool wall.

"Of course, come on in, Daddy!" the doctor hollered.

Alexia's heart lifted, and her cheeks were in pain. The good kind of pain. The one that came from smiling so much for so long. She was again amazed at how this place and these people could teeter-totter her emotions in a way that nowhere and no one else had.

An ambulance finally arrived, escorting the new family of four to a more proper facility to recuperate. And the beach calmed to its normal chaos; people went back to passing out sandwiches, bottles of water and dry clothes.

Alexia then caught another glimpse of the man on the hill.

"Is he with you guys?" she asked, after walking over to the group of journalists. The four men and one woman were now busy uploading their photos and footage on their computers and setting up their BGANs, which they best explained to her as mini-satellites.

The group gave the man a quick glance. "Nope," responded Danny, the American photojournalist. "We pretty much know most of the photogs here, and I've never seen that guy in my life."

"Huh." Alexia crossed her arms. "Okay, thanks."

"Maybe he's a volunteer," the German woman added. "There are so many now."

"Yeah, maybe," Alexia agreed.

Alexia turned her attention back to the mystery man. She watched as he picked his camera back up and started taking snaps of a group of kids playing in the water, still celebrating a safe arrival. An uneasy feeling twisted in her chest, so she finally decided to head over and talk to him.

Driving rocks down with her heels, she climbed up the hill. "Hello," she said, trying to get his attention. But he continued to snap. "Hey there!" She waved her arms. The man eventually brought the camera down to his chest. A sinister scowl painted his face as he glared at Alexia, unabashed and callous, sending an unexpected shivering chill down her spine. "Excuse me!" She continued to walk toward him anyway; she felt protected by the daylight and the crowd below. As she got closer, he spat on the ground before turning his back and setting off. Alexia picked up the pace, but by the time she made it to the top of the ridge, she could only watch as he rushed into the passenger's seat of a taxi.

The yellow car's tires skidded on the gravel, screeching loudly before it sped off, creating a cloud of dust in its wake.

PART III

CHAPTER 17

Tareq packed his backpack and took the nine-hour overnight bus trip from Istanbul to the coastal city of Izmir. His father and sister had a longer, sixteen-hour journey from Gaziantep in southeastern Turkey.

The pain of leaving Musa lifted the second Tareq held his little sister and hugged his father. It had been nearly five months since they had seen each other last. For just one morning they'd decided to forget how scarce money was and splurged on a meal of juicy beef *kofta* and fluffy rice. *They always know now to celebrate*

"*Ayuni.*" Fayed kissed his son's head as they sat at the table with the hot meat steaming in front of them. "I missed you so much! You look thin." His eyes began to tear.

"So do you, Baba." Tareq gave him another embrace while spooning more rice onto his father's plate.

"Farrah and I want Coca-Cola," Susan chimed in, squeezing her doll. "Can we have Coca-Cola?" She pushed her *ayran* yogurt drink to the side. *Still with the doll*

"Yes, *albi.*" Fayed beamed at his daughter and then his

son, grateful they were together. The salt-and-pepper stubble on his face was a new feature, obtained since arriving in Turkey. Tareq's father used to take pride in his dark hair—he would joke that he would live a longer life because of it. A joke he still regrets ever sharing with his wife.

Tareq could see just how much his father had aged, but he didn't realize that he, too, had gray hairs, which pained his father when he spotted them on his teenage son's head.

Already? Why? [handwritten margin note]

When they finished their early lunch, father and son fought over the bill, disregarding the fact that their money came from the same pool of cash.

As they walked around Basmane, a short distance from the coast, Tareq was surprised to see that the area was filled with Syrians. He noticed every other conversation he heard was in Arabic. There were even signs written in Arabic draping the outside of shops with the words *We sell life jackets here.*

The signs seemed redundant to Tareq, since the bright orange vests were blinding enough to the naked eye. In this bustling city, the smuggling trade was out in the open. Human traffickers roamed the streets looking for clients, offering rides to Greece. Some Syrians talked to each other, sharing their stories. Others slept on backpacks wherever they could find a spot—packs filled with all that was left from a life they had left behind.

They'll do it for the money [handwritten margin note]

Tareq quickly learned that anyone carrying a filled black trash bag had life jackets for their journey across the Aegean Sea.

"*Merhaba,*" Fayed said, approaching a man sitting with his family, hugging their rucksacks and leaning on a big black garbage bag.

"*Merhaba*," the older man responded, eyeing him suspiciously. Another soul hardened by the journey.

"I'm sorry to bother you, but my family and I"—Fayed pointed to his children—"are looking for a way to get to Greece, and I was wondering if you knew of a trustworthy person to talk to."

"Hah!" the man grunted. "If you want someone trustworthy, you will die here of old age. They are all thieves with no compassion." *It's the open market*

"I ask," Fayed continued, ignoring the man's gruffness, "because I see that you are prepared to go on the journey." He pointed at the trash bag.

The man peered back to what Fayed was pointing at. "Yes, we've been ready for six days and we are still waiting for our smuggler to call us." He lifted up his black smartphone.

"Do you—" Fayed began again before being cut off.

"Look, I can't help you. I don't recommend our guy. But we are stuck because we've already given him money. All you have to do is walk around; you will find dozens of our own working for these beasts." He turned his head away, shifting his attention to his wife and young children. The kids were fast asleep on both sides of their slouched mother—a woman who was both physically and mentally exhausted from what life had lobbed at her.

"*Yallah*," Fayed said to his children, knowing that there was no more to discuss with that man. They walked across the hectic street, as a soundtrack of car horns and screeching tires filled the air, to what looked like a park jam-packed with people. "I'm sure we can find someone there to help us."

They wandered into Basmane Square, unofficially known as Smuggler's Square.

The next family they approached also brushed them off. That's when Fayed spotted a young man and woman sitting on top of a red-checkered wool blanket in the shadow of an evergreen.

"Merhaba," he began again.

"Merhaba," both the man and woman pleasantly responded.

"My children and I are looking for someone to help us. We want to go to Greece and we just arrived here." The young woman was wearing jeans and an oversized wool sweater. She cracked a gentle smile at Tareq and Susan, who both stared at her like the lost, scared children they were.

"Our guy is coming here to meet us shortly. If you wait, you can talk to him," the young man said, rolling up the sleeves on his flannel shirt. "We've dealt with a lot of terrible folks here. We're not sure if he'll be any better, but a friend who has already made it to Greece recommended him. And we've decided to stick with him before we lose more money in this place."

"Really? Thank you so much, that will be very helpful!" Fayed smiled at the two, relieved to finally take the next step on their journey.

"Of course. We have to help each other," the young man graciously added. "I'm Ammar, and this is Rania."

"Nice to meet you. I am Fayed, and this is Tareq and Susan."

"Pleasure." He nodded to all three.

"Would you like a cup of coffee?" asked Rania. "It's not like the ones you find in the Turkish shops. I'm calling it Syrian coffee now." She winked before she pulled out a plastic thermos and paper cups, beginning to pour without even waiting for their response. "I've mixed in more cardamom. Tastes more like the coffee back home."

"That is so kind, *yislamu*." Fayed took the cup Rania handed up and passed it to Tareq.

The couple unfolded their blanket to make more room for the new family. They passed the time chatting about Syria and the conflict as they waited. Ammar and Rania said they were from Damascus and recently married. Although their neighborhood hadn't gone through the same destruction seen in other Syrian cities, they feared that the time would come soon and then it would be too late for them to leave. Both Fayed and Tareq dreaded the inevitable question, but it came anyway. "What made you decide to finally leave?"

"There was no more flavor to life there," Fayed replied. Both Tareq and his father looked down, not wanting to say more, afraid of the emotions that always followed.

"They killed Mama, Teyta, Farrah, Sameer and Ameer," Susan piped up, counting the names on her fingers. "We never found Salim, but they say he is dead too." She looked at everyone, confused as to why they were suddenly quiet. "This is Farrah." She showed Rania her doll. "She has the same name as my sister. I miss her." She brought the ragged toy in for a hug.

"*Habibti*," Rania said as her eyes began to tear. "I'm sure you do."

Tareq pretended to look at the crowds, hoping to hide the tears swelling in his own eyes.

"I think I see him," Ammar said, breaking the sad silence.

He probably shows empathy too

"That's Abu Laith. The man we've been talking to. He's a Syrian himself."

"*Merhaba!*" A man wearing tight jeans and a white T-shirt came walking toward them. He pulled up his designer sunglasses, resting them on his coifed hair. He was one of the many men who benefited financially from the current crisis. "Good news . . ." He trailed off when he realized new faces were with the couple. "*Merhaba,*" he greeted Fayed.

"These are our new friends, and they need help with their trip too. You can speak freely in front of them," Ammar said, eager to hear more about the good news.

Abu Laith nodded at the three before turning back to Ammar. "We can get you on a boat tonight. Keep your phone on you. I will give you a call and tell you where to meet the car that will take you to the boat."

Ammar and Rania hugged each other, unable to contain their excitement and relief. But the unease of not knowing when they would leave was swiftly replaced with the fear of what the coming trip held, angst they shared with a glance.

Smugglers are hard to trust

"There may be another boat leaving tonight as well." Abu Laith turned his attention toward Fayed, Tareq and Susan. "You can trust me. I promise I will get you to Greece safely. I've done this many times. And I work fast—as you can see with them." He pointed to Ammar and Rania. "Unlike the others who say they will get you on a boat, I care," he added unconvincingly, bringing a hand to his heart. "*Wallahi.*" He pulled out his smartphone. "Look," he said, flipping through the phone before showing the screen to Fayed. It was a video of a rubber boat and a leaner and tanner version of the man in front of them, smiling to the camera as he waved off the passengers.

"What is that?" asked Tareq.

"That's a boat leaving with happy customers to Europe," Abu Laith responded, visibly annoyed. "Look, we are hearing rumors that both the European countries and Turkey will be cracking down on refugees trying to leave. It's in your best interest to leave sooner rather than later. Unless you want to be stuck in Turkey."

For family!

"We want to go," Fayed said desperately. He didn't want his children stuck in Turkey. He wanted them to have hope, and at the moment, that only seemed to be in the stability of Europe's boundaries, where there were no bombs being dropped or people taken hostage in their own cities. He knew Turkey was no longer safe and would get increasingly worse. And he refused to wait until it was too late, not again. "But we want to make sure we are together. We've heard stories of families being separated."

"I can make that happen. And I gave these two a great deal." Abu Laith nodded again to the young couple, who were now holding hands, full of a newfound energy. "Just one thousand, two hundred American dollars per person for the rubber boat. And since she is a child, we will charge just half the price."

"We don't have that much money." Fayed choked on his own words. "We were told that children could ride free."

Abu Laith laughed. "Maybe that is what some people promise, but that is usually the people who are either scamming you or don't care about your safety. They will cram too many people on a boat and won't care if they drown. I care." He brought his hands to his chest again, making it evident that that was part of his sales technique.

"I understand," Fayed said. He felt deflated. This was yet another moment when he felt like he had failed as a father. He looked over to his now gaunt children and felt crushed. "But we really don't have the money." He couldn't meet Tareq's eyes, overcome with the shame of not being able to find more work in the past months and the failure of not providing what his family needed.

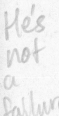

He's not a failure

"Well, how much do you have?" Abu Laith's callous, greedy eyes glowed. "Maybe one of you can go now and send for the rest later. You have a better chance if you send him to Sweden," he said, pointing a finger at Tareq. "And once he makes it, he can apply for asylum and send for the rest of you later. That's what a lot of people are doing. Just make sure you tell them you're sixteen or younger. It'll give you enough time to pass their requirements. They'll give him a host family, he will be fine."

still greedy

"We can afford that." Fayed looked at his son with desperation. The dark circles around his eyes appeared more profound than even a moment before.

Abu Laith's rapacious eyes lit up.

"No, Baba!" Tareq argued. His father put a hand up to silence him.

"But only if both my son and daughter can go together for the twelve hundred," Fayed negotiated.

"No, impossible," Abu Laith said, not budging. "Six hundred more for her."

"But I am telling you," Fayed begged, "we don't have any more. Can you at least call your employer to ask? They are both children—their weight together doesn't even match that of a grown man."

"He's not a child." Abu Laith looked at Tareq.

"He's my child," Fayed pleaded. "Please, just ask."

Abu Laith took a moment before picking up his phone and walking away. Far enough not to be overheard.

"Baba, we can't leave you," Tareq said. "I won't go."

"Rania, my dear, do you mind showing Susan the park?" Fayed asked, turning away from his son. She graciously obliged, taking Susan by the hand.

Ammar smiled weakly at the father and son before walking away to smoke a cigarette. He knew that it was his cue to leave as well.

Fayed waited to make sure they were all far enough away.

"Omri." He turned his attention back to his son. "I know you don't want to leave me. But you won't be leaving me for good. I will save up some money and join you. But what is important right now is that you and Susan get to Europe. This man is right—it will be easier for you and your sister to get started there."

"No!" Tareq raised his voice, something he had never done before toward his father. "I'm sorry, but I can't leave you, not again, not even for a little while." He wouldn't say it out loud, but he wanted to make sure that if they died on the trip, they would all die together. He didn't want to live through more loss.

"You are not leaving me." Fayed stared at his son. His eyes were warm and his heart was full. "You are saving your sister."

"She wants to stay with you too!" he said.

"I know. And God knows I want to stay with you both. But this isn't a place for young Syrian girls." Fayed looked to the distance and watched Susan's curls bounce as her skinny legs, lost in her jeans, ran around the park. "Too many bad things happen to our people here, especially our women and girls. We must protect your sister."

Tareq knew he could no longer argue with his father. He had seen with his own eyes his country's females exploited. He let out one last protest. "But, Baba . . ."

"No more." Fayed held his son's shoulders. "You are her big brother. Your job is to protect her, and my job is to protect you both."

"But who will take care of you?" Tareq asked.

"God," Fayed replied without hesitation. "Don't ever give up on God."

"What has God done but take our family, life and country away from us?" Tareq let his true feelings slip and instantly regretted it, not because he didn't believe it, but because he knew his father would be enraged.

"Stop that!" Fayed was now the one raising his voice. "That wasn't God's doing, that was the devil. The greatest victory the devil has is when you confuse his work with God's."

"I'm sorry, Baba," Tareq muttered.

"I am not the one you should apologize to. Pray for forgiveness and help, every chance you have." Fayed's voice softened. "God has guided you this far and will continue to guide you forward."

Abu Laith walked back toward them, halting their conversation. "Okay, so my boss is being generous because I told him you are good people. They won't charge the little one. But I need you to come with me to deposit the money now." He stuck his phone back in his pocket and looked around. "You too, Ammar!"

"Okay." Fayed looked at his son. "Watch your sister. I'll be back shortly."

"You guys are very lucky." Abu Laith peered at Tareq.

"No one forced to flee their home is ever lucky," Tareq said, under his breath, as he watched the three of them walk away.

"Oh, come on, give him a break." Salim's vision reappeared.

"Why should I do that? He is scum. He's separating our family." Tareq was grateful to see his little brother again.

"He's just trying to feed his family too." Salim looked around. "Wow, so these are all Syrians?" So empathy

"Not all," Tareq said. "There are others as well." He looked at his brother, wearing the same clothes from the last day he saw him. "Am I going crazy? Is this why I can see you?"

"You've always been crazy." Salim smirked.

"I guess so," Tareq said. He didn't mind becoming unhinged as long as it provided more visions of those he lost. He turned his head to the sky and watched a cluster of white seagulls float above. He ached for their wings and freedom. "Look at those birds, so carefree. They don't need passports. They don't have war. They can fly from one place to another without checkpoints, guns or violence. They just need the wind. I want that."

"Be careful, big brother," Salim warned. "You may just get your wish. Angels can do that too."

I like these talks.
Connects with family
and is like his
conscience.

CHAPTER 18

Susan substituted Tareq for her doll. Her little hands wrapped around his neck and her small face lay cradled in the nook under his chin. *Cute*

He could feel her quick warm breaths on his skin, a small relief in the cold dead night.

The van they were traveling in was packed with other refugees. Men, women and children quietly sitting with their isolating fear and regret. A stark contrast to the excitement and noise that packed the hotel lobby where they'd all met, waiting for their rides and their smugglers.

It was in that two-star hotel lobby that Susan had cried loudly, refusing to say goodbye to their father. Fayed stayed strong, as well as he could, reassuring his daughter that they would see each other soon. But the look father and son shared acknowledged the unknown. *It's tough for her*

Tareq nestled his face into Susan's curls, attempting to hide the tears that slowly dripped down his cheeks as he thought of his father. *Already leaving Baba again*

This wasn't how he wanted to do this. In Turkey they were in different cities, but at least they were in the same country. Once he crossed the Greek border, he knew he would be in a different world. He'd already lost so much; he didn't want to lose his father too. *So negative*

Why, God? Why? His mind erupted with the horrible memories from the past six months. After the initial grief poured over him, his blood ran cold. *Why would you do this to us?* The anger was the one thing that turned off the tears.

But then he heard his father's voice:

"The greatest victory the devil has is when you confuse his work with God's."

Good words

"Pray for forgiveness and help, every chance you have."

"God has guided you this far and will continue to guide you forward."

As angry as he was with God, Tareq didn't want to betray his father. So without further hesitation he began reciting his prayers, softly whispering them to Susan so she could hear them too. With each prayer he felt her breath settle.

It was the teen's prayers that set off a chain of quiet worship in the bouncing van—both Muslim and Christian—a soothing distraction from the trepidation and fear. Even the atheist in the group reeled off the prayers he remembered from childhood.

Hours passed, but Tareq didn't know how many. Susan had fallen asleep, and as he scanned the van, he noticed others had too.

One man was still flicking his prayer beads when Tareq caught his eyes. The man nodded and went back to his beads as his wife and baby dozed next to him. For the first time, Tareq noticed he didn't see Ammar or Rania. He wondered if they were sent to another location or if they had decided no longer to take the trip, which people had been known to do.

Tareq leaned his head back, hoping to fall asleep. He knew he needed the energy for the coming boat ride. The trip wouldn't take the twenty minutes Abu Laith had assured them, he was certain of that. "On a clear day, the trip is so fast!" the tenacious smuggler had said—but Tareq had done his research in the months leading up to this day. He'd also heard other Syrians talking in and around Basmane. Many had friends and family who had taken the journey and were told it could take several hours. Some of those people even said they had lost loved ones to the waters, yet they still decided to continue—they said it wasn't a choice, it was about survival.

Right as Tareq's eyes were beginning to get heavy, the car jolted to a stop. Short moments later the back doors flew open and a man whispered sharply, "*Yallah! Yallah!* And stay quiet!"

Tareq didn't let go of his baby sister. Instead, he used all his might to pull himself, Susan and their backpacks up with one jolt. He then grabbed the black garbage bag that contained their vests.

Susan woke up, again petrified. She strengthened her grip around her big brother's neck. As he stepped out, the man who had opened the van door shoved him and told him to find a bush to hide in.

"When it's time to load the boats, we will come get you." He needlessly jostled him again. Tareq decided not to snap or fight back because he didn't have the leverage here. He was helpless.

The misty sea air let Tareq know that they were very close to the water, but his eyes could only see so far in the dark. He saw branches and lifeless trees as he walked down the sandy path strewn with rocks, abandoned clothing, trash and feces. They were not the first and would not be the last to use this beach as their point of embarkation. The refugee trail is always lined with the haggard, bloody footsteps of those who came before. The brush they were standing in has felt many feet and heard many languages. It has also been the spot where many soulless bodies have washed ashore.

As Tareq's eyes adjusted to the darkness, he noticed that the grove was filled with people. He walked slowly, afraid of tripping over fallen branches, scattered rocks or dispersed families. When he finally found a patch of empty sand, Tareq dropped the bag and attempted to put Susan down slowly. But she wouldn't budge.

"*Ayuni*, it's okay," he assured her.

"It's dirty," she whispered.

"I will fix it," Tareq promised her. "Just let me put you down."

He gently placed her on the ground, slowly peeling her hands off his neck. He then pulled out their life jackets and flattened the trash bag they were stored in before placing it on the ground.

"See, like the blanket by the tree." He kissed her cheek before sitting down. She tucked in next to him.

"I'm scared," she said. Her blue eyes looked gray with the night sky above.

"Don't be, *hayati*. I will protect you," Tareq said, convincing her but not himself. He began running his shaky hand through his sister's soft curls.

The fear that continued to build inside made him dream up horrible scenarios, all ending with his sister lying dead on the beach like the little Syrian-Kurdish boy he saw a picture of not too long ago. For all Tareq knew, it could have been at this exact beach.

Three-year-old Alan Kurdi was taking this same route with his parents and five-year-old brother when their boat capsized. The boys' father tried saving them but could only grab one of the boys. Thinking he'd saved one son, he left him floating so he could swim to the other, only to find him dead. When he swam back, he couldn't find the one he left behind. He lost his whole family, all on a dream to give them a better life. The sole survivor of a family stolen by the waters.

Newspapers and TV stations ran the picture of Alan wearing a red T-shirt and blue shorts, lying dead on the beach, looking as though he were napping and dreaming, like little boys all over the world do. Hearts broke collectively around the globe. Discussions gained steam on how to help these refugees so they wouldn't have to risk their lives or their children's lives for a warless future. It seemed that, for a moment, people cared about the plight of the refugee. But it was fleeting. Since that day, thousands more children, women and men have died for the same reason without making it into the papers or on television screens. And now Tareq feared that he or Susan would be another tally mark added to that statistic. Another dead refugee that people would turn their backs on because it's just too depressing to click on the link and read their story.

Susan finally fell back asleep, using her backpack as a pillow. Tareq refused to let himself compare her peaceful slumber to the images of little Alan, his eyes closed on the sand.

The cold sea breeze had Tareq's nose running. He used his sleeve to wipe it before picking up his life vest and placing it on Susan's curled-up body, an attempt to protect her from the lowering temperature.

It didn't take long for more people to find their spot and squeeze in near them. To distract himself from his thoughts, Tareq listened to the whispered conversations around him.

There was a mother trying to feed her children snacks—what he couldn't hear were the empty growls in her own stomach. He heard a father scolding his sons for squabbling—but his mind was punishing him with thoughts of blame for bringing them there. And all around, Tareq caught words of reassurance from adults to their kids that everything would be fine and that a better life awaited them with new toys, schools and friends, when really they were trying to convince themselves of the same.

He could also hear the lies that were said with love. They were words meant to comfort by gentle deceit. "It's just going to be a very short trip. Then everything will be easy. *Wallahi!*" Using the same words that the traffickers from Izmir used on them, but this time with tender rationale.

He fell asleep with Susan in possession

No matter his efforts, Tareq's mind raced, making it hard for him to fall asleep. He stared at the black sky, salted with specks of blurry bright stars, and made wishes on the shiniest one he could find. He concentrated on the sounds of the crashing waves as he huffed his warm breath into the chilly thick air. It was a game he used to play as a child. He'd slowly exhale and watch as small clouds would form, then float away. The goal was to help build a real cloud, letting the condensation from his mouth soar to the sky. The distraction worked, but not long enough, as the morbid images of death kept assaulting his thoughts. Corpses floating on blue water—including his own. But eventually his body and mind gave in, no longer able to handle his morose imagination. *foreshadowing?*

This stress could bring down even the strongest of humans; a weakened teenager stood little chance.

He held his sister's hand and finally dozed off.

When Tareq woke up, he knew he hadn't slept very long, but it felt like his body had recuperated. His hands were no longer trembling and his head was less dizzy. The blurry stars he had wished on earlier looked sharper.

It helped that he didn't dream.

He heard more voices around him, new voices.

There were two young females—one around his age, the other slightly older—on the left side of them now. They had arrived while Tareq was sleeping.

For the girls, Tareq, Susan and the family on the other

end of the brush were safe. After searching for a place to hide, they deemed this spot the most secure for two girls traveling alone. *Worse for them*

In your world, the burden of softness and vulnerability is an extra weight a segment of the population carries. The daily decisions of where to stand and walk are always a gamble, much more so for a female than for a male.

Tareq tried to listen to what the sisters were talking about, but he couldn't recognize the language. It wasn't Arabic or Turkish. He knew there were many different nationalities that were making this journey. But he hadn't yet spoken to anyone other than Syrians, Iraqis and Turks.

The girl in the yellow headscarf noticed Tareq looking at them. She lifted the small bag she was holding toward him, offering some dried fruit.

As much as he wanted to be polite and decline, he was starving. And the snacks they brought were in Susan's backpack, her current pillow.

"Thank you," Tareq said, trying to remember his rusty English. He pulled out one dried apricot.

"You can have more." The girl shook the bag.

"I am sorry," he said as he took another one out. "We bring food, but my sister sleeping on bag holdings it."

The girls smiled. Partly at Susan, but mostly from the relief that they felt that Tareq was not a threat, unlike the many men they'd met along their journey.

"Where you are from?" Tareq asked.

"We are from Afghanistan," the girl in the gray

headscarf responded. "We are sisters. I am Najiba, and this is Jamila."

"Nice meeting you. I am Tareq, and this sleeping girl is Susan," he said, suddenly very self-conscious about his English. He took courses in school, but he learned more of the language from movies and TV shows.

Najiba and Jamila smiled as they watched Susan sleep. Her little mouth was open as she took in deep breaths, looking like an angel.

"From Syria." Tareq patted his chest. "We escape war. You too?"

"Yes," replied Najiba. "Afghanistan, also not so safe and is very difficult for women and girls. So we leave for Germany to find our *khala*—uh . . . aunt. Sorry."

"Yes, you have Taliban," Tareq said. He didn't know much about Afghanistan but what he had seen on news programs. And it always involved Taliban, the all-covering blue burkas and international forces.

"Yes, and you have Daesh," Jamila responded. Her eyes didn't mask her annoyance. She was fed up with the world associating Afghanistan only with the Taliban. She hated that group and didn't want them to own her country's image.

"Yes, we do. And many more bad people, including government." Tareq was confused by why she was agitated.

Najiba tried to cut the tension. "We hear Syria was very beautiful before wartime."

"It was." Tareq gazed down. "It was too much beautiful, very different now."

"Afghanistan is still beautiful," Jamila said. "But because we are women, we have no freedom." She peeked down at Susan. "Are you two alone?"

"Yes, first we will go to Europe and then our father will come." Tareq's hand quivered again as he took a bite of his apricot.

"What about your mother?" Jamila asked.

Tareq shook his head. "She is dead." The words felt like razors in his mouth. He hated saying them out loud. And rarely did. It felt even more corrosive to his tongue in another language.

"From the war?" Jamila asked.

Tareq nodded.

"I'm so sorry." She put her head down, feeling shame for how she responded to him before. She didn't expect a stranger from another land to understand her pain.

"Many people have died in Syria. But you know, many people have died in Afghanistan too." Tareq took another bite to distract from his emotions.

The girls nodded and avoided each other's eyes as they thought of their own parents.

"There is never a day when people don't die from war in Afghanistan," Najiba said, feeling the pangs of their loss. "It's been almost forty years of dying. Everyone say it will get better, but it never get better. All we know is life of war."

"For Syria, this is new. Our lives were very good," Tareq told them. "We went to school, played outside, went to park. On Friday our parents always take us somewhere to spend time as family and have fun. No danger."

"Lovely," Najiba said, glancing at her sister.

"In Afghanistan you must have the same, yes?" Tareq asked. He couldn't believe that any country could have a nonstop war for forty years.

"No." Jamila looked at him blankly. "We were born refugees in Pakistan. Our parents went as refugees there when they were children. When the US came to Afghanistan, we went back. We thought things will be better. But they were not. It's still very dangerous. Still bombs. Still bad gangs—some Taliban, some government, now even Daesh."

"I am sorry," Tareq said.

"It is life," Jamila said, shrugging. She didn't want to share their story. Her best defense against weakness was to not think or talk about the past. "We were just born in unlucky circumstances. It is our destiny to be like this."

"It is not our destiny anymore." Najiba put a hand on her younger sister's shoulder. "We are making a better future. It's what our mother and father would want."

Jamila shot her eyes away from her sister as she shrugged her palm off. "Or our destiny is to die in cold water."

"Stop that!" Najiba scolded her sister. *"Bas!"*

"We can't deny that is possible." Jamila glared at her. She then looked up at Tareq, who saw not defiance but a scared girl looking for reassurance. It reminded him of how Susan sometimes looked at him.

"It will be okay," he said, unblinking. "Hundreds of thousands people have made it safe. We will all be fine."

"We cannot swim," she muttered.

"I can. If, God forbid, something should happen, I help."

"We won't be on same boat. Afghans and Arabs on different boats."

"Stop looking for reasons to make yourself sad. And now you will upset him." Najiba shoved her sister. "This is why we bought life jackets. How hard is it to kick our feet to land?"

"But . . ." Jamila tried to continue before Najiba cut her off, speaking in Dari. Tareq tried to see if he could pick out any words, but he couldn't; they were talking too fast. He could just tell that they were squabbling like teenage sisters did in Syria, and in Turkey, and probably all over the world.

"Okay, we will now try and get some rest," Najiba said to Tareq. "We are sorry if we upset you."

"I am not upset." Tareq smiled. For the first time since the *koftas* and rice with his father and sister, he felt a happiness that wasn't forced.

But it was short-lived.

Did they foreshadow something bad in the waters to come?

CHAPTER 19

As the sun began to rise, lighting up the landscape, the coastline of the Aegean Sea was visible through the shrubbery.

The water glistened, soft, tranquil and yet dazzling–summoning the desperate like a siren song calling for Odysseus (a man I crossed paths with years ago). *What great description*

The hills and mountains of Greece held the dreams of a warless Europe in plain sight, now that the veil of the night sky had been lifted. Tareq could see a bright future for his sister past these waters, something he didn't believe he could give her here or at home. *Sad to believe but true*

It was hard for Tareq to imagine that thousands of people had died trying to cross the stretch of water in front of him. His eyes focused on the terrain past the blue expanse, a place that looked like freedom. But he knew all too well from the images–bodies washing up on this exact shoreline–that the land could just as easily hold destruction.

Tareq envisioned his brother Salim sitting next to him, feeling his brother's excited energy.

"You weren't in my dream last night."

"You missed me?" Salim's image smiled.

"Of course I did." Tareq's heart sank. "I always do."

"Good." He grinned at his older brother. "I took the night off to rest. We have a big day today."

"Yes, we do."

"I will race you there." He ran toward the sea, yelling back, "You get on the boat and take care of Susan, and I will swim!"

Tareq wanted to run after him, but his heart quickly dropped as Salim vanished into the sea's mist.

I live these moments with his brother

A motor buzzed in the distance, too burly to be from a boat or a car.

Tareq picked himself up. Slapping the dirt off his hands, he watched a tractor haul a large, rusty wagon. Lying on the carriage bed were giant cardboard boxes.

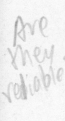

Are they reliable?

"That must be the dinghies," the man next to him said softly. An unlit cigarette hung from his cracked lips, just under his graying mustache. He didn't want his family to hear.

"You mean the inflatable boats?" asked Tareq.

"Eh." The man nodded as he pulled out a lighter and sparked his cigarette. He took a deep drag before offering it to Tareq.

"Lah, shukran," Tareq declined, realizing that with this simple offer he was, for the first time, considered a man in the eyes of those around him.

"There should be more boats on that truck." He shook his

head. Both men glanced at the dozens of people around them. "We really are on a journey of death."

That's reassuring

The words stung as Tareq looked at his little sister, still asleep.

"Crazy." The man blew a cloud of smoke toward the sky. "All of these people." He extended his arms, displaying what was in front of them. "We are all the same. But we are all from different places."

Togetherness - form a bond

Tareq was astonished as he examined the crowd around him. He could tell who was Syrian and who was not by their clothes alone—from the way a hijab was wrapped to the wash of their jeans. But the expression around their eyes connected all the souls in front of him. All wounded, all hopeful, all afraid.

He peeked back at the smugglers, who were finally using their scrawny muscles rather than their forceful tongues. The skinny Syrian and Afghan trafficking operatives dragged the boxes off the truck and pulled out new dinghies.

"Let's hope it's the Russian-made ones," the man said, lifting up three fingers. "I hear the order that you want is Russian"—he pulled down his middle finger—"then Turkish"—he pulled down his index finger, leaving only his thumb—"and you better hope it's not the Chinese-made ones, because then we are, how do they say? Ah yes, screwed." He turned his thumb upside down.

Tareq swallowed hard as he watched the gaunt men start to inflate a dinghy. Another sunburned smuggler dropped a motor next to it. The engine didn't come out of fresh packaging. It looked worn and beaten up.

From past trips

"God help us," said the man next to Tareq.

"Are we going soon?" Susan's voice broke through Tareq's escalating terror.

"I think so, *hayati*." Tareq bent down while eyeing his smoking neighbor, who nodded in understanding. This wasn't for juvenile ears.

He brushed the side of his sister's plump cheek, the only part of her body that hadn't withered in the past months.

"I miss Baba," she whispered through tears.

"I know, so do I." Tareq kissed the top of her head. "But before you know it, he will be with us. Right now I need you to be brave and strong." He caressed her hair. "We are going to go on the boat ride soon. It might make you scared at times, but I promise we'll be fine. I will protect you."

"Like Salim with Farrah?" She looked up. Tareq couldn't believe she remembered how Salim used to protect Farrah from the neighborhood boys. He didn't think Susan was old enough to recall the scolding Salim had received for beating up the boy who scared their sister.

"Yes, just like that." He studied her face tenderly. "I won't let anyone or anything hurt you. Do you trust me?"

Susan bobbed her head. "I'm hungry."

Tareq gave her head another kiss and then grabbed her pack, pulling out some cereal bars and bananas for both of them. He didn't know when they would eat next, but he made sure to stick a cereal bar in each pocket for the boat ride.

"Drink this," he said, grabbing the bottle of water from the bag. He didn't want her to get dehydrated on the trip. "I need you to finish all of it."

The older Afghan sister opened her eyes. She jolted up and glanced at her watch.

"Good morning," Tareq said.

"Good morning," Najiba tugged on her sister's jacket. *"Behdar sho, oh dokhtar."*

Jamila rubbed her eyes before slapping her sister's hand off. She sat up when she saw Susan. "She's so beautiful! *Namekhuda!* May God always protect her!"

"Who are they?" Susan asked her brother in Arabic, tucking her face into his knee.

"They're our new friends. They're really nice," Tareq assured his little sister with a warm rub on the back.

Jamila opened her bag of dried fruit and offered it to the bashful child. Susan eventually stuck her hand in and selected some dried cherries, examining her pickings before smiling up at her new friend.

"Yislamu," Susan thanked Jamila before sticking the tart fruit into her mouth.

The introduction was cut short as people clattered about around them.

"Yallah!" One of the smugglers' voices echoed over the scuttling. "It's time. Put your vests on if you haven't already!"

Another man yelled in Dari, directing his group to do the same.

Jamila stuffed the snacks back into her sack. Both sisters pulled out their life vests with quivering arms. Throughout the trip from Afghanistan through Iran, and then to Turkey, the sisters' energy came from each other. Their eyes steadied on each *theme for mom + Tarea* [handwritten note]

other's as they refueled. When you truly love someone, their life means more to you than your own. When it is difficult to find strength in yourself, it's often more easily found by focusing on the survival of your loved one. The fight to keep them alive holds immeasurable power.

Foreshadowing? [handwritten note]
Odds against them [handwritten note]

Tareq hastily blew up Susan's vest. It was a yellow inflatable meant only as a swimming aid for pools. The warning label stated THIS IS NOT A LIFESAVING DEVICE—WILL NOT PREVENT DROWNING. But the store clerk had promised Tareq that it was better than most of the life jackets being sold, including the ones he would offer him. The Turkish clerk had pulled out an orange vest and said Tareq could purchase an authentic Yamaha vest for $150 or the black-and-red fake one for $20. The clerk told him it was the best of the fakes on the market as he squeezed the vest. "Not stuffed with paper, see? It has foam inside." He guaranteed the vest wouldn't let Tareq drown, a hollow warranty. *If I drown, how do I get my money back?* Tareq wanted to ask the pushy salesman just to hear his response. But he held his tongue in front of his father, who was already tense and afraid.

After buckling Susan up, Tareq slipped into his black-and-red "Yamaxa" vest.

"Good luck," Jamila said to Tareq as she conjured a tiny smile for Susan.

"And you," Tareq reciprocated, noticing her speckled jade eyes for the first time. He wanted to say more, but his breath got caught in his throat as his heart skipped a beat. His body suddenly felt lighter. He wondered if this is what Musa had felt when he met Shayma. If so, he understood maybe a tiny bit more why his cousin wanted to stay in Istanbul.

"Thank you, we meet again in Greece. *Inshallah,*" Najiba said, noticing the spark that was just lit. She whispered something to her sister.

Jamila blushed before shoving her, her rosy cheeks more noticeable next to her bright orange life vest. She turned to Tareq, no longer able to make eye contact. "Goodbye and good luck," she said.

His stomach tingled. Tareq now grasped the term *butterflies in your stomach.* *Something's going on*

The tragic irony was not lost on him. The first time he felt these pangs could be the last. But what he didn't know is that sometimes the most beautiful love happens at the most unforeseen times with the most unexpected people. And those unanticipated moments can provide the flicker of strength, courage and faith to survive against all odds. *Funny how they find love*

Tareq quickly tried to brush the feelings aside; he needed to focus on the journey ahead. Though now he did it with a *in weird* newfound energy. *times*

The two groups, Arab and Afghan, marched their separate ways.

Tareq spotted only the two dinghies with dilapidated motors and more than 100 bodies to fill them.

He held his sister's little hand. "Whatever you do, don't let go of me," he commanded. Susan squeezed his hand back but remained quiet. She wasn't scared. She knew as long as she had her big brother, she was safe. *A great assurance for her*

Tareq followed the man he'd met earlier that morning and his family. They all spent the night next to each other. He felt they were connected now. A sense of familiarity in this uncertain situation. *They all are together (same voice)*

The Arabic-speaking trafficker began to give instructions and orders. His sleeves were rolled up, revealing lanky arms and a scarlet T-shirt tan.

"Women and children will board first!" he hollered. "Do not panic when you are on the boat, that is what causes it to capsize! Stay calm and you will be in Greece fast. You cause a commotion, you put everyone's life in danger."

As he dragged on, Tareq couldn't help but peek over at the mass of Afghans. He watched them boarding. As the boat filled, the panic rose. There were too many of them. Their faces held trepidation and horror. *good word*

There was an old lady with a white scarf currently being pushed into the boat, clearly in tears. The smuggler holding her walking stick threw it toward the beach. The young man with her began to yell at him before putting his hands up and backing away. At that moment howls erupted.

The Syrians could hear the terror coming from their neighbors.

Tareq tried to make out what was in the Turkish smuggler's hand, but the panicked crowd was blocking the object.

He searched for Jamila and Najiba among the group. He finally located Najiba. She had been squashed toward the front of the dinghy, her face red as her bulging eyes searched desperately for her sister.

Tareq couldn't find Jamila either. He scanned the boat back and forth until he finally caught a glimpse. She'd been pushed to the back of the crowd still on the shoreline. Behind the men. *She should be first*, he thought, panicked.

One by one the frightened Afghans were put on the boat. Tareq kept his eyes glued, waiting for Jamila to step in.

That's when he spotted it.

The Turkish smuggler had been thrusting a pistol into the body of each passenger as he crammed them into the raft.

Jamila was the last to board before he yanked her off.

A sense of foreboding permeated Tareq's body, followed by an adrenaline surge. He edged forward, only to be held back by the Syrian behind him.

"No. This isn't our problem," the young man said.

"She is a girl by herself! She needs our help!" Tareq tried to fight through his arms.

"Look." He gestured to the Afghans on the back of the boat who'd started screaming, catching the attention of the other smugglers. "They will take care of it. We can't ruin our trip across because of them."

The Afghan smuggler ran to the back of the boat. He and the Turkish smuggler had a tense exchange before the Afghan man grabbed Jamila's arm while pushing the Turkish man with the gun away. The Turk clambered away from the dinghy and blew kisses toward Jamila as the Afghan led her away, saving her from a doom far too many women suffer in these circumstances.

Tareq struggled to stay in place. His instinct was to run over and beat the man until blood poured out of his disgusting mouth. But a tiny arm wrapped around his leg brought him back.

The Afghan man dragged a resisting Jamila toward the Syrian group. She kept her head turned, searching for her sister, who was being held down, prevented from jumping out of the already tottering vessel.

When they made the fifty yards to the Syrian dinghy, the Afghan trafficker handed her to his colleague in charge of the Syrians. The two men discussed something, and the Afghan left without her, despite her protests. She tried to run, but the Syrian smuggler pulled out his own pistol.

"Shut up!" he spat as he squeezed her arm. "You're with us now." He turned to the frightened group in front of him. "Okay, it's time to board our boat. Women, children and families first!"

"I need to be with my sister!" yelled Jamila.

"I said shut up! You go on this boat or stay in Turkey!"

Tareq sprinted toward the front with Susan. Desperately kicking the rocks and sand behind them. The crowd began to move to let him go forward. He made it to Jamila and grabbed her hand.

The smuggler glared at him before pushing them through.

"Are you okay?" Tareq whispered. But he knew the answer from looking at her damp eyes.

"My sister," she mumbled.

"Do not worry, we will find her when we arrive to Greece." He tried to comfort her. "We will find her," he said with determination. "Okay?"

Jamila nodded and looked down at Susan, who was staring at her, petrified. The doe eyes forced Jamila to wipe her tears.

They tumbled into the rubber inflatable.

The Afghan boat had already departed from the shore and bobbed in the water ahead. The Syrians watched as their own dinghy—built for ten passengers—was flooded with forty-four men, women and children.

As Tareq situated his sister, he saw the symbols on the black rubber. Chinese. The thumbs-down. He looked up and saw the man with the gray mustache shake his head. *This one will sink*

Once everyone was on board, the daunted skipper scanned the passengers. He was a computer technician, not a seaman, and he didn't even know how to swim. He had just completed a five-minute tutorial on how to navigate a dinghy. This was his free ride.

He got a quick refresher from a shirtless crook in his underwear. The man in his boxer shorts patted the skipper on the back before he dove off the boat into the cold water.

"You're all in God's hands now," he shouted back at them with a perverse grin. "And the sea's."

Luck's game in a way

CHAPTER 20

"No one move!" a woman shrieked. "Stop moving, for God's sake!"

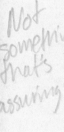

The boat tumbled from side to side, bringing in gallons of water. At any moment it could capsize. The fragility of the lives on board depended on one strong sneeze or one scared child jumping onto their father's lap.

The rhythmic beat of the sea pounding on the slippery rubber tubing serenaded the devil as he waited for the right moment. The salty water in the air fell like daggers on the sunken faces aboard. Right then, it was a familiar horror that kept them warm.

"Don't everyone sit in the middle," shouted another passenger. "Sit on the sides! Sit on the sides!"

Their lungs may not have been taking in water yet, but they were all drowning in fear.

We're going to die. The shared thought zipped through the minds of the men and women on board. But no one dared to verbalize it.

"Is the water coming from a hole or from the waves?" asked

a middle-aged woman who had her arms wrapped around her crying toddler. Her other daughter sat in front of them, staring blankly ahead.

"The waves," a young man responded while trying to smile at the girl, an attempt to comfort the terrified child—and her mother. "Don't worry, this boat is like a balloon, it won't sink." He looked directly at the little girl, raising his eyebrows in assurance. "Balloons don't sink." *At least, he's comforting*

"Slow down!" a man yelled to the young driver, who carried the burden of knowing that one misstep on his part could kill them all. He imagined forty-four bodies floating toward the shores as he gripped the red plastic gas tank with the soles of his feet. He didn't want to be responsible for the deaths of more Syrians; he had enough ghosts terrorizing his dreams. *Sad reality to live with*

Tareq was mustering up as much courage as he could as he stared at his little sister, who was sitting in front of him with three other children.

There was a woman nursing a three-month-old baby next to him. She concentrated on the infant's round cheeks and attentive eyes, attempting to avoid the chaos around her. She began tucking the pink knitted blanket under the baby's soft neck before kissing her forehead. Thoughts of Ameer and Sameer seeped into Tareq's mind.

Not now. Tareq shook his head. He knew he needed to focus.

Jamila had not let go of his hand. Her eyes scanned the horizon, as her thoughts were lost, thinking of her sister, afraid of losing the only family she had left.

"I do not see them," she said to Tareq. "Where did they go?"

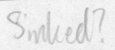
Smiled?

"Do not worry," he tried to reassure her. "They are probably near to Greece." His insides felt an uncontrollable urge to protect her, similar to Susan but also completely different.

A shrill voice cut through the conversations on the boat. "Does anyone have a map?"

"We don't need a map, we just need to get there." A man pointed to the land that seemed so much closer when they were on the beach than it did now from the undulating waters.

"We have to get to the island of Lesvos." She looked at him, annoyed. "My cousins are there!"

"Who cares where in Greece we land, as long as it's Europe. You can meet your cousin in Athens." He then turned his attention to his young son, who was stretching his neck and legs to see what was going on. "Sit down!"

"I want to see, Baba." The kid looked slightly older than Susan.

"He's veering too much. Tell him," the map woman told her husband.

"You tell him," he mumbled back, hugging his blue backpack, paralyzed with fear and unable to look his wife in the eyes.

"Fine!" she replied, agitated, before turning her attention to the skipper. "You're veering! Keep it steady!"

The driver's quivering arms began to wobble.

"Relax, *habibi*." An older man with gray stubble tried to console the man at the helm. "You're doing fine. Just take control of your nerves. We trust you."

The words tempered his anxiety a bit.

"Let's sink the boat so the Greek Coast Guard will have to save us," a young man with gelled black curls suggested.

[handwritten margin note: Tough to deal with all the different words thrown at you]

"No!" a chorus of voices yelled back. "Do not sink the boat!"

"I can't do this trip again," the young man said in defense of his proposal. "This is my third time. Something always goes wrong, and we always have to go back. Not again!"

"We are barely a kilometer from the Turkish shore." The old man pointed to the beach they just departed. "If any coast guard will come, it will be the Turks. And they will take us back only to give us deportation papers!"

"And what if no one comes?" The woman holding on to her daughter glared at the young man. "If the boat sinks, we will all die." She scanned around, now directing her words to everyone. "No one sinks the boat! We can't all swim!" She kissed her toddler while cursing the young man under her breath. "Ahmaq."

The young man rolled his eyes, giving up on his deadly suggestion. "I've been told that it works."

"Who told you that? The ghosts below us?" She shifted her eyes.

"No," he said. "I read it on Facebook."

"There are many rumors and lies that have been spread," Tareq heard the man from last night say as he cradled his wife and daughters. "They have cost lives. We won't risk that today."

"Well then, let's just hope the bandits don't stop us," the young man continued. "And that's not a rumor or lie. They're out there."

"Bandits?" Tareq asked.

"Yes, the bandits." The young man leaned toward him from the back of the boat. He positioned his head between two bodies, making sure the scared teen could see him. "On one of my trips, a small boat came toward us and we were so excited, thinking a fishing boat would help us. Instead, these bastards took all our bags, phones and money. They knew that we could carry only our most important possessions with us. They even took the fuel! May God punish them all. So we had to turn back to the shore and paddle with our hands. Those who could swim pushed the boat ashore." He leaned back again.

Tareq gulped down a newly added fear. His terror was not lost on the old man.

"You are not allowed to talk anymore," the man with gray stubble said.

"What? I can't tell the truth?"

"You need to stop this now." He scolded him with his index finger, like a father to a naughty child. "There are children here who are frightened enough."

An hour passed. But Greece still seemed farther away than Turkey.

"Look!" A woman yelled. "A ship!"

A white vessel with an orange stripe sped toward them.

"God is great!" she screamed in delight.

The group burst with excitement.

"*Akalna khara!*" the young man cursed. "It's the Turks! Speed up the engine! We have to get past the Turkish waters!"

"How do you know?" the skipper asked. "If I go faster, we will take in more of the sea."

"He's right," said the old man. "Those are the Turkish Coast Guard colors."

The enthusiasm on the boat transformed to unrest. Tareq could feel his heart pounding through his head as the crammed bodies shifted and turned.

"Stop moving, everyone!" The old man tried to take charge as he directed his attention to the skipper. "Speed up the motor."

He increased the acceleration, but that only caused the dinghy to take in more water.

"Slow it down! We don't want to die!" yelled a young woman in a purple hijab.

"What is going on?" Jamila asked Tareq, unable to understand the Arabic that was being spoken around her.

"Everything is fine." He tried to put her at ease. "But it look like that ship is Turkish Coast Guard."

"Oh no." Her eyes began to fill up as fast as the boat. "I have to get to Greece. I have to go to my sister!"

"Do not worry, they will let us pass," he said, squeezing her hand. *"Inshallah."* He then kissed the top of his sister's head, who was now sitting between his legs. "Are you okay, *ayuni?*"

"It's cold," she responded, hugging her backpack tighter.

Tareq clamped her stiffening body between his legs. "Does this help?" Her wet curls flapped as she nodded. She could no longer feel her bottom as it sat in the icy pool filling the raft.

As the Turkish vessel neared, it caused their inflatable to wobble even more. The wrathful sea flew up and crashed down, saturating the passengers further. The approaching cutter's sirens blared as its lights flashed. A voice bellowed out of the megaphone.

"Dur! Dur! Stop! Stop!" it commanded first in Turkish, then in English.

"Don't stop!" the young man shouted at the driver.

"Stop!" the megaphone roared again. "Turn around. You must turn around now!"

"We can't outrun them with our tiny boat," the old man yelled.

"We can't go back," the young man retorted.

Prayers could be heard throughout the pack.

"Recite after me," the old man screamed out. "God is great. God is great. God is great." The throng repeated. "The one who has placed this vessel at our service. Oh God, facilitate our journey . . ."

Bang. Bang. *Believe!*

The unmistakable bursts came from the Turkish boat. The prayers were now replaced by shrieks of horror. The commander on board the Turkish ship gripped a pistol pointed to the sky.

"Stop! And turn your boat around!" The orders were repeated.

"Don't do it!" The young man looked at the skipper and then turned his attention to the old man. "We have to keep pushing through."

The old man looked around at the terrified faces and wanted to give in. "We can't risk it," he said.

"We've made it this far, we have to keep going!" he begged. "We have no lives there. What's the risk in dying if we are already dead?" *It's the bad in Turkey !!*

The old man scanned the hollow eyes around him and finally nodded in agreement. "Keep going, *habibi*," he said to the wobbly-armed driver, who was waiting for his command.

"Yallah!" the other passengers joined in, encouraging the young skipper. Their lives had been in peril for years now. They truly believed Europe would change that, as long as they made it.

"To go faster, we have to drop anything we don't need," the young man added as he threw his backpack into the water. "They will have clothes and blankets in Greece. That's what I've been told. And if not, all we need is the clothes on our backs!" He looked at the grim faces. "Our lives are far more precious than what we have in these bags." *Very true + wise*

They all started opening their sacks, quickly pulling out their small valuables and money.

Map woman yanked away her husband's grip of their pack and drew out a resealable freezer bag that held old family photos along with their money. She knew it was not much, but they would need it. "Get a grip." She poked his shoulder before chucking the rest of the bag's contents. *Tough to do but good sacrifice*

The old man gently looked at his wife, who kept a raggedy old baby blanket before handing the bag to her husband to drop into the unforgiving waters. His eyebrows curled and he stared at her with pained eyes. The blanket once belonged to their grown daughter, who had died three months prior. She was having lunch at a park near her university when a bomb fell from the sky, blowing up all their lives. This torn blanket was all they had left of her. He took the blanket from his wife and tucked it under his shirt to keep it as safe as possible. *Would know this story if 1st person*

The mother of the two girls was pulling out diapers and a bottle before her husband stopped her. "We need this!" she yelled at him.

"They will have bottles in Europe," he said calmly as he touched her shoulder. "We just need to make sure we get there alive."

"I'm keeping one." She grabbed a diaper and stuck it in a plastic grocery bag, which she tied tightly.

"Okay." Her husband smiled gently while grabbing the other items and throwing them over.

Jamila picked up on what was going on. She pulled out a handkerchief her mother had embroidered with doves for her when she was a young child. She had used scarlet, emerald and black string—the colors of the Afghan flag. The cloth was wrapped into a square, holding her only valuables inside.

She quickly stuck it in her shirt, tucking it into her bra before tossing her bag behind her.

Tareq pulled out Susan's doll and a waterproof pouch holding his phone and the little leftover cash his father had given them.

He handed Susan the doll. "Hold on to Farrah, *habibti*," he said before flinging both their bags over. He noticed a message had come through on his phone but quickly wrapped the string of the bag over his head and around his neck. This was not the time to check it. *It wasn't*

And just like that, one by one, the passengers threw the remnants of their past lives into the Aegean Sea, like a payment to Poseidon as they tumbled through his world. A new chapter in their lives began the moment they set foot on that rubber boat. This was why I was there too.

They're working together

Under those deep dark waters are so many priceless

mementos of those I traveled with. A life etched now only in memories. But those on the raft knew that the sacrifices they were making to the sea were not as priceless as the lives lost to the same waters.

Tareq thought of the thousands of lives lost that now haunted these waters. *Please help us,* he asked their ghosts. Breathing in the mist of both life and death that lingered in the air. *I know it's not fair that you didn't make it. But please help.*

The dinghy grew lighter and started moving at a quicker pace. Smiles of relief spread throughout the boat. The deafening pounding in Tareq's ears steadied. The delighted passengers looked at each other with glistening eyes.

It was a moment of bliss that quickly crashed into a surge of panic.

Charging at them came another dinghy. It whizzed forward, shooting off water on both its sides. This rubber inflatable was smaller than theirs but also stronger and faster. It carried three men—all members of the Turkish Coast Guard. The man up front was holding on to a large metal stick in the shape of an arrow. He aimed for the motor.

Boof! Clank!

He hit the side of the rubber dinghy, causing the boat to vigorously sway back and forth, taking in more of the sea.

"He is going to pop the boat!" the woman holding her infant cried out.

"Stop it! You're going to kill us!" yelled her husband. But the coast guards ignored his pleas. The man pried his baby out of its mother's arms despite her protests and tears. He held the screaming child to the coast guard as his wife continued to slap at the back of his head.

The baby's wails were only drowned out by her mother's. "Give her back to me!"

"My baby! We have babies!" the man shrieked to deaf ears.

The coast guards continued to try and puncture the boat and its motor.

"They are trying to kill us!" Jamila snapped. "Why does everyone want to kill us?" she shouted before continuing in Dari. Tareq didn't understand what she was saying, but he recognized the anger. So did everyone on the boat. Their pleas turned to rage. Screaming at the coast guard to get lost.

But the chaos and fear only fueled the men on the other boat. They rammed the rod again but this time missed the boat and hit the skipper's right arm.

The old man caught him before he could fall into the sea.

Suddenly the father holding his baby got up and held his daughter over the edge of the boat. "I will drop her!" he shouted loud enough for the Turkish men on the other dinghy to hear. "I swear I will drop her if you don't let us pass!" The boat went silent, except for the screaming mother. She pounded her fists on her husband's vest, but she was too weak and her body gave in, collapsing to the floor of the dinghy, her face splashing on the water that had sloshed in. She whimpered like a hurt puppy as she lay next to the children.

The man pushed his arms forward as if he was going to drop the infant.

The young man, now angrier than before, pulled out

his phone and started filming. He directed his words to the Turkish dinghy, speaking in English: "If you don't let us through, I will send this film to my friends now! They will take it to the media, and you will be the reason why the baby died." He then panned his phone toward them. "I just zoomed on your faces." *Still an awful sacrifice*

There was an exchange of words among the Turks before they pulled out their radio and signaled to the cutter. Without looking back, the Turkish dinghy sped away.

They had given up on this group but knew they would have plenty more throughout the day, another chance to prove to the international community that they were doing enough to prevent refugees from making it to European soil. *People do not agree with refugees*

"*Allah akbar!* God is great!" the chants began, thanking God and hugging each other.

The only person not celebrating was the mother of the infant, who feebly got back up and grabbed her daughter. She tried to slap her husband but could only muster the energy for small taps.

"What?" He put his hands up to protect his face. "I wasn't really going to do it! It was just to make them leave! And it worked."

Tareq grabbed Susan from behind and gave her a big hug. He looked at Jamila.

"You are okay?" he asked.

"I'm just very tired," she muttered. "They treated us like animals in Iran, and now Turkey. How do we know it will be better in Europe?"

You just hope

"We don't. And we should not pretend it will be." Tareq clasped her hand in his.

Be together [handwritten]

Brrmph brmph puuuuff . . .

"What just happened?" the old man turned to the skipper. The thumping of the motor had stopped.

"The engine is dead."

"*Ya Allah!*" Exhausted wails circulated. "Oh God!"

"Well, we can't call the Turkish Coast Guard," the young man joked, still high on endorphins.

Seems likely since everything has gone wrong [handwritten]

No one laughed. They just glared.

The old man ignored him. "Who can swim?"

Tareq searched around the boat but found downcast eyes. Two men raised their hands and he joined them.

"I'm not very good, but I used to swim in the Euphrates with my cousin," he said.

"Any help will do, son." The old man gave him a steadfast nod. "Just keep your vest on."

"The vest will do him no good. It's a fake," the young man said. "It will be as heavy as having cement around your body when it soaks up the water. Take one of the tubes." He tossed a black inflated ring in his direction.

"We are still taking in water." Tareq flinched. The level had risen sharply, covering Susan's stomach. "*Omri*, are you okay?"

She clung to her doll as her body shivered. Jamila grabbed Susan and held her close.

"All the men, whether you can swim or not, we have to get out of the boat." The old man stared widely at the pool in front of him. "We will hold on to the sides. The swimmers will lead us."

No one argued. They grabbed the black inner tubes on the boat and dove into the frigid water, feeling it prick every inch of their body.

"Well, now I know how water feels when it turns to i-i-i-ice," the young man said through rattling teeth. *It's the sea. I would expect it to be cold*

Tareq held on to the side of the dinghy with one arm as he kicked his feet and paddled with the other arm. His body felt heavy from the cold, but the tube around his neck kept him afloat. He chose to keep the vest on, mostly for the small bit of protection it provided from the stinging water. He labored through the freezing temperature. They all did. *"For Susan. For my father. For Jamila,"* he repeated to himself. *"For Susan. For my father. For Jamila."* *You do end up doing it for family (theme)!*

The women, in an almost futile but spirited effort, used their hands to scoop out the water in the boat while encouraging their husbands, fathers, sons and brothers. "We are getting nearer! We are almost there!"

But as time passed, so did their energy. The women's arms became sore and Tareq's leg spasms more painful and intense. Confidence and hope began to drain as their hands and limbs went numb. *The stamina aspect is why people drown!*

Tareq steadied his sight on the landmass ahead. It still felt impossibly far. He shifted over to the man who had been paddling next to him, the infant's father. His face was pale and lips blue. *"Ammo, are you okay?"* But there was no response. *"Ammo?"* He tapped the man's stiff shoulder, which only made him float back like a buoy. *Oh no! He died! Gives the swimmers fear*

He pulled the young father closer and immediately knew. He'd seen that look before. The empty gaze from the eyes of a body whose soul had already slipped away.

He turned to the man's wife, who was now staring down at them. She'd heard Tareq trying to wake him. She shoved her baby into Jamila's already crowded arms and splashed into the water.

"Hussam!" she grabbed her husband by the top of his life jacket as she swallowed the frigid salt water, trying to stay afloat. "Hussam! Wake up! Wake up!" Tareq tried to grab her, but she was in a hypnotic state and slapped the boy away. "*Hayati!* Wake up!" She cried.

Grief swept the boat.

Death had followed them from Syria.

Some cried. Others didn't have the tears left.

A woman on the boat yelled out to her, "Please, sister, come back on the boat, your daughter needs you."

"Hussam!" she continued, lost in the moment, not hearing or thinking of anything else. Her body bobbed frantically as her lungs took in more of the choppy water, choking on it. She kicked but didn't know how to swim. The unforgiving sea sucked her in, separating her from her husband's frozen body. Tareq held on to her vest as tight as he could. He, too, felt the pull of the forceful water as they were jerked under. He gripped on to her desperately, trying to kick up, but instead was dragged deeper down.

They were face-to-face under the deep blue sea. Her head-scarf slowly unwrapped, revealing her highlighted chestnut hair.

The rose-colored fabric gently fluttered and floated toward the surface.

Their eyes locked through the crystal blue water. The bubbles stopped pouring from her mouth. And like the decamped piece of fabric, her soul drifted from her lifeless green eyes.

She died with her husband.

Risk dying + being with your husband or try for freedom + a new life?

I feel empathy for her.

Her emotions came over her + it costed her her life (unless she meant to for him—to see him)

CHAPTER 21

Some of the most beautiful parts of humanity are seen in strangers—as are some of the most vile.

The helpers and the hunters.

A helper can be someone who saves lives, like a Neonatal Intensive Care Unit nurse who revives a premature baby. It can be a person who smiles at you as you walk past each other on the street, sharing joy and positivity. It can be the man who holds the door open for a mother lugging her crying child. And the woman in line at the store's register who gives some change to the homeless man in front of her when she notices he doesn't have enough for food.

Helpers come in many forms.

As do the hunters.

The killer who takes away the divine gift of life. Or the rapist who stains the existence of their victim by brutally violating not only their body but also their soul. A hunter can be that person who spits in your direction as you walk down the street. Or the man who sees the mother approaching the door with her child and decides to slam it in her face. Or the woman who snickers behind a homeless man's back because he can't afford a sandwich.

There are obviously extremes to both.

Not every hunter is a Charles Manson and not every helper is a saint. In fact, most humans have aspects of both inside their hearts and minds. It's a battle within to see which one is exposed at what moments. *It's your choice – you can control that*

I love my work when you make the caring choices.

You see, words fade through time, as do faces. But it's actions that linger, yours and those of others. They stay in the mind and the heart even as your body grows old and fragile. They transform into regrets and gratitude. Their effects outlive your brief stay on this planet. *Some people never get over it*

The best you can do is pray that your deeds lead, in some way, to making someone's life better—if even for a moment. Especially at a time when their lives have been all but destroyed by the hunters.

I hate my work when you make the dark choices.

It makes me sick when I have to stay with the souls who lurk in the shadows as they wait for the weak and wounded, feeding on the vulnerable and pouncing on the destitute.

They often disguise themselves, and their victims don't notice—at least not until it's too late.

They can be dangerous

CHAPTER 22

Mundane moments are no longer simple once your eyes have seen too much or your heart has felt too much. Even when the human body survives another trying day, its brain holds on to the memory. And like a movie set on a loop, it replays over and over.

As the steam rose from Alexia's cup in the crisp Molyvos air, she could see the days behind her and wondered what the day ahead would bring. She contemplated whether or not her fleece would be warm enough for today's slapping wind. *It doesn't really matter,* she thought. She knew that once the boats arrived and she was knee-deep in the frigid sea pulling refugees to safety, no piece of fabric would keep her warm. The stings of the bitter temperature and situation would slay her body—and her spirit.

She thought of the Greek and Turkish coast guards who had grown more vigilant even as the weather had cooled. Fewer boats had been making the journey across the riskier winter waters, but they were still coming by the thousands. She knew she had to be prepared—both physically and emotionally.

Alexia sipped her cappuccino, allowing the warmth to fill her body. The foam was not too thick or too thin, just the way she liked it. She pressed her long fingers around the cup, keeping her hands warm, trying to focus on the cup and not the faces in her mind. But the more she focused on not seeing them, the more they would appear.

This time it was the little boy in the Spider-Man sweatshirt. His mother and father carrying him off the boat. Happy but exhausted—they had made it. Their clothes still dripped from the salty seawater. The mother, hair pulled back in a bun, smiled before kissing her husband on the cheek and then leaned down to kiss the sleeping son, who couldn't have been more than four. She went to embrace her son again, but her smile quickly faded. The memory of the piercing shrieks of terror made Alexia flinch still. The medical team ran over to help. The mother fell from her husband's arms. The little boy was dead, frozen on the journey to freedom. Alexia swore she could see the hope and joy drain from his parents' eyes. An irrecoverable loss. *She has empathy*

"Here you is." The waitress dropped some sugar in front of Alexia, bringing her back.

"Efcharistó," she thanked her.

Beep. Beep. Beep. Beep. Beep.

Alexia took a look at her cheap black Casio and jumped. Her shift started in fifteen minutes. She quickly stirred in the sugar and chugged her coffee, feeling it burn her throat.

She snapped on her helmet and rode off on her rented red scooter.

Is that big there?

Nothing felt more European to her than riding her scooter. She zipped through the swerving roads but reduced her speed when she got to the entrance of the beach.

Alexia bounced down the gravel and dirt path that led to the rocky shores. She squeezed the brake handle just enough to prevent a flip, not wanting to waste the medical team's efforts and supplies on a careless volunteer. *smart*

As the sea came into view, she took a deep breath, calmed by the crisp sapphire water as it faded to turquoise near the shores. She admired the sun's morning blaze, which sent sharp rays through the marshmallow clouds. Alexia loved everything she saw. She imagined diamonds cascading across the seafloor, creating the sparkles that glistened all around. One would even call it heavenly, if they didn't know the darkness and death that lurked in its depths.

Such a happy place w/ darkness in it

Alexia parked her scooter next to the clothing tent.

She pulled out her phone, took a snapshot of the morning landscape and texted it to her parents with a short message: Love you both, and miss you ♥.

"Hey, guys." Alexia slid her phone into her pocket. She crunched on the pebbles, walking toward the team lounging on broken plastic chairs by the shore. Fewer boats meant more downtime. The small team of lifeguards and volunteers greeted her back. "Any pings yet?"

"There have been some," Famke, a Dutch volunteer, said. The dirty-blond-haired social worker had been with them for a week now. Her fit body was a testament to the bicycle she rode everywhere. "But they weren't headed in this direction. I'm sure the Greek Coast Guard will pick them up." She pointed her hands toward the water. "We did see the Turkish Coast Guard roaming around. They're likely sending many boats back."

They're the hunters -heartless but doing their job

"Heartless bastards," Dave, one of the lifeguards, scoffed.

"How about the waters?" Alexia asked.

"They're bad," Dave said, his hands tucked inside his sweat-pants for warmth. "Just look. So choppy. It's actually almost better if they are sent back. Or they should at least wait until later to take off. If the freakin' smugglers have any kinda heart, they'd wait a few hours."

Alexia studied the rough waters. To the untrained eye, it would still look tranquil and inviting, but the volunteers knew what even the slightest change in current meant to a boat stuffed like a tin can of sardines—though tin was stronger than the flimsy rubber of the dinghies.

"Geez. Let's hope they have a heart." She glanced at her watch. "I'm gonna go relieve Hilda."

Bad for Tareq. Foreshadowing their help to him

Alexia flipped open the tarp of the clothing tent but couldn't spot Hilda.

"Hello?" she called out, then heard scattering.

"Yah!" Hilda shouted from the back.

Alexia walked over and found the nearly six-foot German girl lying down on the hemp mat that covered the tent floor. Her hair was in a messy ponytail as she leaned her head on a garbage bag full of donated clothes.

"Sleep well?" Alexia joked.

"Oh, shut up!" Hilda retorted. "It was a very boring night and I finished the work. Well, except this bag." She looked at it sheepishly. "It was too comfortable."

"Okay, okay." Alexia grabbed her hand, struggling to help her stand. "Go home and get some real rest."

"This pillow is better than the one I have in my hotel." Hilda blew a kiss to the flimsy black bag. "But I leave it for you to sort, okay?"

"Yeah, I got it. Don't worry." Alexia contemplated taking a nap on it too. If the day was as slow as yesterday, she might. "It'll help pass some time."

Hilda was no longer listening, exhausted from her night of trying to stay awake. "Okay, I will see you then. Goodbye." She scurried out of the tent.

They are helpers—people with kind hearts

Alexia surveyed the room of donated clothes, all divided by gender and size, an undertaking she'd initiated. She liked to think of all the people who donated each and every item.

This room was a testament to humanity. A reminder that not everyone was ignoring the plight of the refugees, or fearing them. After the recent media coverage of the crisis, more and more handouts came flooding in. There were outgrown baby onesies; jackets that had belonged to husbands, sons and fathers; and dresses that were worn by wives, mothers, daughters. Though these families couldn't be there physically, they wanted to help.

What I like to see!
Warms my heart

She walked over to her favorite item and slid her fingers along the beat-up lime-green wool coat that belonged to another decade but miraculously had made its way to the here and now. The jacket still smelled of mothballs, and no amount of detergent could get rid of the odor. It was so old that even those still dripping from the frigid sea quickly scanned past it for something more modern. Or at least pretty.

But the original owner never cared about the style or color. He just loved that his wife picked the strongest jacket to keep him warm as he tilled his crops and drove around in his pickup with a broken heater. He wore it everywhere. Everyone in his small town knew he was around when they saw the jacket in the distance. They'd spot him at the drugstore. They'd spot him at church. "There's Terry!" It's the jacket he wore when he took his grandchildren to the park and his wife to the movies. And when he died, it was the one thing his family couldn't throw out or give away. It was too precious to let go. Unless it was to someone deserving.

Despite its ugly appearance, Alexia knew that one day someone would grab it. They would put their arms through the sleeves and wrap their body in its warmth. And during one of the hardest days of their lives, they'd place their trembling hands into the pocket of the beaten coat to find a note that would make them feel loved, oceans away from its sender.

Alexia pulled out the ripped-up piece of notebook paper during every shift to remind herself that the world wasn't all bad.

Hi! I know you may not speak or read English, but in the case that you do, please continue reading. I want you to know that people are rooting for you. There are people in the world fighting for your safety and equality. People are doing this because despite what you've been made to believe, you are an important person in this world and you are going to do great things. This jacket you are wearing belonged to my grandfather Terry Jenkins. He grew up and lived his whole life in Iowa. Now you are wearing his jacket in Greece, after going through something most people in the world can't bear to think about. Terry would be proud to have known that someone with courage and patience such as yours is wearing his jacket. I would love to hear from you and hear your personal story because you matter to me. When you get access to a computer, please email me: sally.martin@trendmail.com

Love, Sally Martin

Alexia folded the paper and stuck it back into the pocket. She was always tempted to email and thank her. But she knew Sally didn't want to hear from her, at least not until she knew that someone was kept warm because of her grandfather's jacket. All Alexia could do was continue to display the jacket

[handwritten annotations: "What an encouraging, heartful message"; "They have empathy — allows to do nice things (be kind)"; "I would want the same"]

in front, in the hope that someone would grab it. *Maybe today will be the day*, she thought.

Alexia headed back to the crates packed with baby meal bags, all purchased with donated money and flown in from the UK by volunteers. Hilda had already filled and tied dozens of plastic bags full of pouches and fruit. To pass time, Alexia decided to make more.

She stuffed the bags like she was a one-person assembly line. Two fruit squeeze packets, a banana and apple juice. Squeeze packets, banana, juice. Squeeze packets, banana, juice . . .

Time to check her watch; only fourteen minutes had passed. Alexia sighed.

Squeeze packets, banana, juice . . .

Time check. Another eleven minutes. *Damn.*

Phone break. Alexia opened the Snapchat app. By now, drunk pictures of her friends back home were posted. She scrolled through laughing and slightly missing a life that seemed so far away, and not just by distance.

Back to the bags.

Alexia's daily temptation to try the strawberries-and-apple baby food pouch surfaced. She never gave in. *Those are for hungry babies!* she'd tell herself, promising to buy one at Target when she got back to Connecticut. It was one of her many missions lined up for when she went home, just behind a hot bowl of meatball pho from her favorite Vietnamese restaurant and devouring a Boston Kreme from Dunkin' Donuts.

Alexia heard footsteps crunching outside, breaking the monotony of the food bagging.

As the white plastic cover lifted, two women walked through, one a brunette and the other a blonde.

"Hello! We have come to help today," said the golden-haired one, extending a hand. "My name is Sivan, and this is Mariam."

Alexia shook both of their hands, noticing that they were slightly older than her. "Alexia. Nice to meet you."

"We are here for medical assistance." Mariam examined the tent with her piercing caramel eyes. "We are medics. But while we wait for the boats, we can help here."

"Welcome. This is the clothing tent, as you can see." Alexia tied up a bag. "We just make sure they get out of their wet clothes and put on some dry ones after they make it to shore. We also have some food items for babies." She lifted the bag before dropping it into the plastic crate. "You are more than welcome to join me."

The two girls nodded. "We'd love to. It'll help pass the time."

"Not as much as you'd think." Alexia smiled. "So, where are you guys from?"

"We are from Israel. I'm from Tel Aviv," Sivan said. "And Mariam is from Nazareth. You?"

"America." Alexia's eyes bounced between the two girls. She knew that Israel and Syria were technically at war.

"You are wondering why Israelis have come here?" Mariam said.

"I guess I'd assumed that most Arabs and Israelis . . . don't really get along," Alexia said as Mariam and Sivan smirked. "Do the refugees give you a hard time when they find out where you're from?"

"No, they are kind and grateful," said Mariam. *Agreed*

"We are just here to help, like you," Sivan said. "And if during that time people realize that there is more than meets the eye with any country, including ours, then okay." She shrugged.

"How about the Palestinians that arrive from places like Yarmouk—how are they with you? Do you avoid telling them where you're from?" Alexia asked.

"I am Palestinian," Mariam said. "An Arab-Israeli. I can talk to them if there are problems. But really, we haven't had any."

"Yes, Mariam is right," Sivan added. "Everyone is just so relieved when they make it, or are so scared that they don't see politics. We receive hugs, not hate."

"And they, of all people, know that governments don't always represent all the people," Mariam said. "Even when it seems to be black-and-white, you will always find those specks of gray."

"Now"—Sivan looked at the crates in front of her—"will you tell us how to pack these bags?"

In times of need, they'll look past the unimportant details

Less than a kilometer from the beach, more volunteers were on shift at the Athena Hotel, including the young man who would soon save the lives of those on Tareq's boat just by using his eyes. It's not always brawn and muscles that save ships and, in turn, the people on them. *Ummm... foreshadowing*

The building they were staying in offered the perfect vantage point. And it was definitely more comfortable than the other lookout points on top of dirt hills, with only cars and earth to rest on.

The popular family-run resort's sun-and-fun-seeking guests stopped coming as the refugees continued to land en masse. At the moment, their business was afloat because of the numerous volunteers. But the owners were worried, like all the villagers, that when the refugees stopped landing on their shores and the volunteers left, the tourists wouldn't come back.

Michael, a Singaporean volunteer, was at the helm of the lookout team. He peered through state-of-the-art scopes situated on brand-new tripods.

He scanned the water and the Turkish coastline carefully.

The rest of his team was having breakfast outside the room. They ate scrambled eggs and sipped their coffee while taking in the morning view. But they couldn't fully relax, instinctively examining the waters with each bite.

Michael had been monitoring the Turkish Coast Guard vessel. He knew that they, too, were searching the waters for boats. And the encounters between the coast guard and the refugees were not always pleasant.

Every once in a while the refugees would get past them without being noticed, or at times they were flat-out ignored. During the busiest months, the coast guards didn't have enough boats to stop the thousands of people who were transiting through every day. And until the European Union handed out more concessions to the Turkish government, their vigilance was as unpredictable as the waves.

Every few minutes, Michael took another scan through the scope.

Between each sweep, he tried to organize the room. His

[handwritten marginalia: It is something to think about]

military training had instilled in him a need to have everything orderly and ready.

He positioned the map of the Aegean, with both coastlines, so it was visible from the scope's position. The map marked the most common departure and landing points with the given names of each beach. Michael had constructed it.

Back to the scope.

Then he checked to make sure the portable battery packs were charged. The last thing they needed was a volunteer with a dead phone, their preferred way to communicate. The generational gap between the volunteers was always visible when someone asked for a walkie-talkie. They didn't have any. And teaching someone how to use WhatsApp was much cheaper than purchasing them.

Back to the scope.

This time, he spotted movement from the coast guard vessel. He panned to the right, and there it was.

A black object with orange dots.

Do these volunteers ever get stopped by a political force?

CHAPTER 23

"We got a ping from Mike!" Famke announced. *"They see a boat!"* She showed the group the message.

MIKE: Boat spotted.

Turk Coast Guard approaching. 8:40AM

Joel, a blond Australian, grabbed the binoculars and stepped onto the rocks. "I see the coast guard. I can't spot the boat. Is it a dinghy?"

MIKE: Boat spotted.

Turk Coast Guard approaching. 8:40AM

> **FAMKE:** Copy. What kind of boat? Can you tell how many on board? 8:40AM

MIKE: It's an inflatable. Dinghy. Unclear on numbers. But it's packed. Will keep you posted. 8:41AM

Good comms

> **FAMKE:** We will get ready and keep watch. 8:41AM

MIKE: Us too. 8:41AM

The group's adrenaline soared as they hit preparation mode.

Joel and the lifeguards got their boards ready just in case they had to help navigate them in.

Sivan and Mariam, the two Israeli medics, had their bags beside them. Their arms crossed as they searched the water.

"Mariam, can you serve as translator if it's an Arabic-speaking boat?" Dave asked.

She nodded. "Of course."

Alexia and Tina, a volunteer from China, brought out the sack filled with the fluorescent space blankets, thin metal-coated sheets often given to marathon runners after they finish a race. The blanket reflected a person's own body heat back toward them, retaining warmth.

Alexia could feel her pulse vibrating through her throat.

They all knew the intensity that was about to hit them when and if the boat landed on their beach.

Thoughts of past landings rushed through Alexia's head. Regrets and mistakes that she didn't want to make again. *What ifs* that will forever linger in her heart.

What if we had pulled her out sooner? Would she have survived?

What if I'd given him my jacket? Would that have prevented his hypothermia?

What if I'd hugged her? Would she have stopped crying?

The demons continued to taunt her. She tried to push them out of her mind. But as she waited for the wave that slowly came crashing her way, it was hard for her not to get lost in shadowy thoughts.

Your being helpful. Don't worry. Just try your best + give it all you got.

MIKE: Coast guard puncturing boat.
Sent out their own dinghy. Boat may
turn back. 8:53AM

FAMKE: Bastards. 8:53AM

MIKE: Not turning back.
Coast guard left them. 9:02AM

FAMKE: Wow. How'd they get
away with that? 9:02AM

MIKE: No clue. Headed toward
lighthouse beach. Be ready. 9:02AM

FAMKE: Standing by. 9:02AM

The team anxiously waited, all eyes glued on the deep blue-green water.

And that's when they saw a black speck very slowly expanding into a black-and-orange spot.

"Boat's barely moving," Alexia yelled out.

"Probably the engine." Dave looked up at Joel. "Jackasses probably sent them out with a half tank."

"Can't really tell." Joel's eyes were attached to the binoculars. "They're too far out. But they look really panicked."

They all strained to see more. They knew that panic led to disaster.

"All we can do is be ready," Sivan added. "The more they are panicking, the calmer we need to be." Everyone nodded in agreement. Sometimes the obvious is exactly what one needs to hear.

"There are a lot of women and children on this one," Joel said.

"Any boats out there to help?" asked Alexia.

Must be very stressful

"None that I can see." He peeled the binoculars off and looked distressed.

"Mike said he can't see any boats nearby either," Famke added, looking up from her phone. "One is on the way. They're just not sure how long it will take them. But he said he can see some of the refugees in the water paddling and pushing the dinghy."

"Let's be ready for possible hypothermia," Mariam said to Sivan, who tilted her head in agreement before bending down to take inventory of their supplies.

"There are people floating on the sides," Joel added. "I see them. They must be taking in water. That's it." He looked at the other two volunteer lifeguards. "I'm goin' out. We don't know how long they've had to paddle."

And without another word, all three peeled off their red sweatshirts and zipped up their wet suits. Within minutes they were in the cutting water, swimming out.

"Here!" Famke rushed an infant to Alexia, who was also knee-deep in the translucent Aegean. The frigid temperature sent stings shooting up and down her legs. But the chaos of the moment numbed her from taking in the pain.

The baby's body was rattling. Alexia held her close to her chest and instinctively started to huff warm breath on the tiny crimson face. Carefully she navigated the slimy rocks as she pounded toward the beach.

"Mariam! Sivan!" she called out, looking for the two medics. The volunteers had multiplied on the beach as those from the hotel rushed down when they saw the lifeguards steer the boat there. One of the new women ran a shiny space blanket toward Alexia and wrapped it around the baby.

"Mariam! Sivan!" Alexia continued to scream. Her nerves were taking over. *The baby's not crying. She's just shivering. This can't be good.*

She spotted Sivan and ran over to her. The medic was trying to calm a woman dripping from the sea and tears. "Please tell her she is okay," Sivan asked an Arabic-speaking volunteer who had joined them. "She is having an anxiety attack."

"Sivan!" Alexia yelled. "Help!"

Sivan snapped her head. "What?" She immediately saw the bundle in Alexia's arms. "Give her to me!" She grabbed the baby. "You go and find her mother!"

Alexia nodded, her eyes still glued to the baby as she stumbled backward. She took a second and swallowed her emotions. *They need me. No time to let my emotions control me.* The choice between fight and flight had come too often on these shores.

She turned back to the madness. There were children being passed from refugee to volunteer. And there were shrieks of fear from the deflating rubber boat.

Most of the passengers didn't know how to swim. The few yards left were just as frightening as the miles they'd just passed.

That's when Alexia saw her.

CHAPTER 24

Must be tough for him

Susan's eyes were dazed and her lips pale. Her teeth had stopped chattering. Terror ripped through Tareq as he hesitated before handing over his baby sister to the stranger that grabbed for her. He watched as a woman with blond hair passed her over to a woman with brown hair who looked like she was only a few years older than Tareq himself.

The brunette locked eyes with Tareq, who held tighter to his sister's doll.

His eyes screamed, *Please help her!*

The young woman's replied, *You can trust me.*

Unspoken connections happen when souls become intertwined. Most last for fractions of a second, but some a lifetime—and beyond. *In tough times, yes*

Alexia's foot banged against a rock underneath the water, a pain that immediately throbbed. She felt herself begin to tip, unable to balance the little body she was carrying. She scrabbled her feet, adjusting her legs to find balance. *Not now, God.* Her demand was met as she regained stability.

"I need help!" she yelled, splashing back to the beach as Tareq watched desperately. He waded his way through the water and slippery rocks.

"Tareq!" He heard Jamila's voice crack behind him. He turned to find her struggling to keep afoot.

"Here, take my hand." He turned back.

Mariam spotted Alexia and the little girl. "Bring her here." Mariam dropped to the ground.

Alexia carried the young girl, with clothes still streaming, and laid her down on the rock-strewn surface.

"Help me take her clothes off."

Alexia tugged on the little girl's soaked jeans as Mariam unzipped her jacket and stripped off her heavy damp shirt, quickly wrapping her in a space blanket.

Alexia listened as Mariam tried to comfort the little girl in Arabic before turning back to her. "Can you carry her to the clothing tent? It's warmer in there."

Without another word, Alexia picked her up—she was lighter without the sea-drenched clothing—and made her way to the tent. Mariam found a wool blanket and wrapped that around the space blanket.

"Keep these on her," Mariam ordered. "I'm going to get an IV. If she starts shivering again, that's a good sign," she said before running out.

. . .

"Susan!" Tareq screamed. "Susan!" He looked at Jamila and saw the worry on her face mirroring his. "She was there." He pointed to a patch of gravel.

"She is here." Jamila's green eyes searched through the disarray around her. Wondering if her own sister was there as well. "Somewhere."

Tareq frantically stomped through the crowds of volunteers and refugees, scanning every square inch. Ignoring the chill that blanketed his body from his sopping clothes.

"*Okhteh!* My sister! I cannot see her!" he yelled into the face of a volunteer who was wearing a fluorescent yellow vest. "Susan!"

"Come on, sweetheart," Alexia whispered through the wet blond curls. "Please be okay." She hugged her tighter. Hoping it would help warm her. "Come on, darling."

She rocked the little girl for what felt like an eternity, staring at the pale pink lips and colorless cheeks. She started huffing warm breath onto her cold skin, like she had with the tiny baby. Watching as her own tears fell onto the small beautiful face, one that her mind was already tattooing into her brain.

Then she saw it.

A twitch.

"That's it! Come on." She held the girl closer.

Another twitch. Then tiny jolts. Followed by quivers.

And then the most beautiful chatters Alexia had ever heard.

Mariam ran back in. "How is she?"

Let's go Destiny

"She's shivering," Alexia said with tears of joy flooding her face.

"Good. Great." Mariam's face was stoic and professional as she continued her work. She located a vein and inserted a sterile needle into the girl's arm. "Hopefully this will help too. It's warm intravenous fluid. Keep it elevated." She handed Alexia the clear bag of liquid. "I have to go triage the arrivals." She ran out without waiting for a response.

As Alexia gently rocked the little girl, she could hear the chaos continue through the tent's thin walls.

"Mein bihajeh la'dactor?" She could hear Mariam's voice calling out to see if anyone needed a doctor. *"Mein bihajeh la'dactor?"* She knew Mariam had found someone when she could no longer hear the shouts.

"Allah akbar," others screamed, thanking God for making it alive. "God is great!" They continued to repeat.

Alexia moved the little girl, carefully, to the area where Hilda had been sleeping, placing her shivering head on the makeshift beanbag.

She knew soon enough the volunteers would be coming in to get dry clothes for the arrivals. Women and girls would be rushing in to change in a place where they could have at least a semblance of privacy.

She listened to the hustle and bustle as volunteers passed out bottles of water and bread to the dehydrated and starving arrivals. *"Mai! Mai!"* Often they landed after days without food as they hid in the brush waiting for their departure.

Alexia peered down and stroked the little girl's cheek as

she saw a pinkish color return. *It's warmer.* She looked up to the white ceiling in relief as she listened to the chattering ease. *Thank you, God.*

Through the commotion she could hear yelling. *"Okhteh! Okhteh!"* The man's voice changed to English. "My sister! Where is my sister?" He yelled. "Susan!"

Alexia glanced down at the little girl in front of her. "So, your name is Susan, sweet girl. Nice to meet you. I'm Alexia."

"In here. Susan's in here," a voice yelled through the white tarp.

Tareq's panic turned to joy as he lifted the plastic and ran in.

"You can't go in there!" He ignored the voice of a volunteer blaring behind him. "Get back!"

"Susan!" he yelled. His eyes darted from one corner of the tent to another. All he could see were lines of clothing.

"She's over here," a woman's voice called from the back. He stumbled forward, almost tripping over a crate.

"Susan." His heart dropped. "Is she . . ."

"She's going to be fine," the young woman said. "She just needs to warm up right now."

The volunteer from outside stormed in. "I said, you can't come in here!"

"Who says?" Alexia shot back.

"We are about to have the women come in and change!"

"Well, he needs to be with his sister. Stop being so callous."

"You're the one who is being callous if you allow these poor women and children to freeze in their soaked clothing."

warming moment! !!

Tareq stroked his sister's hair as the two volunteers continued at it. *"Ayuni,* I'm so sorry." He kissed her forehead, making her eyes flicker. "That's it. Wake up, *habibti."*

As her eyes slowly opened, she stared at her brother and faintly smiled.

"Omri." He kissed her again. This time his lips landed on her soft cheek.

"Farrah?" she said, her smile beginning to fade.

"Don't worry. She's right here." He lifted the beat-up doll, which was still drenched, bringing back the joy in his sister's face.

"Susan?" Jamila's voice popped through. "She is okay?"

Tareq turned and smiled. "She is very okay. We are all okay. God is great."

Yes, he is

CHAPTER 25

Relieved of the trip

Outside the tent and on the beach, things had quieted down some. The initial chaos passed. Pulses calmed and the adrenaline settled. Some refugees had already left to make the trek into the city. Others waited for the bus that would take them to a transit camp, while a few decided not to stop and started the thirty-seven-mile journey to Mytilene.

A volunteer held up a map, explaining the next steps to a family of five. Most arrivals didn't even know where they had landed. They weren't sure if they were on Lesvos or Kos or Chios. It always helped to have an Arabic-speaking volunteer to *And comforting* talk with them; hearing their language was almost as important as figuring out the next move. A small deed but a tremendous comfort. It was harder with the people on the Afghan boats; most of them didn't speak English and there weren't enough Dari- or Pashto-speaking translators to help.

Alexia smiled when she spotted Sivan laughing as a much older Syrian man was kissing her head and thanking her. *"Mashallah! Mashallah!"* He passed his phone to another volunteer and took a picture with her, holding his thumb up. His wife chuckled and went to grab Sivan too, enveloping her into a warm hug. Sivan locked eyes with Alexia, smiled and gave an *I told you so* look.

Both women laughed. A warm moment and a reminder of the power of the human heart. In this case, they were no longer Israeli or Syrian, Jewish or Muslim, they were what they were intended to be—human.

Alexia's relief was short-lived when she spotted Tina holding the infant Alexia had grabbed off the dinghy earlier. The Chinese volunteer's eyes were full of tears.

She died! Alexia's heart stopped as her mind flushed with darkness.

Quickly running over, Alexia asked urgently, "What happened?"

Tina looked at Alexia with swollen weepy eyes. "She's fine. See." The little baby was gazing at Tina with her big brown eyes, cooing as she pushed her arms up.

"Thank God," Alexia sighed, noticing the baby was dressed in oversized but warm pajamas. "Hey, little one!" She tickled the little girl, setting her off in gurgled giggles.

"Her parents." Tina hesitated. "They— They— They d-died," Tina stuttered, trying to wipe her tears before they streamed completely down her face.

"What?" Alexia asked. "Where?" She scanned around the beach and didn't spot any body bags.

"They drowned," Tina answered. "Their bodies aren't here. Not yet."

"Oh God." Alexia's heart fell to her stomach. "Does she have any other family here?"

Tina shook her head. "I don't think so. What do we do?"

"I don't know." Alexia's eyes twitched. The stress of the day was adding up. "Have you asked anyone else?"

"No." Tina took in a slow deep breath. "One of the guys from the boat told me when I asked where her parents were." She pursed her lips, trying to hold back the extra tears that were forming puddles in her eyes. "He thinks her name is Heba." She let out a sob before sucking it back in.

"Excuse me." The old man who had been with Sivan interrupted the two volunteers. He was with his wife. Their faces were mournful, a stark contrast from what Alexia had seen just moments ago.

That's the thing with these journeys. One minute can be filled with pure happiness, the next somber and morose.

"I am Dr. Ismail Kassem. How is she?" he asked.

"She is healthy." Tina choked on her words.

"What will happen to her?" His eyes strained as he stared at the little baby. Tina looked at Alexia.

"We don't know," Alexia eventually answered, unable to look at the rosy-faced baby. "I guess she will be given to the Greek authorities and they will have to figure it out. Maybe an orphanage?"

The husband and wife looked at each other, distraught, before speaking in Arabic. Alexia watched as they conversed with words and gestures that she couldn't read, except for their eyes—which were drowning in despair.

"We can't let her go to an orphanage and get lost." Dr. Kassem turned his attention back to Tina and Alexia. "We knew her parents, albeit briefly, but they would not want that either."

"I'm sorry for your loss," Alexia said. She noticed how immaculate his English was. "But there's no other option but to tell the authorities."

"Yes, there is," the doctor said as he looked at his wife and released a long breath. "We will take her with us. She is a Syrian child and she should be raised with a Syrian family."

"But—" Alexia began before she was cut off.

"I know we are asking much of you, but we must all do what is best for the baby. And an orphanage is not it. Her parents said the only reason they left was to give her a better life in Europe. It would be like killing them again if we let her grow up in a place where she would feel unloved, abandoned and without a family. God knows what can happen to her. We will be her family."

Tina stared at Alexia. "We don't have to tell anyone. You see the way the authorities treat refugees. Do you think it will be any different for her? A Syrian orphan?"

Alexia examined the six desperate eyes in front of her. She didn't know Greek law, but she did know that allowing this to happen would make her a criminal. "We could go to jail," she said to Tina.

"Not if we don't tell anyone." Tina passed the baby to Dr. Kassem's wife. "Children have gone missing throughout

Europe because of traffickers. At least this one will be in the right hands." *It's the right thing to do*

Alexia watched as the little girl wrapped her hand around the older woman's finger and squeaked with delight. She saw the warmth in the lady's eyes, kindness, love.

"Okay." She fixed her eyes on the doctor. "We didn't know her circumstances and you told us you were her family. *Khalas*." She cut the air with her hands.

"Finished," said the doctor. "You did not know."

"Please take care of her," Tina begged, her voice soft and sweet.

"We will, with our lives." He looked at her. "We will love her the way we loved our own daughter."

They saw his eyes well up, letting the volunteers know he was sincere, before the couple turned away.

Alexia shifted her attention to the sea, looking for a distraction. And that's when she spotted another black-and-orange dot in the distance.

"Here we go again." *Another big haul — it's what they're prepared for*

Five boats. Two hundred twenty-four people. Those were the shift's statistics for the day.

After the chaotic morning landing of the deflated dinghy, there were 182 more people who came and went, all in need of some sort of assistance. Alexia's shoulders were as wet as her shoes. She held and cried—both joyous and somber tears—with six different women and three children. None of whom she could communicate with verbally, just through smiles and damp eyes.

But as the day came to an end, the volunteers had their moment to reflect. Alexia turned to the water. Her body felt heavy from the weight of the day and the burden of memories reflecting off the sea. She kept picturing the faces she'd met on these shores—the happiness, sadness, fear and confusion. All of it overtook her body right then and there, no matter how hard she tried to push it away.

She headed for the empty tent, needing to be alone, and collapsed inside. She covered her mouth with the sleeve of her sweatshirt and released the emotions that had built up. Once the sobbing started, she couldn't stop it. The tears washed away her pain. The flexing of her lungs sent pulsating relief through her body. Alexia pressed her face into the inside of her elbow and kept crying. As her tear ducts drained, her breathing steadied too.

She looked up and quickly become distracted. *Where is it?* She thought. Her eyes searched for the lime-green wool jacket. Her jacket. Terry's jacket.

Laughter broke through as she realized that the beautifully hideous coat had found its new owner.

CHAPTER 26

The drive from the beach was shorter than they expected. Tareq carried his sister out the door of the white van that held a big yellow sticker with a black arrow on it. The weather sliced at their raw skin. The cold was made increasingly bitter by their hair, still wet with seawater.

The group was directed to stand in a line that had already formed, zigzagging outside the camp. They were the last of their boat to make it here. But there were more people than just those from their dinghy.

"You guys can come with me," said one of the volunteers from the beach, pointing at Tareq. She had driven over with them in the van. "We can deal with check-in later. I want your sister to get to the clinic."

"Is she not better?" Tareq worried.

"She is fine," the friendly woman said. "But I just want her to get checked out properly with real equipment. You have nothing to worry about."

"My sister," Jamila whispered to Tareq.

Family! Togetherness - themes

"Other people from different boats are here," he said, staring at the group ahead.

"Yes, but they are not Afghan." A solitary tear slid down her left cheek.

"Come with us. We will find someone to help us locate her. I promise." The truth was, he wasn't sure what had happened to Najiba, but he also didn't want to see Jamila upset, not until they figured out where her sister could be.

"Hey!" yelled the young man from the boat. "How did you get first class?" He laughed as they passed. *Did he take the jacket (thinking)*

Tareq couldn't help but taste the festive air in the crowd. Despite the horror of the journey, it really was delicious to be alive. *We are alive. Susan's okay!* So he threw the man a bone. "Nice jacket!" He smirked as they made their way past the group. *You feel successful to accomplish a goal and a life-changing one*

"What? It's warm." The young man brushed his hands down into the pockets of his lime-green wool coat. He looked at the other men next to him, who were also laughing. "It's warm!"

Tareq gripped his sister tightly as they navigated their way through the rock-strewn camp, following the brown swinging ponytail of the volunteer ahead of them. She finally stopped at a small white tent; the sign read CLINIC in English, Arabic and Persian. The building was sturdier than the one at the beach. There was a sign of the Red Cross plastered to the side of the door. They trudged through gravel to make their way to the entrance, watching as the volunteer talked to the doctor, explaining Susan's situation.

"Okay." She finally turned back to them. "You will be in good hands here. This is Dr. Raquel. She will check Susan out."

"Thank you." Tareq passed his sister to a pretty woman in a red long-sleeved shirt. "You go with the doctor, *habibti*. I won't be more than a minute," he promised before turning to Jamila. "I need to go in with Susan. But tell her about your sister." He tilted his head toward the young woman who had walked them over.

Jamila looked at him, her eyes filled with guilt and regret, wondering what she could have done differently to have remained by Najiba's side. Tareq detected other emotions there too, though. He felt like he was an expert on reading eyes now, schooled in the most horrible of circumstances. He could see a deep pain in hers. He wanted to unlock her past, her fears, her joys and her dreams. He wanted to know everything about her. But he knew, for now, he had to wait. He held his heart and his body back. *Jamila needs her sister. And I need to take care of mine.*

"It is okay. Tell her what happened. I feel she will be able to help," Tareq said.

Jamila knew he was right. The fact that the volunteer was a woman made it easier. *She can't hurt me.* She calmed herself with that thought. She turned back to Tareq and said, "Just make sure Susan is okay."

"Thank you." Tareq didn't want to abandon Jamila. "Find us," he said before pivoting back toward the clinic.

As he stepped into the heated room, he felt relief. The burning chill on his nose and ears began to abate. He could smell the scent of fresh timber rise from the thin wooden flooring. Dr. Raquel was taking Susan's temperature and had given her a box of orange juice to hold.

"Hello." The curly-haired woman smiled at Tareq as he walked in. "She is absolutely perfect."

He stared at the two, amazed. She looked like an older version of Susan—the hair, the eyes and the smile. In a flash he pictured his sister fully grown, having had the opportunity to be as successful as this doctor in their new lives, away from war—a dream that was no longer possible in Syria, at least not for them. "Thank you," he said.

Good Visions from Destiny

"*Shoof*, juice!" Susan picked the box up higher for her brother to get a better look.

"*Merhaba.*" A voice came from the side. A man walked out from behind a box, pulling out a gray blanket.

"Hello," Tareq answered.

"You can take this with you." The Arab man lifted the blanket. "You will get more when you get to the tent with non-food items." Tareq looked at him quizzically. And the man caught on. "When we are done, I'll get you checked in and take you there."

"Are you Syrian?" Tareq asked. The man's dialect was curious.

"Yes," he replied. "I'm Hashem. My parents were from Syria, but I grew up in London."

Tareq nodded. "That explains the accent, almost Syrian but a little different."

Hashem laughed. "I guess that is how my parents would describe me too."

"You're a doctor?" *Empathy*

"No, I'm just here to help out." The man tossed the blanket to Tareq. "Wrap that around your sister." Tareq obliged. "Dr. Raquel is from Spain. We have another doctor from Denmark.

Neither of them speak Arabic but they both speak English. So I am translating."

"That is very helpful," Tareq said as he wrapped the heavy wool blanket around his sister's shoulders.

"Yeah, until you have a bus of Afghans that come in." He shook his head. "Then I'm useless."

"The sign, it looks familiar. Red Cross?"

"You're probably used to it as Red Crescent. The group operates all over the world."

"Yes, yes." Tareq remembered the ambulances he saw around his city. "There seems to be so much more help here than back home. If we had help there, we wouldn't have to be here." He let his thoughts pour out. *Govt. still really bad*

Hashem looked down. "Yes, well, there are a lot of people who care. But you're not wrong. There isn't enough being done in Syria. Or here either, to be honest."

"And there are a lot of people who hate us." Tareq stared boldly at Hashem's dark brown eyes.

Susan put her juice box down and glanced up at her brother. Hashem took notice. "It's not hate as much as it is fear," he tried to explain. "You see–" *They fear them but show it*

"I know the difference between hate and fear," Tareq cut *through* him off. *hate*

Hashem pushed himself off the stool and walked to a stack of orange juice boxes. He pulled one off the top of the pile. "Here." Hashem passed him a box. "You must be hungry."

Tareq took it but kept his eyes glued to the man in front of him. "You know, if you were in Syria, you would have been forced to fight. Either for the government or for an opposition group—if you weren't dead by now."

"Excuse me?" Hashem studied the boy in front of him.

"My point is, we are the ones afraid. We are the ones who have suffered. How can complete strangers be afraid of those of us who have seen what real suffering is? They can't be afraid of the weak. We should call it what it is: *hate*."

"I don't disagree with you. But there are people from all over the world who still care."

Tareq was too exhausted to continue the conversation. He knew it wasn't fair to Hashem, who actually came to help. Instead, he studied his juice box and unwrapped the plastic around the straw, poking it through the hole at the top. With two giant sips he had swallowed it all down.

"Would you like another?" Hashem looked at the crushed box.

"*Lah, shukran.*" Tareq thanked him for the offer, but it was time to get ahold of his father. Removing his phone from the waterproof pouch, he cursed under his breath when it wouldn't turn on. "Do you have a place I can charge my phone?" he asked. He wanted to let his father know they'd arrived and they were safe. He wouldn't go into details. Not today. He didn't want him to worry.

"Yes, of course." Hashem pointed to a white table with outlets around it. "That's our charging station. It should have any type of cable you need."

"Thank you." Tareq was amazed by the preparation and organization, luxuries that arrivals in the months before didn't have. He walked over to the table, knowing it would take time for his phone to charge. But he sat next to it anyway, waiting.

"Why don't we go check you two in while it charges?" Hashem walked over with another box of juice, placing it in front of the drained teen, who himself needed a reboot.

Hashem couldn't do that, but he could share a juice.

Will it get stolen?

↑

prediction

CHAPTER 27

"Yes, we are safe," Tareq shouted into the phone. *He still had his* Turkish SIM card in, and it barely got any reception. He had to walk up the hill from the camp to find even the one bar. There were others around him sending messages and making calls to family. "When do you think you can join us?"

"I don't know, *rohi,*" his father's voice crackled through. "I need to save up enough money, and then I will join you. I swear."

Tareq could hear another voice in the background. "Who is that?"

"Ah, that's my new friend Anas." Fayed laughed. "He is telling me to tell you to say hi to all the Syrians in Europe."

"Well, there are a lot, but I will do my best." Tareq let out a chuckle. "Where are you right now?"

"What? I'm sorry, *ibni,* your voice is breaking up."

"I said," Tareq said louder, while moving the direction of his phone, "where are you?"

"I'm near the square. Working with Anas. We sell cigarettes.

He has been doing this for a while now and he is letting me assist him."

"Cigarettes?" *Bad for their health*

"Yes, there are so many Syrians in Basmane. They can live without food but not without their cigarettes."

Fair point, Tareq thought. *Their homes have been taken, their lives flipped upside down, the least they should have is their cigarettes.* "Baba, have you heard from Musa?" There was silence at the end of the line, so he angled his phone around again. "Baba?"

"Yes, *omri,* I'm here."

"I said, how is Musa?" Tareq repeated. He could hear the car horns in the background as his father breathed heavily. "Is he okay—did something happen?" His heart began to race.

"Musa is okay." Fayed sighed. "It's your uncle and aunt."

Tareq's stomach turned. "What happened?" There was silence again. "Baba!" *That's terrible. Their beliefs are too*

"Daesh found out that Musa left. So men came. Grabbed them. *extreme* Painted on their house, claiming they were spies for America."

"Where are they?" Tareq's body tensed up.

"They're no more." The words punched him in the gut, stopping the air from going in and out of his lungs. "I'm sorry." Tareq could hear his father sniffle even through the bad connection. "Musa won't answer his phone."

"I . . . I have to go." Tareq knew if he continued to talk, he would fall apart, and he didn't have the luxury to mourn—not at the moment. Right now, he needed all the strength he could gather. "I miss you—please join us soon."

"Yes, of course." Fayed's voice feigned strength again. "Kiss my Susan for me."

"I will. Bye." Tareq put his phone back into his pocket and searched across the water in front of him. For what? He wasn't sure.

The hills and mountains of Turkey and its speckled city lights ahead looked no different from when he was on the other side of the sea, looking toward Greece. After taking in a long deep breath of the crisp air, he released another cloud.

He pulled his phone out and texted Musa.

TAREQ: I'm sorry.

He didn't expect a response. But he saw that Musa started typing right away.

Poor Musa. Hope he's okay

MUSA: We've never been so different, you and I. Now we both have lost our families.

TAREQ: I didn't want you to know this pain . . . ever.

He waited, but Musa didn't message him again. Tareq clicked to go back to the home screen when he noticed another missed ping. He opened the app but only saw symbols—his updated app didn't have the right fonts to cover whatever language it was written in.

TAREQ: Who is this? My number will change soon, message now please.

Tareq sat on the dirt and lingered longer. He watched the sky fade from a rusty orange to a bruised blue. For a moment he thought the sea looked so picturesque, so beautiful. But then his mind flashed to the woman's lifeless eyes as they stared at him through the crystal blue waters. His body shivered, and not from the cold. He wondered if her corpse had washed up yet, or if it ever would. *Would it bloat? Does skin on a dead body shrivel when it has been in the water for too long?* He shook his head. *Fall from my ears. I don't need this right now.* He didn't want to stay another minute; the sea kept tormenting him. No matter how much he rattled his head, the memories were far stronger. They were all he could see.

And the truth is, they will never fully fade. He will continue to have flashbacks and nightmares throughout his life. The memories will fill him, making him anxious. Some humans can shrug off stress better than others. But when your soul feels too much, that trauma makes a home in your heart. But it's not a weakness or even an illness. To feel so much means you can find empathy—when you can sense the pain of others, that is a power to hold on to. That is a power that can change the world you live in. But it's also a power that comes with burden and pain.

Tareq made his way back to the camp.

As he walked through, he saw the young man from the boat again. "Hey," the man yelled out to Tareq. "We're here for the night. Could be worse. They say the other camp, Moria, is full, so we have to wait."

"That's what I was told might happen," Tareq responded.

The man stuck his hands into his pockets. "Guess what," he said. "You all made fun of this jacket, but now I have a new friend." He pulled out the note. "There are good people who still care." He winked at Tareq before moving on.

Tareq found his sister and Jamila at the children's tent,

where he'd left them. Susan was drawing with some crayons as Jamila sat next to her. *Even distressed, she's beautiful.* Tareq fixed onto the Afghan girl's jade eyes again. "They tell you more?" he asked.

Like Musa, he found someone

Jamila shook her head and continued to rub her hands together. "They say boat with Afghans got to Moria camp this morning. But no more information."

"This is good news," he tried to comfort her.

"Just one boat." She looked up at him, tormented. "Too many boats come today. How only one Afghan?"

"God will help." Tareq tried desperately to believe his own words. He turned to his sister. "How are you, *rohi*?"

"I'm drawing." She lifted her red crayon up. "This is home." Tareq strained to figure out what the picture was of. He saw faces, but one corner was blue and the other red.

"What is this supposed to be?"

She pointed to the blue. "Us in the water." Then she pointed to the red. "Mama, Teyta, Salim, Farrah, Ameer, Sameer in blood." Susan looked up at her brother, concerned. "I don't know where to draw Baba."

Tareq could feel his tears on the edge of bursting like a broken drainpipe, but he tried hard to hold them in. "Put Baba with us," he finally said. "He is with us."

< They all are!
She has sophisticated thoughts
that alarm me!

CHAPTER 28

As Alexia scanned the grounds of the transit camp, she came to a stark realization. For many months she had helped the people who passed through, but she'd never had a real conversation with any of them. ~~Interesting~~

She'd hugged them, she'd cried with them, she'd sat in silence holding their hands. But she'd never been able to sit down and get to know them. There was never time. They landed, celebrated being alive, and then moved on to the next step. But now she was realizing that she was still trying to protect herself.

Distance often safeguards the heart. It preserves and shields you from letting the pain enter your spirit, changing you forever. Bridging that distance can make you hurt. But that isn't a sign of weakness; it's the power of compassion and love—the two elements that can save a world.

On this day, Alexia decided to take an active step in bridging the gap between herself and the refugees she helped to save.

[handwritten: Way to get out of comfort zone? She can help them let out their emotions]

"Hi!" Her voice made Tareq jump.

He was waiting for Susan and Jamila outside the bath-room facilities with the mustached man he met on the beach in Turkey—who he learned was named Kamel.

"Hello." He looked at the volunteer, puzzled. She was with a blond-haired male volunteer. He reminded Tareq of a poster he once saw of a man surfing.

"I'm sorry to interrupt." Alexia swung her attention to the older man with the mustache.

"You are most welcome," Kamel said, lifting his hand to his chest.

"I don't know if you remember me. From the beach?" She turned back to Tareq.

He studied her face but couldn't place it.

"I was the one in the tent with your sister," Alexia said, almost hurt that she was so forgettable.

"Ah, yes!" Tareq reached out and shook her hand. "Thank you so much. So very much, for help, for my sister."

"It was my pleasure. I'm Alexia, and this is Joel," she said, pointing at her friend. ~~prediction: good friends~~

"Hey there." Joel shook both the men's hands.

"How is she, your sister?" Alexia asked.

"Better, thank you. She is with Jamila in toilets." He watched as Kamel threw his cigarette to the ground and dug it into the gravel. "Here they come." Tareq shifted his gaze as Susan ran and jumped into his arms.

"Playroom?" begged Susan.

"*Hayati*, we need to get some rest. Besides, that room is closed."

"*Yallah*, please." She pouted.

"Isn't Farrah sleepy?"

"Maybe?" Susan clenched tighter to her damp doll.

"*Yallah*, let's go." Tareq turned to Alexia. "Very nice to see you. Thank you for helping my sister." He started to walk away.

"Wait," Alexia blurted. "What are you guys doing for dinner?"

Tareq looked at Jamila. "The camp, they gave us meal."

"Are you still hungry?"

"We are always hungry," Kamel grunted as he pulled out another cigarette and placed it between his lips.

"How about we bring you more food?" She looked at Joel, raising an eyebrow.

She's using food as a talking mechanism [handwritten annotation]

Alexia and Joel purchased a mix of thirty chicken and falafel sandwiches from the food truck outside the camp, a portable restaurant catering to the on-site volunteers more than the refugees. Tareq welcomed them to the tent, where he, Susan and Jamila would be spending the night along with Kamel's family, like they did on the Turkish beach the night before—this time with blankets and heat.

The two volunteers took off their shoes and entered with bags in hand. "We got sandwiches and chips."

"You did not have to do this," Tareq said.

Nice of them [handwritten annotation]

"We wanted to." Alexia beamed at everyone inside.

"We brought extra, we figured others would be hungry too," Joel added.

"*Yislamu*," Kamel said. Then he turned to his oldest and

told her to go distribute the generous gift to the tents next to them.

"Just be careful," warned Joel. "The people working here aren't keen on having us here. So we snuck in with the food." The father translated to his daughter. "Safety and all."

As they ate, two other female volunteers came to join them.

"Not easy to sneak in here," Famke said, putting down a bag full of soda bottles. "But not hard either." She smirked.

Alexia introduced Famke and Hilda to the group. Tareq learned that they were from the Netherlands and Germany.

Famke looked back at Alexia. "This wasn't what I was expecting when I texted you about having dinner. I figured you would have some dolmades and a beer. This is so much more interesting."

"Definitely." Hilda smiled as she opened a bag of potato chips to share with the young Syrian girl next to her.

As the night progressed, everyone felt more open. The children fell asleep on their blue mats and were covered with blankets. The Syrians brought in tea from the transit tent and began asking questions about Europe and sharing their experiences. *A good way to learn*

"Syria is thousands of years old, with so much history and great people," Kamel said as he scratched his growing stubble. "But it was destroyed in a moment. Nobody wants to leave their country and risk having their family die at sea. But when it is impossible to live in your own land, people will do many desperate things. We started together, we finish together. If we must, we should die together." Alexia's eyes glanced over to his three

together!!!

daughters, who were fast asleep. Innocents who only knew to listen and trust their parents.

"But you knew before you came that many families did die. How come you would want to take that risk rather than stay in Turkey?" asked Hilda. "They are not at war."

"Turkey was not living with hope. Not for a Syrian. What is life without hope?" Kamel asked back. "We had bombs falling on us. Why I should be afraid of some waves? Let us die, at least then we can finally rest. In our graves at least we can sleep forever."

"I did not mean to insult." *Tough refugee crisis*

"I am not insulted. But I tell you. This is hardest test of my life." He looked at his family. "And most important."

As the night progressed, the Syrians and the one Afghan shared their stories from home. They talked about the beauty of their cities and the destruction of their lives and loved ones. *Truly said* Both volunteers and refugees shed tears, salty droplets of relief as they set free the stories that were trapped in their hearts and minds. Talk truly is therapy. Just having someone listen and care can cure so much. Sharing the burden of your past makes your load that much lighter as you continue into your future. But it's not always easy. *Everyone's story can be shocking / bad*

Even Tareq was shocked when he heard about Jamila's parents and little brother being killed on a routine trip to the supermarket in Kabul. "They were shopping for food for my birthday. I did not know. It was to be a surprise." She wiped her eyes. "The police said the suicide bomber first shoot with machine gun at shoppers and store workers. Then he explode his vest. A big fire burned." She covered her face as the tears streamed

[handwritten: Tough for them to say]

down. After a minute she regained her composure. "Their bodies were burned black. Like when you leave chicken too long on fire. Charred, I think is what the English news called it. We could not even do religious cleaning for burial, too much charred. Like thin black paper." She pulled out a folded hand-kerchief, slowly unwrapping it. Inside was a wedding ring with black stains and a locket. "My mother's. Both of these. All I have left." She opened the heart-shaped locket and shared the pictures of her parents on their wedding day. "I didn't want party, I just want them."

The stories continued from person to person, until they were too exhausted to remember any more.

"What's next?" Joel asked no one in particular.

[handwritten: should he get caught?] "I need to check Facebook," Kamel answered. "There are groups on there who advertise smugglers, where to go and how. Some smugglers even post promotions. This is human traffick-ing, but it is so easy for them. My cousin met one in Athens. He arrived with suitcase full of passports. I guess if you have money, it is no problem." He heaved a laugh.

"And for you?" Alexia looked at Tareq.

"I don't know," he whispered, staring at Susan, whose head was nuzzled in his lap as she slept. "I don't know."

[handwritten: I wouldn't either]

[handwritten: I love how they share their experiences, learn + feel from them]

CHAPTER 29

Tareq waited till the water filled his cupped hands and then splashed it onto his face. The cold felt good on his hot skin and tired eyes.

Earlier that morning, they had left the transit camp and a bus dropped them off at Moria, a larger camp in Mytilene. The Internet chat pages hadn't had many nice things to say about the former detention facility, but so far Tareq didn't have any complaints. They'd been fingerprinted, registered and assigned a trailer with bunks that lined the inner perimeter. They had some problems with Jamila's papers because she was Afghan, but once they found the right person to help them, they got lucky.

Tareq stepped out of the trailer's bathroom to a chorus of babies crying and a toddler giggling as he rolled around on a rough mat. His exhausted mother sat on the floor next to him with a hand to her forehead. The Kurdish woman was just grateful the boy's energy was currently confined to this small room. Tareq found Jamila and Susan still sitting on his bed, but now laughing. "What is so funny?" he asked.

You can find relief in your little siblings joy

"Your ears." Susan giggled and then placed her hands behind her own, sticking them out. And for added measure, she blew air into her cheeks.

"It's not that bad." Jamila covered her sniggering with a hand that disguised nothing.

"This is my picture for Europe." Tareq picked up the registration papers they were looking at, his ticket for the ferry to Athens. He knew it wasn't the best picture he'd ever taken, but seeing Jamila's smile again made it worth it. She was finally reunited with her sister after someone working at this new camp located Najiba's name under those who'd registered the day before. It was an emotional reunion with many tears and kisses before they returned to their bickering. Najiba was in her trailer showering, so Jamila came to spend time with her new friends.

"What do we do now?" asked Jamila.

"We explore our home for the night and take ferry tomorrow." Tareq watched Jamila shiver. "I think no one wants to go back in water. But this time it will be on big ship." He stretched his arms out. "We will be safe, *inshallah*."

"Yes, God willing," she agreed.

Where are they trying to go?

Tareq heard the chime of his phone and picked it up. The camp had Wi-Fi, albeit intermittently, so he had been able to speak with his father and finally tried calling Musa—who didn't pick up. This time it was a message from the American girl. She and her friend were here and wanted to see them.

"*Yallah*, let's go." He patted Susan. "It's too crowded in here. And our new friends want to meet with us." Tareq felt almost normal. He'd met new people last night that he liked.

They made the hard journey

And he was finally regaining some hope that things would get better.

good things to come

Jamila popped up too. "Let us get Najiba. Afghan Hill has tea and soup. It will keep us warm."

They stepped out the trailer door and onto the white concrete. The fence in front of them was lined with clothes left to dry by those who were transported straight from the beaches they landed on. The bright blue sky began fading to a bruised purple and its balls of thick white clouds were turning gray as the sun started to set. "I'm cold," Susan said, looking up at her brother.

"We will get you a better jacket, *rohi*." A promise he intended to fulfill immediately, after so many he had made and couldn't. He was told there was a clothing tent on Afghan Hill, the makeshift camp next to Moria.

Be careful with promises to children

They stopped at Najiba's trailer. "I will get her." Jamila opened the door and called out for her sister, who ran to the entrance and promptly lifted her gray headscarf, covering most of her hair, when she saw Tareq. Something Jamila had stopped doing.

"Hello," Najiba said to Tareq and Susan before turning back to her sister to speak in Dari. Tareq peeked in through the door and saw a girl around Jamila's age curled up into a ball, staring at the sisters. She had sunk her body into her long dress, hiding from the world. Only her pale face was exposed, holding a vacant expression. She flinched and quickly hid her head when she saw the boy peering in. Jamila eventually looked at Tareq, her expression filled with distress. She nodded at her sister and turned back.

Tareq is a helper

"I need to help my sister." Her eyes shifted down. "There is a person with trouble here."

"Can I help?" Tareq leaned forward.

Helpful, kind, hopeful

"No." She shook her head and put her hands on his chest to block him. The simple touch shot goose bumps throughout his body. "This is not for man."

"Okay. We talk later?" he asked, deflated at the thought of leaving her. Tareq had been enjoying his moments with Jamila. She gave him energy in a way he'd never felt before. He wanted her to join them. He wanted to spend every moment with her.

"Yes, of course." She smiled, then turned back, closing the door behind her.

He's like Musa

Tareq and Susan walked toward the entrance of the camp. Susan kicked a golf-ball-sized rock she found on the ground, knocking it down the concrete steps and past the white brick buildings where the police and registration officials were. She chased it when it went astray, only to bring it back to where her brother was. As they made it out of the gate, the street was lined with cars. An indigo filter had veiled this part of the island as day faded to night. The forested hills became a silhouette without the sun's rays hitting them.

"Hold my hand." Tareq reached out to Susan. The little girl promptly grabbed her brother's palm with a tight squeeze.

Alexia's message said to meet them near the food trucks, requiring them to walk past the barrier walls lined with barbed-wire fences. Tareq now understood why many were not fond of Moria; it made you feel like a criminal. But the graffiti on the barricades lifted his spirits a bit. NO BORDERS, NO NATIONS.

You never want to feel like a criminal when in distress

SOLIDARITY WITH MIGRANTS. NO ONE IS ILLEGAL. He began
to think that maybe the reports he had seen and read about
refugees being unwelcome might have been exaggerated. That
was, until he finally made it to Afghan Hill.

The muddy olive grove was packed with tents and people. *Wow!*
Many of those there were not even allowed into Moria because
they were not considered the right *type* of refugee, the ones
they considered economic migrants, not asylum seekers. And
once, that had been mostly Afghans—the hill's namesake—
despite the war that still raged there. But recently, it was mostly
Moroccans, Iranians, Palestinians and many other nationalities
who were left in limbo. After risking their lives to make it here,
they now faced deportation. In the hierarchy of who got their
papers registered by European Union officials, Syrians were
priority while others shimmied up, down and off the list in the
eyes of EU law on any given day. *That seems biased*

Tareq spotted the food trucks across from the line of yellow
taxis, the cabbies waiting for the wealthier refugees who opted
out of the shared buses to the port. He saw Alexia, who enthusiastically waved at him. Next to her, ordering a coffee, was Joel.

She splashed through the mud. "Hi, guys!" she said. "And
how are you?" She nudged Susan, who giggled at the chipper
American lady. Joel made his way over, holding a hot cup.

"G'day," he said. "How you goin' on, mate?" Tareq eyed him,
confused. "Hello." Joel slowed down, realizing his accent could
confuse even fluent English speakers. "How are you doing?"
Tareq lifted his head and eyebrows, understanding now.

"We are good, thank you." He looked at Susan. "We

received the registration papers and we leave tomorrow, *inshallah*."

"Great news, mate!" Joel said. "You want one?" He lifted his coffee cup.

Tareq shook his head. "We need to get Susan another coat. This one, not warm enough."

"Good call," Alexia said. "She'll need it for the coming journey. I'll go with you guys."

"Thank you." Tareq was grateful for the friendly girl's help.

"Tareq?" Susan tugged on her brother's hand. "I'm really cold."

"Here, *habibti*." Tareq took off the puffy down jacket he'd received at the first camp, wrapping it around her little body. "Is this better?"

"*Eh*," she tittered, knowing how silly she looked in the oversized coat as she stuck the bottom half of her face under the collar.

Tareq was often struck by his sister's beauty. And this moment was no different. Her light curls and blue eyes contrasted against his black jacket. Instinctively he kissed her forehead. "*Ana behebek*."

"I love you too." She smiled, grabbing his hand to kiss before rubbing it on her cheek.

"I can get 'er a hot choco' if she's nippy," Joel suggested. He saw the confused stare again. "I can get her a hot *choc-o-late* if she is *cold*," he repeated slowly. "While you guys find another coat."

Tareq frowned on taking handouts, but right now he was not in the position to say no to them either. Denying his sister something that would make her happy and warm wasn't what he wanted to do. But he also didn't want to leave her alone with a stranger.

"It's okay. I will get her something hot after," Tareq responded.

"There might be a line," Alexia said. "A lot of people aren't in love with the clothes they've received. So they keep lining up for something else." *Picky - need to be greatly*

Tareq scratched the back of his head as he glanced at his sister dancing around in his oversized jacket. "Okay," he gave in and knelt down. "He's going to get you something warm to drink. I want you to stay here." He stared at his sister's innocent eyes, amazed that they'd stayed that way after all they'd seen. "Do you understand?"

She nodded, clutching his jacket.

"We go now?" Tareq shifted his gaze to Alexia. "Let us be fast, please."

"Yeah, of course, let's go." She winked at Susan.

The two trudged through the mud, squelching and squerching with each step. Around them were families and groups of young men and boys looking for anyone to bum a cigarette from.

"This is very . . ." Tareq tried to find the right words. "Not so nice." The faces around him drooped as they shivered in the cold damp air. The bleak and unwelcoming surroundings matched their pasts, their presents and their near futures.

"Yeah, it's a bit dreary." Alexia scanned the field full of white tents and mud. "But believe me when I say, it's so much better than what it used to be. These tents weren't here before. And if

Very wearing and dreading setting

you think it's crowded now"–she blew out some air–"you should have seen it in the fall."

They reached the clothing tent and were relieved to see that the line wasn't as long as they'd expected. As they approached, they noticed an older couple watching two volunteers who were arguing with each other.

"Well, get your lazy butt back in there and find her something better, goddammit!" a ball of fire with chestnut hair roared.

"You can't . . . I mean–" The man in a gray beanie behind the table tried to fight back. "You have no right to tell me what to do." He slammed a foot into the wet ground, splashing mud onto his own pants.

"What did you say?" she snapped back. Her brown eyes seared through him. "We are here to serve. Now go in there and get her new shoes and pants." The horrified man glanced at the Afghan couple who were watching, but gave in and disappeared into the giant white pavilion. The brunette then turned to the husband and wife and spoke to them in Dari. The older lady, in a brown headscarf, planted a wet kiss on both sides of the woman's face.

"That certainly was a display," Alexia said to the woman. "Maybe you can help us when you're done helping them."

"Sometimes you have to remind these people why we all came. To help." She put a hand out. "I'm Siddiqa from New York, by way of Afghanistan thirty-five years ago."

"She best!" the lady next to her said enthusiastically. She clapped her hands before smooching her again. She started speaking to Alexia in Dari.

Siddiqa smirked while looking at the bewilderment on the pretty American girl's face, so she decided to translate. "She said God gave her short legs and these guys in the tent gave her long pants." As Siddiqa explained, the older woman opened up her long winter coat to reveal a pair of stonewashed jeans that belonged in a heavy metal concert from the 1980s. "Her nickname among the Afghans has become 'young momma.'" They chuckled together.

"It's great that you speak the language," said Alexia.

"Not enough people speak Dari around here, just me and my son right now for the hundreds of Afghans and Iranians who come through every day. There are more Arabic translators, but I notice many of the Arabic speakers can speak some English anyway. Although I think this week there is another Afghan American doctor in the medical tent." She pointed in its direction. "What do you guys need? This guy is bad at his job, and his answer is always no." She rolled her eyes. "But he knows not to say no to me." She grinned. Alexia was relieved to have Siddiqa there. She knew that she wouldn't have the fortitude to fight, and she never dealt well with confrontation.

Alexia told her all about Susan, from her size to her pudgy-cheeked smile, and how they needed a warm jacket for the journey.

"Got it. We'll get her something perfect."

Tareq enjoyed the confident Afghan American woman. She reminded him of his *teyta*—the same feisty spirit, the same big heart, just a tad younger.

The man in the gray beanie stumbled out of the tent.

"Here! But that's it!" He slashed his hand in the air, feigning authority.

"Thank you so much!" Siddiqa squealed, beaming rays of sunshine his way, making him cringe. He knew it wasn't over. "Now, my Syrian friend needs help for his little sister . . ."

After six trips in and out of the tent and Siddiqa's analysis of the quality of each jacket, she finally decided on a red wool hooded coat. She also provided knitted gloves and two scarves. "Stick one down to cover her chest and wrap the other around her face. You know what?" She grabbed the scarves back from Tareq. "Take me to her, I will show you how to do it." She blew a kiss to the man in the gray beanie, who dropped his head in exhaustion and relief as he watched her walk away.

"This place just doesn't seem to get better," Alexia said as they prepared to walk back toward the food trucks.

"Yes," Siddiqa said. "It's also frequented by some dodgy people who say they're volunteering or that they're refugees themselves—but we don't think they're either. We're looking for these young teenage Moroccan boys who were here for a week, trying to get out of Greece. We think they gave up and left with some traffickers." She shook her head. "You just never know who is lurking around the camps looking to exploit these desperate people. I'm most afraid for the children. So many travel alone and trust anyone who offers them a sandwich or cigarette."

Tareq listened in, but he was focused on getting back to his sister and showing her the new coat. He couldn't wait to see her curls against the red wool, and there was enough room for her to squeeze Farrah inside. He knew she was going to be excited.

"Do you guys want to stop and get some soup or hot tea?" Siddiqa looked at Tareq as they walked, trying to change the subject.

"No, thank you," Tareq said. "We give my sister this coat first, then soup."

"Of course." Siddiqa nodded.

As they approached the food trucks, they saw Joel sitting on the curb, chomping on a chicken burger. Tareq scanned the area but didn't see Susan. "Susan. Where is Susan?" Tareq asked as the anxiety built inside him. *Was his worry right?*

Joel turned around, wiping his mouth. "Hey, no dramas, mate. She was cold, so a cabbie offered her a heated seat."

"Where?" asked Siddiqa, already tense from her conversation.

Joel looked up at the new woman. "Right th–" He scratched his head. "Hold up."

"Where is she?" Tareq's heart pounded and his breaths became heavy. "What taxi?" He couldn't tell if it was his body spinning or the camp.

"I swear it was right there." Joel stood up and dropped his sandwich. "She was right there."

Oh no! The guy messed up big time! I would panic so much right there

His worry foreshadowed this

CHAPTER 30

They ran up and down the line of taxis. None of the drivers knew about the little girl with blond curls. Siddiqa took charge and ordered Alexia and Tareq to go with her son, Dean. "Drive toward Mytilene center, look everywhere and start with the port. A lot of those being trafficked will be taken by ferry," she said, avoiding Tareq's eyes as she tossed keys to her muscular son, who towered over them all. "Bluetooth me her picture now." She finally gave Tareq a solid, reassuring stare. "We *will* find her." He scrambled through his phone, unable to speak. "And you"—she turned to Joel—"you're coming with me to report this to the police." Her gaze was void of the gentleness she'd shared with the rest of the group, despite her cognizance of the inexperienced volunteers who came to help.

"I'm so s-s-sorry," Joel stuttered. Even Alexia couldn't focus on comforting him as she asked Dean which car was his.

"Got it," Siddiqa said, her eyebrows furrowed as she stared at the picture of the little girl on her phone. She shifted back to Joel. "Do you remember anything from the taxi that can help differentiate it from the others?"

The young surfer strained his eyes shut. "I just remember the man was fat and bald with gray wings of hair on the sides and a dark mustache. Almost as if he dyes it black." His eyes popped open. "There was a sticker that caught my attention. On the driver's side of the windscreen. A red flag. At first I thought it was the Nazi symbol, that's why I checked it out. Then I realized it was just a line, kind of like a zigzag but folded into a square or rectangle. I didn't think it was a big deal."

"The Golden Dawn." Siddiqa's stomach sank as the eyes around her anxiously waited for more. "They're the fascist party." She shook her head as she continued, but then darted her head up. "Go now!" she ordered. *Are they a bad group?*

The three started running toward the white hatchback parked on the main road. "Try the port first and the docks around it! It's easy to hide in a crowd," Siddiqa yelled from behind. "We will *But there is* force the police to get involved and spread the word!" *so many people— too hard to find*

Dean clicked his key fob to unlock the doors before jumping into the driver's seat. He started the engine as Tareq and Alexia were still jumping in. He turned to Tareq in the passenger's seat. "Buckle your seat belt, guys. We are going to find your sister. And I'm going to kick that guy's ass." Alexia watched his chiseled jaw flex. *love the determination*

"Please, let's g—" Tareq's head hit the back of his seat as the car sped down the road. Dean repeatedly slammed his hand on the horn, saving his swivels for those who didn't jump off the road fast enough.

"Probably best if we don't kill anyone on the way," Alexia said. "Including us." She looked at the tanned jock and became annoyed with herself for thinking he was attractive at a moment like this. *Bruh*

"No, fast is good," Tareq slipped in before returning to his thoughts. His body was still, but his insides were flailing and his mind churning. *I will kill myself if anything happens. I was supposed to protect her. What do I tell Baba?* *That's what I thought*

Alexia kept her eyes on the cars riding down the highway, looking for any splash of yellow. They whizzed past one. "Will you slow down when we get near taxis, at least?" she said, glaring at Dean.

"Shit, sorry," said the twenty-three-year-old. "I was so focused on getting to the city, I didn't pay attention."

"Well, do now," Alexia snapped. "I'm pretty sure I saw the driver had a full head of hair in the one we just passed."

"Here's another," Dean said. All three tensed up as he let go of the accelerator, slowing the car down. "He's bald!"

"Not him," Alexia said, deflated. "No flag, no mustache, and no one in the back."

Dean slammed his foot on the accelerator again. Tareq kept his face turned to his window as his tears dripped down. "Don't worry, bud," Dean said, reaching into the side pocket of his door and pulling out a small packet of tissues. He handed it to Tareq. "We're going to find her." As they pulled in closer to the city's narrow and sharp roads, there were more cabs and more disappointment. The restaurants and stores bustled with carefree shoppers and bored clerks. An energy that had felt foreign to Tareq for some time now. *Its impossible*

He began negotiating with God, promising he would be

fine with all he had lost and would start being grateful, as long as he could have his sister back. The only sibling he had left. Flashes of Salim, Farrah, Sameer and Ameer popped into his head. It was followed by a vision of Susan also in the rubble as dust piled onto her face. He shook his head. Neither Alexia nor Dean said anything. *Fears/bad dreams*

"We're close to where the ferries are." Dean yanked the steering wheel, avoiding a motorcycle. "We can start there."

The cloudless sky was black, most of the stars lost in the city's luminosity. Parts of the city were softly glowing, others abandoned and sleeping. Deceivingly peaceful. The ferry was docked for the next day's voyage, but no passengers were waiting. A few stragglers strolled the empty alleys. But no taxis. *All of these people directing the search are helpers.*

Alexia dropped her head. But Tareq perked up. "I know she is nearby."

"Do you see something?" Dean asked as they parked and stepped out of the car. *are helpers. the stealers is au tiel hunter*

"I feel it." Tareq stared ahead. *Please, God, don't let this be the devil tricking me again*, he thought as his stomach tightened. He picked up his pace and started to jog. Nothing. His jog transitioned to a sprint. But still nothing. Tareq frantically whirled his body, looking for anything yellow and anyone with blond hair, but he was met with emptiness. *Helpers feel empathy, right thing to do*

He ran to where some cars were parked in the nearby lot. No taxi. He jolted down an alleyway. Nobody. He wobbled back, straining his face, and grabbed his hair with both hands, yanking as he let out silent sobs. *There is no God*, he cried to himself. *I would lose it too*

He felt a hand on his shoulder, which he quickly nudged off. "Let's just get back in the car," Dean said. "We won't give up. There are other places to search."

But Tareq spread his body on the ground, feeling the rough black asphalt on his face. He imagined his corpse lying on this cold concrete slab. *This is death. This is what it feels like to be dead. Just let me die right here.*

The awful thoughts
- and imagery he
   experiences
(hurts me)

CHAPTER 31

The description of it being filled makes it more hopeless [handwritten annotation]

Alexia, unable to watch, kept striding ahead. As her feet pounded the pavement, she headed in the direction of Kountourioti, the main road of Port Lesvos. The street was illuminated by the blinking red taillights of cars crowding their way around, looping the city's waterfront. On one side of the traffic sat stores and restaurants that were still open. On the other, she walked on the empty pathway lined with wooden benches, parked motorcycles and streetlamps pouring a faint golden glow onto the cracked bleached concrete. She passed boats cloaked in the darkness of night, lined securely to the dock, both professional and personal vessels.

She thought she was alone. Until she spotted a man standing on his boat. His face was familiar, but she couldn't quite place it. Assuming it was one of the volunteers she had met during her months on the island, she pushed forward toward him. *Maybe he can help—he has to have friends nearby. We need all hands on deck.* She pardoned her own pun. As she inched closer, her stomach instantly fell and her feet skid to a stop. That face.

It's him? feels dangerous [handwritten annotation]

She felt the same unforgettable chill that had traveled down her spine the first time she saw him at the beach, when he'd leered at her with menacing eyes. This time there was no camera in his hands. She quickly turned before he could see her watching him. She shifted her attention toward Saint Therapon, the nineteenth-century church radiant under the night sky. *He will just think I'm a tourist.* With a side glance, she knew he hadn't noticed her.

Alexia watched as he jumped off the stern of one of the smaller boats onto the dock. He lit a cigarette by the traffic before walking through the stream of moving cars, flipping off the drivers who honked at him, and even those who didn't. She followed from across the road and watched as he spat on the sidewalk and opened the glass door of a restaurant, sitting at the window table. There was another man with him whose back was against the window. The waiter placed a beer down in front of him, and she saw a snarl form on his wretched face. He kept taking drags from his cigarette and guzzled down his drink. Alexia waited. The hefty man with him finally turned his head to glance out the window. These people seem like hunters

Oh my God! Frightened, Alexia guarded her body behind a line of parked motorcycles. She paused to regain her composure before lifting her head high enough to peek past the bikes. She felt the acidic bile crawl up her throat when she identified the black mustache and gray wings of hair that Joel had described. *It's him. They're together. Susan! Poor Susan!*

She turned to the red-and-white vessel he had leaped from. Although it was dwarfed by the local ferries that surrounded it, it was still quite large. On the bow she saw the name *Euphoria* painted in white over the red background. The irony was not lost on her.

Looking back, she saw that another round of beers had been placed on their table. *Now or never* went on repeat in her mind as she took in the cold damp air and sprinted before flinging her body onto the surface of the rickety boat. Her elbows caught part of her fall, but she still slammed the side of her face against the deck. "That's gonna leave a bruise," she said, slowly peeling her head off and lifting it to peek over the starboard side of the ship. She took a deep breath and let it out slowly. They were still drinking.

Ignoring her aching elbows, she army-crawled her way around the deck. "Susan," she called under her breath, fearful of causing too much attention. "Susan!" She slipped out her phone to text Tareq.

ALEXIA: Look for Euphoria boat. Red and white.

She pressed send. But the message wouldn't deliver. And she remembered his Turkish SIM card didn't work in Greece; he needed Wi-Fi. *Dammit!* She kicked herself for not taking down Dean's number or the local police's during the ride over. "Idiot," she whispered to herself before deciding to press onward alone.

Sliding her way down to the lower deck, she recoiled at the stench of mold and dirty sweat socks. The surroundings looked no better than they smelled. The wooden vessel was stained with tarnish and broken timber. Crusted canisters of food littered the floor along with discarded cans of beer and bottles of alcohol.

"Susan!" she said, louder this time, kicking away the trash on the floor. She heard pounding and shouting. "Keep kicking!" she hollered back. The voices didn't belong to Susan. If hers was there, others on board drowned it out. Alexia pinpointed a door with wooden paneling, vibrating from the thuds. As she ran forward, she screamed, "Hello!"—this time at the top of her lungs, slapping her hands on the moldy timber.

"Help us, you, please!" She heard the voice of a boy struggling to speak English while others were speaking in both Arabic and Dari. She yanked on the door handle, but it wouldn't open.

"Hold on," she yelled. Searching the cabin, she tried to find something, anything that might help. The banging continued as she unzipped a black duffel bag, pulling everything out. All she found were dirty clothes and cigarettes. Focusing now on the boat's seat boxes, she was able to flip some open and rummage through them. But again, useless. She ran over to the cabinets. In the first one she opened, she found an old fire extinguisher. She grabbed the small metal canister and ran back to the door. "Okay." She tried to stay calm. "Don't touch the door. Do you understand? Do not touch door. Move back."

"Yes, okay, yes. Please. Hurry," the English speaker begged.

"One. Two. Three!" Alexia slammed the extinguisher down, breaking the handle off. Quickly grabbing the door's side, she tried to pry it open with her fingers. "Dammit!"

"It is no move," the voice said through the screams.

"Shit!" Alexia yelled. She continued pounding the extinguisher on the area where the handle used to be, using all her strength. "Come on!"

"What is dis?" The bellowing sound frightened Alexia. She spun around to find herself face-to-face with the creepy man from the beach.

His foul eyes studied the girl standing in front of him.

Alexia started to scream, "HE–," but he blazed forward, sticking his grimy hands on her open mouth. She could taste the saltiness of the filth and smell the beer and cigarettes he had just ingested. *Hunter*

He clucked his tongue at her. "No, no scream, little girl." She felt his thick breath on her ear. "I have gun, and I like to use."

"Help!" the voices continued through the door.

"Shut up!" the man yelled, promptly silencing the clanging and calls for help. "You see"–he threw Alexia forward–"dey know to listen. You will be wise to follow dem." Alexia couldn't place his accent. "Do I know you?" He tilted his head, examining her face.

"No," she muttered.

"What?" He put a hand behind his ear. "I did not hear you?" he said with a sadistic smile.

"I said, no." Alexia raised her voice. She didn't think reminding him of the beach would work in her favor. "We don't know each other."

"An American, huh?" He began leering at Alexia's body. "Good money for you." She could feel his hot dirty breath moistening her face. "Young and juicy too." He revealed decaying teeth, the front one missing.

"You're disgusting," she spat, but was met with a sour chortle. "You can't get away with this."

This is how he makes money! Sick !!

He grimaced.

She lifted herself up and tried to make a run for it. Instantly, he threw her down to the floor with little effort, as if she were a rag doll. "Where you go? You tink you will leave? You tink you will be saved? Who will save you? Captain America is not real, just movies." He growled. "Maybe I test-drive? See if engine good. Yes?" He moved closer and bent down, placing the tip of his pistol on her shoulder, slowly sliding it down her arm. His breath reeked of decaying gums. He leaned in, letting the weapon rub her thigh as he smelled her hair. "Mmm . . . like flower."

"Get off me." She grabbed his face and shoved it to the side, which set him off in a rage. He lifted a hand to slap her when they both heard a thump from above and felt the boat shake.

"What da hell is dis?" He stuck the gun to her forehead, pressing it in. "You do not move." He then stood up and ran to the top deck.

Alexia picked up the fire extinguisher and went back to work. She refused to leave whoever was in there behind, and she could use their help in overpowering him. "He will kill us," a weak voice said from the other end.

"Then we die trying," Alexia said without flinching. She heard scuffling atop. But she refused to stop. She kept pounding until she broke through the rotten wood and finally released the latch. A group of four boys came tumbling out of the cramped space that held a soiled toilet and sink. "Where's the girl? Is there a girl?" She searched frantically past the boys.

"There." A boy pointed to a ball curled up next to the toilet.

"Susan," Alexia whispered through watery eyes. "Susan, darling." She knelt down and put a hand on the little girl's back. "Yallah, habibti. We need to go." She mixed in the few words of Arabic she had picked up. Alexia pulled the little body toward her and took Susan into her arms. Susan held on tight, sticking her wet face into Alexia's neck. "It will be okay." She rubbed the little girl's back. "I got you now."

Bang!

Alexia's body jolted when she heard the gunshot, then froze when she heard the footsteps that followed, slamming down the steps. She quickly regained control and positioned her body to block Susan from the oncoming attack. But when she looked up, she saw a wide-eyed Tareq. The boys ran past him and out of the galley.

"Susan," he moaned with anguished eyes.

"Tareq?" She looked up. "Tareq!" She jumped from Alexia's arms into her big brother's. He cradled his baby sister as they both sobbed. *A great helper*

"Th-th-thank you," Tareq finally forced out. Alexia wiped her own tears, unable to answer, afraid she would lose it even more if she did.

She ran up to the top deck instead. She knew she couldn't let these men get lost in the crowd.

"You piece of–" Dean said, lunging into a punch and cracking the man's face. "Who do you think you are?" Blood gushed from the guy's nose as he continued to thrash.

The sound of distant sirens quickly approached.

"I think that's enough." Alexia grabbed one of Dean's brawny arms, making him flinch. "Are you okay?" she asked. The man was now lying unconscious before them.

"Yeah, it's just a graze," he said, crouched on the floor. "But it still burns." He held up his right arm, which oozed blood from a deep scratch on its side.

"I'm sorry." She winced with him. "I should find the police."

"They're on their way." He looked up at her.

"How did you guys find us?" She gazed at his soft brown eyes, noticing the kindness there.

"We couldn't find you, so we went looking. I turned on my hotspot for Tareq just in case you would think to call him or something. And that's when we found the cab. It was parked right down there." He pointed at the main road. "He wasn't even scared that someone would catch him. I saw the sticker in the front, and Tareq saw his jacket in the backseat. As we started running around, he got your text. So I pinned our location and sent it to my mom." He cringed with pain as he gesticulated. "She called the cops."

"The cab's gone." Alexia peered down the road. "I don't see a taxi!"

"It's okay," Dean said. "I took a picture of the plate numbers. I'll give it to the police. We're not going to let either of these douchebags get away with this. Is Susan—"

"She's with her brother," Alexia said. "Here they come." She pointed her head toward the police cars. "For this guy's sake"— she pointed to the lowlife—"let's hope your mom's not here."

"Yeah." Dean grinned. "Last thing we need to deal with is a murder tonight."

"I'm gonna . . ." She gestured at the young boys who had run out of the boat and now stood terrified on the sidewalk.

"Yeah, go." Dean raised an eyebrow as he took a moment to stare at her blue eyes. "I'm going to stay here to make sure he doesn't pull a horror movie and get up and attack one last time."

Alexia turned to the approaching blue and red police lights.

She looked down and found that this time, she was met by the hands of refugees wanting to help her as she hopped off a boat, following her own terrifying experience.

Good job! She is a sailor now!

CHAPTER 32

Several days had passed since the moments when he had almost lost Susan forever. After some rest, they decided it was time to leave. It was difficult for Tareq to see the port again, but they had no choice. In the daylight, it was a different place for Susan. A four-year-old has extra opportunities to escape her thoughts, although not often enough, but more than the young man who felt like he had failed her. Tareq firmly held on to Susan, wearing his sister around him, tight, as if she were a part of his skin.

Alexia, Siddiqa and Dean joined to say their farewells. Siddiqa purchased a lightweight stroller—"A small gift. I know you will want to keep her close. And there will be times you will feel tired and weak. I thought about one of those baby-carrier backpacks, but I figured she'd be too heavy for that." She insisted Tareq take the stroller, despite his protests. Finally, he conceded. Tareq thanked her as she pulled him in for a hug. For a moment, he imagined that she was his *teyta*, resting his head on her shoulder.

"Take care." Dean patted him on the back with his unbandaged arm. "Let us know how things go."

Tareq couldn't find the words for his gratitude and didn't think another thank-you would suffice, so he gave Dean a nod. A gesture understood, and returned.

He then turned to Alexia, who held her arms out for Susan. The little girl jumped into them, and the two shared a warm hug. When Alexia finally opened her eyes, she stared at the boy in front of her. He had the face of a pained man, one who had aged in even the short days since they'd met. She wondered how that face would continue to morph in the coming weeks, months and years. His trials were far from over. This was just the beginning.

"You know, my favorite childhood show growing up was with this guy called Mr. Rogers," she said. "He was a gentle man with a soft voice, and he made me understand the world in a way others couldn't. He taught me things, like, you can eat an orange and then take the seeds and plant an orange tree. He taught kids how to handle emotions and things like that." She handed Susan back to him. "I'll never forget the advice he said he got from his mother. 'Always look for the helpers.' Like, during a fire, there are firefighters. That kind of thing," she explained. "Look, you've had a pretty horrible journey so far. And it's not even close to being over. But when you think that the world is against you, please just take a moment and look for them—the helpers." She shrugged. "I don't know, it may make things better."

Tareq thanked her. "I will try and do this." He buckled his sister into the new stroller, already recognizing the benefits as it lightened the weight in his arms but still kept him connected to her. "We need to go now."

Alexia failed to keep her tears at bay as she watched.
"Goodbye."

Bonds to get him through

He didn't want to make eye contact. It pained him to leave
the people who seemed to care about him and Susan. At the same
time, he wanted nothing more to do with this island—he just
wanted to get to Germany, where he believed his sister could
be safe.

Joining the long line of refugees waiting for the ferry, his
gaze kept falling on the children, particularly those traveling
alone. All were as vulnerable as Susan, some more so. But he knew
dwelling on that would drive him mad. So he tried only to focus
on the little girl in front of him.

It would be a twelve-hour journey from Mytilene to Athens. But
this time they boarded a sturdy vessel with dry feet, not sloshing
through the icy sea as they climbed into an overflowing rubber
dinghy.

The mood on the ship was mainly cheerful, as everyone was
ready to move on. One step closer to starting their warless new
lives. Tareq eventually found Jamila and Najiba on the port side
of the deck. They had Muzhgan, the girl from the trailer, with
them. Tareq learned that her smuggler in Turkey had repeatedly raped her before he finally set her free. She had no one
to turn to but them, girls she had just met, but whom she was
connected to by a shared language and homeland. The camps
didn't have the capabilities to help with these circumstances,
so she was left to cope on her own. The best they could hope for

Tough sad, terrible hunter

was help when they landed in their final destination—but even that was unlikely. *like the comparison*

"The sea is two-faced," Jamila said, standing next to Tareq. Her eyes reflected the waves she stared at from the moving vessel.

"Yes. But in the end, it did not deceive us." Tareq kept a firm grip on the stroller. Susan was fast asleep. He had made a promise to God to be grateful for what he had if he got her back. He intended to keep it.

"But it has deceived so many." Jamila turned back to look at him. "The promise of what lay beyond it cheated many. It ruined her." She pointed in the direction of the shell of a girl standing next to Najiba. "Muzhgan will never be same. And look what almost happened to your sister."

"If we think this way, we will not make it far." Tareq stared ahead. He knew they were both right. "This is not over."

Once in Athens, the refugees were rounded up and made to wait for buses that eventually shuttled them to the border with the Republic of Macedonia. An overnight journey that many refugees before them had to do by foot, even if they were using walkers or in wheelchairs. They were dropped off at the village of Idomeni. At first, the frozen earth was a blessing in disguise, offering solid ground for the stroller's wheels as they passed through hills and rumbled along train tracks. But that blessing only lasted for the tiring walk to the border between Greece and Macedonia.

When they arrived at the border, they were met by thousands

of others trying to survive the frigid temperatures. There weren't enough tents or food. Refugees were burning cardboard, branches and scraps of wood to keep warm.

The Afghan girls found shelter under a plastic tarp as Tareq decided to find warmth from the few makeshift fires.

"They have closed the border," the old man from the boat, Dr. Kassem, told Tareq. He had arrived a day earlier but was still stuck. "The Macedonians say for security reasons." He sniffled.

"For how long?" Tareq asked, tucking an extra blanket around Susan as they stood near a burning wooden crate.

"I don't know." Dr. Kassem's pale face was thinner than before. "I am worried for the baby. She won't take a bottle very well. She's been used to nursing."

"You have her?" Tareq looked surprised. His stomach twisted at the memory of her parents. He could still picture the blue lips and the lifeless eyes.

"Yes, we are telling the authorities she is our grand-daughter. I trust you will not share anything different." He lifted his brow.

"Of course," promised Tareq. "This is not a time for a child to be alone." He quickly shook his head, throwing out thoughts of the other evening. "Where is she now?"

"In that awning." He pointed with his head to a blue tarp held up with sticks as he rubbed his hands over the flames. "My wife is trying to get her to drink the little milk we have. Do you have some?"

Tareq shook his head.

"Her parents called her Heba." He crinkled his nose. "But

my wife keeps calling her Ruqia, like our daughter. All I pray is that she has a better fate." *There have been many*

Both men, young and old, extended their gaze to the sky as *kind people and* they heard the rhythmic beating of helicopter rotors overhead. *many bad*

"If this were Syria, they would be dropping cluster bombs," said Tareq. *throughout this journey*

"A faster death than what they are putting us through here."

"What do you think they're doing up there?"

"Finding people who are trying to cross the border illegally." Dr. Kassem saw Tareq's eyes beam. "Don't even think about it. Two young men were electrocuted earlier. They had climbed on a truck to see the surrounding area, plotting to find a way through, when we heard the explosion. I saw one before the Red Cross doctors made it to him." He shuddered. "His skin had peeled right off from the electricity." *What's wrong with letting people in?*

Tareq shivered as he shifted his feet closer to the fire, but they still felt like they were encased in ice.

He excused himself in order to walk off the cold. He hoped that movement of his toes would do the trick. The concern of losing his big toes to frostbite increased with every step. Trying to keep his mind off the frosty weather, he studied his surroundings. He saw the same emotions reflected in every face—they were all desperate, all tired. Even those asleep looked exhausted. It made him think of an old proverb: *Sleep doesn't help if it's your soul that is tired.* All around him were exhausted souls.

A man walked toward him. "Here." The thinly bearded stranger handed Tareq a burned ear of corn. "It's not much, it doesn't taste good, but it's food," he said as he looked down at Susan, asleep again in her stroller. Tareq spotted miniature icicles on the side of the man's mouth. "They used to say back home, 'No one dies of hunger.' It turns out you do."

The Syrian-Palestinian man, Khalil, shared his story with Tareq. He called himself a "permanent refugee." His parents had fled the Golan Heights in 1967, following the Israeli occupation. They settled in Yarmouk, a southern Damascus neighborhood, home to the largest Palestinian refugee community in Syria. In this current war, the regime saw them as supporters of rebel fighters. *Seems bad like it was meant to be*

At first they were targeted with bombs and ground troops. Then their food supply was cut off. "Hunger is the most powerful weapon," he said. "When a sniper starts shooting or helicopters fly overhead, you look for cover. When the troops and tanks flood the streets, you can try and fight them back. But hunger, it is not something you can run from or combat. It's a slow, painful death. But what is worse is surviving while you watch your mother's lips shrivel and her skin flake until one day . . ." He sighed. "We are young, and we can't even handle this cold weather. For the children and elderly, it means certain death." He walked away, not in the mood to talk or remember any more. *It's a terrible torturous death*

Tareq chipped away at the burned black bits of corn, kernel by kernel. He hoped that it would look somewhat appetizing by the time Susan woke. But it didn't matter. When she opened her eyes, her stomach growled, craving anything that could stave off the hollow pain. She looked at the rock-hard maize like he had just given her the juiciest steak in all of Greece.

. . .

Helpers

As Tareq held his sister close, volunteers came by with paper cups and thermoses of tea. *The helpers,* he told himself as he let the warm liquid filter down his throat, through his chest and into his vacant belly.

First, it was the old man who shared his fire. Then Khalil, who gave him corn. And now these strangers who were offering tea. *The helpers.*

After several more hours, the border finally reopened. Not out of mercy and kindness, but out of fear of bad press attention in Western Europe. *These people make me mad*

Two children and one adult died that night. Including baby Heba and Dr. Kassem's wife. The infant froze, her lungs burned by the icy air she had inhaled. The woman's heart gave out soon after witnessing the baby's pale lips and cold gaze. The doctors said it, too, was because of the weather, but her husband knew differently.

There isn't one heart among these people that isn't cracked or broken, but when it's shattered to sand . . . Well, if you have ever questioned if one can die from a broken heart, the answer is yes. I've seen it happen more often than it should.

Tareq watched the old man wrap a blanket around his wife with dry eyes. His body was too dehydrated to produce even one tear. Some of you may be wondering whether the baby would have survived had she been given to the authorities. Possibly. Possibly not. She may have also become another victim of the darkness that lurks in the shadows.

It's a long, tough process

Once in Macedonia, Tareq and Susan, along with Jamila, Najiba and Muzhgan, were sent to another camp for registration. More fingerprints and pictures were taken and it included hours of waiting. Eventually they were allowed to purchase a train ticket, which the Macedonian railway company raised from seven euros to twenty-five euros a ticket—helping it acquire millions in profit, taking advantage of already desperate people who needed to transit through their country.

The rest of the journey was much the same. Freezing weather, cold buses and run-down trains. Serbia, Croatia and Slovenia did not follow Macedonia's financial lead and instead provided free transportation. Although that was of little merit when they were met at every border by military and police, some beating them, others yelling as if they were stray dogs chomping on a pie left on the windowsill.

Tareq kept in touch with Alexia, texting her updates along the way.

What's Baba doing

TAREQ: Sometimes I feel like we've committed a crime because of the way they treat us. But I don't know what we did wrong. We are not welcome, I know this. Every country we arrive in also wants to make us

leave fast. They say, "Just keep
going north, there you will figure out."

       ALEXIA: I'm sorry . . .

TAREQ: But you are correct. I see
helpers too. Red Cross meets us
at every border, looking for sick.
That yellow sticker from first camp, IRC?

       ALEXIA: The International Rescue
       Committee

TAREQ: Yes, them. I see their sticker
in some camps. And the UNHCR,
Save the Children.

       ALEXIA: That's great. I'm glad you
       are noticing them.

TAREQ: Yes, but it is more. I see many
good people from the countries who
come to say hello. They smile at us and
make us human again after being yelled
at by their military and police. They make
me remember, every country has good
people and bad people. Just like mine.

At times the journey was made tougher for continuing to
travel with the Afghan girls—some days the places they went
would accept Syrians but not Afghans. As much as Jamila and
Najiba insisted that Tareq and Susan push on, Tareq refused to
leave them stranded and alone.

Until the day that he had to.

those people warm my heart

Bonds make you stronger

What happened?

CHAPTER 33

The land was encircled by stunning lush green hills. Alexia saw the beauty even in the island's makeshift landfill.

This one held the skeletal remains of boats and deflated rubber vessels. A landfill without garbage, just the memories of traumatizing escapes. It was nicknamed the Life Jacket Graveyard.

Alexia felt like she was drowning in the images that enveloped her; ghostly images of the people she met, the survivors who lived to see another day, kept appearing. But she couldn't help but weep for them as she took in the ocean of discarded life vests—orange, black, red and sprinkles of blue and yellow.

She knew she should be celebrating the victories of those who made it, who reached Europe. But instead she mourned. Yes, they lived through what many did not. They were not lying abandoned in dirt mounds with simple, often nameless headstone markers. But a part of all the people who once wore these vests had died. They were no longer the people they had worked their lives to become. They were no longer the people they were born as. At the will of a war, they went from being doctors,

It is good to remember the dead

lawyers, storekeepers, students, mothers, fathers, daughters and sons to refugees, foreigners, freeloaders, terrorists, enemies. Labels that didn't represent their true selves.

Alexia spotted a yellow inflatable and thought of Susan. It was just like what she was wearing when Alexia carried her still body off the dinghy. Next to it was a Spider-Man vest. *Maybe these belonged to a brother and sister?* She turned her head away only to see a pair of blue velvet pants with bunnies on the hem—she then tried to imagine what that toddler went through.

"Are you okay?" asked Dean, slightly regretting bringing her here after witnessing her tears.

"It's just hard." She looked at the man she'd grown to like a lot (as a friend—she thought of him only as a friend—though she wouldn't think that way for long). This wasn't the first heap of life vests she had seen in her time here. She was trying not to get mad at herself for letting it get to her. "You know?"

What she liked most about Dean was that he seemed to understand what it was like to feel lost in all of this, the way she did. He was the comforting moon that stayed in view during both the day and the night.

"Yeah." He took a deep breath while sticking his hands in his jean pockets. "It's heavy, man." He picked up a life vest and effortlessly ripped off the synthetic cover, flipping through sheets of thin foam. "You see this? Fake. This mountain has more counterfeit vests than authentic."

"I'll never understand those who profit off suffering."

"*Big money game!*" Dean imitated Annis, Alexia's local

friend—she had shared the story with him about her. He saw his intention worked when she snorted.

"Cute." He lifted an eyebrow.

"Shut up." Her cheeks flushed. "I'm trying to be serious here."

"Sorry, my bad. You were saying."

"I don't know. I just thought that by the end of my time here, I wouldn't feel this . . . disappointed."

"I know." He looked at her sincerely. "You've done as much as you could and gave all your heart." He glimpsed at the hundreds of thousands of abandoned vests ahead of him. "The thing is, with something like this, even your absolute best will always just be a drop in the—"

"Bucket."

"No. Something like this is so much bigger. What we've done here is just a single drop in the ocean. It's hard to be satisfied. But you have to remember that there would be no ocean without every drop."

Alexia grabbed his arm, now healed. He always knew what to say to pull her out of her funk. "Looks like your muscles didn't atrophy much from that bullet graze."

Dean started flexing. "Careful, now, or I'm gonna start to think you like me." He held on to her hand as they walked back to his car.

As they crossed Austria, Tareq and Jamila knew their time together would be coming to an end. A relationship forged in the harshest of times. *A gift from God while trapped in hell,* Tareq thought. The idea of separating from her ripped at his insides. Because of her, the worst time in his life still held beauty.

"We will see each other." Jamila's eyes glistened with the tears that were building. She didn't want Najiba to see. She knew she'd give her flack for it later. "We will be in the same country."

"Yes, of course." Tareq stared at the strand of hair that wrapped around the side of her face. "Soon. Susan will miss you very much." *I wanted a good ending*

"I will miss her too," she said, staring at the beautiful little girl sitting quietly in her stroller.

Tareq evaded her eyes. "*I* will miss you very much."

"Me too." Jamila was now smiling. Those six words let her know that he felt the same way she did. Tareq returned his gaze to Jamila's face, also smiling, as he felt fireworks exploding in his heart.

Watching Jamila, Najiba and Muzhgan board their train to meet the girls' aunt pained him. He prayed this wasn't another permanent goodbye. As the train pulled out, he took out his phone. *Callback*

TAREQ: I had to say goodbye to
Jamila and her sister. It was
very difficult.

ALEXIA: I'm so sorry. I'm sure it
was. How did Susan take it?

TAREQ: She does not understand
yet. But she will soon, and
I know will cry. Silent cry.
She no longer have loud cry.

ALEXIA: Poor girl. Tell her I miss
her. I miss you both. And we will
all see each other again one
day and we will remember these
days as long-ago memories. We
will be happy and laughing and
drinking tea.

TAREQ: I look forward to this.
God willing.

ALEXIA: Yes, inshallah :)

BABA CALLING

TAREQ: I must go, my father
is calling.

ALEXIA: Okay, chat soon. Send
me pix of Su! Xo

"Baba?" Tareq felt relief after trying to reach his father for
days. He was frightened when he didn't hear back. "Baba, are
you okay?"

"Tareq," the familiar voice whispered. A voice that didn't
belong to his dad. A voice he thought he would never hear again.
It was a person he thought was dead.

"Salim?"

*He did live! It was
foreshadowed! A better
ending!*

EPILOGUE

When Tareq finally reached Germany, no one was clapping, there were no welcome signs at the train station, and no teddy bears were being distributed to small children. Those news clips were from a different time—even if that was just several months before they had arrived. *art*

Smiles were replaced with suspicion. Especially after various traumatizing incidents in Europe—including the coordinated terror attacks in Paris that killed more than one hundred people and the horrendous reports of sexual assaults on New Year's Eve in various German cities. *Is it going to be like Turkey?*

He no longer blamed them for being afraid. He shared their fear. He lived it.

Tareq wished he could tell them, *Please don't be scared of us. We are more terrified of your reactions. We are broken people who are haunted by our past, our future and our dreams. We narrowly escaped death, the war, the rapes, the murders and the killers—we have family who didn't—please don't think those monsters represent us. We swam through our country's blood* and corpses barely keeping our heads afloat to breathe, to survive and to live another day. We left our homes, we left our history. We left our loved ones without the time to mourn them. We brought our hearts, but they have been shattered into tiny pieces. We didn't come here to harm you, we've come to heal.

But he stayed quiet.

Instead, he spent his days at the facility where the German government had placed him, trying to relax in the absence of soldiers, rebels, Daesh, bullets, shells and missiles. He was grateful for the many helpers he met there. One even helped him submit an application to reunite them with his father and Salim—the brother God had given back to him.

His younger brother had his own story to share and traumas he endured. He didn't talk much about it but had divulged the vaguest of details. He was sent to a different hospital after the bombing, where he was then taken by a rebel group who wanted him to fight. When he escaped from their clutches, he was grabbed by Daesh. They sent him to a camp that tried to indoctrinate him; he said it almost worked, but he kept seeing Farrah in his head and could never treat her the way they were being taught that women should be treated. He had been caught using someone's phone to reach Tareq and was beaten. He eventually made contact with their father and found his way to Turkey. Fayed told Tareq that Salim didn't sleep well, and when he did, he screamed in the night.

"Give it time, he will be better," Tareq told his father, unsure if he was lying again.

Musa found a decent job in Istanbul and was planning to

ask for Shayma's hand in marriage once he saved up enough money. Now more than ever, he wanted to be a part of her family to take away some of his loneliness. *Good for him!*

Tareq kept in touch with Jamila, who lived with Najiba and their aunt in Frankfurt as they waited to see whether their asylum application would go through. Muzhgan was sent to a facility for minors—she never received counseling and was terrified every day. *Oh brother—not good!*

Tareq looked forward to the next weekend when Jamila would drive down and visit with her family. He couldn't stop thinking about the girl with the speckled eyes and beautiful smile.

Susan was happy; she started kindergarten at a local school and was picking up German faster than her older brother. She didn't talk about the trip very much; when she did, she would cry. Farrah, the doll, no longer came with her everywhere—but it still brought her comfort in the night.

I don't understand how the human eye works. It seems so impaired at times. So, for a moment, let me lend you mine.

These people—the refugees or migrants or whatever you choose to call them—are fragile vessels, almost like eggshells, empty and isolated. Drained. And just as a newborn baby is brought into the world quite the same, each vessel needs to be filled properly. When kindness, love and understanding are poured into them, a solid foundation is created, building sturdy citizens who can do wonders for those around them.

They've gone through so much that something little goes a long way

They've been through it already so they take it in

But when they are filled with hate, hostility, mercilessness—something different happens. They don't necessarily break, though some do. More often they become hard, filled with shadows and despair. But that darkness is nothing compared to what is deep in the hearts of those it reflects—the ones who use their fear and hatred on the blameless.

Tareq's heart is very kind. Since he was a young baby, he loved everyone. He wanted everyone to be happy, and now he wants them all to live safely and peacefully—whether that be in Germany or in Syria, in America or in China. Most of all, he doesn't want anyone to experience his loss.

He's done a good job not changing his ideals too much

Making it to Germany ended Tareq's crossing and escape from war, but his new life as a refugee is just beginning. There are millions of Tareqs, Susans and Fayeds, all in search of safety and kindness.

I hope you will provide that warmth, be that helper, do what you can to make that world a better place. Because when I meet you—and I will—there will be a reckoning. There always is.

Author's purpose—Inform about the refugee crisis and their struggles/feelings during their experiences

GLOSSARY

As with all languages, there are many figurative meanings as well as literal meanings to words and expressions. There are also varied regional and local dialects. This glossary is to share simple definitions in the context the terms were used for in the book.

ARABIC:

aa rasi–thank you

ahlan wa sahlan–hello; welcome

ahmaq–idiot

akalna khara–(curse word)

Al Defa'a al Madani–Syrian Civil Defense

albi–my heart (term of endearment)

alhamdulillah–praise be to God

Allah akbar–God is great

Allah ieshfeek–God heal you

Allah yerhamo–God have mercy (on him)

ammo–uncle

ana behebek–I love you

ayuni–my eyes (term of endearment)

baba–father

binti–my daughter

ebqa huna–stay here

habibi–my beloved (masculine)

habibti–my beloved (feminine)

halawe' tahine–a type of sweet food

hayati–my life

Hisbah–Daesh religious police

ibni–my son

ii'dam–execution

inshallah–God willing

inte ghabi–you're stupid

kafer–nonbeliever; infidel

khalas–enough

khale–aunt

kofta–a rolled ground meat dish

lah–no

mabrook–congratulations

mai–water

mama–mother

mart'ammo–aunt (wife of father's brother)

mashallah–what God bestowed

massalame–goodbye; peace be with you

mein bihajeh la'dactor?–does anyone need a
doctor?

merhaba–hello

molokhiyya–green leaf vegetable

okhteh–sister

omri–my life

rohi–my soul

salaam alaykum–hello; peace be unto you

shabiha–pro-Assad militia group

shahada–declaration of faith

shoof–look

shukran–thank you

teyta–grandmother

walaykum asalaam–and upon you be peace
(response to *salaam alaykum*)

wallahi–I swear (to God)

ya Allah–oh God

yallah–hurry; come on; let's go

yislamu–thank you

TURKISH:

ayran–cold salty yogurt drink

buyrun–here you are

dur–stop

evet–yes

hayır–no

hoş bulduk–thanks (in response to being
welcomed)

hoş geldiniz–welcome

simit–circular Turkish bread

teşekkürler–thanks

GREEK:

ágnostos–unknown

efcharistó–thank you

DARI:

bas–enough

behdar sho, oh dokhtar–wake up, girl

khala–aunt

namekhuda–in the name of God

ACKNOWLEDGMENTS

Some people have a knack for writing and do it effortlessly. I'm not one of them. A weight of responsibility weighs on my shoulders to try and give justice to a story where none can be found.

Luckily, I have been blessed to have amazing people who have supported me every step of the way.

My incredibly talented editor, Jill Santopolo, and gifted publisher, Michael Green, are angels on earth for allowing me to share my stories. Thank you to Talia Benamy, Brian Geffen, Elaine Demasco, Bridget Hartzler, Theresa Evangelista, Elyse Marshall, Cindy Howle, Ellice Lee and the entire Philomel and Penguin team for their continued hard work and kindness. I am so lucky to be a part of your incredible book phamily.

A big thanks to my extraordinary agent, Stephen Barbara, and the entire team at InkWell Management, not least of which includes Lyndsey Blessing and Claire Draper.

This has been quite an emotional book to research and write. Countless tears have been shed tackling such an important and devastating topic. No book can touch the true scope of what real people, nations and families have been suffering through, but I took the responsibility for trying to share even some of it very seriously.

I want to express heartfelt appreciation for all the people from various nationalities who shared their personal stories with me. It was a privilege and an honor to meet and speak with them all. I am beyond grateful to Feras Hanosh for taking the time to share his accounts, memories and expertise. My only way into Raqqa was through his experiences. Thanks to Sarah Dadduch, who introduced me to Syrian life in Istanbul, and in particular to Samer Alkadri and her friends at the bakery for letting me into their world. There are so many more who deserve acknowledgment but had asked to remain anonymous for fear of putting their families in jeopardy.

I was able to communicate with many of them thanks to the great Raja Razek. She's the friend who you can call and say, "I'm flying to Greece for research. Can you meet me there and help?" And without hesitation, you hear, "Of course! When do you need me there?"

The volunteers we met from around the world had taken precious time out of their lives to help those in need and still managed to find time to assist in my research. Thank you to Kristy Lam, Erika Sherman, Clare Roberts and Julianna Nagy for sharing your homes and your lives in Lesvos with us. Thank you to the Woodhouse family, Dr. Lina Amini, Arzo Wardak, Usman Khan from Save the Children Norway, Colleen Sinsky, Lucy Carrigan and Dennis Moroni from International Rescue Committee, Max Humpf and David Ang with Starfish, Dr. Sanne

Hofstede and Dr. Samir Achbab of the Boat Refugee Foundation, and everyone we met and talked to.

I appreciate the welcome and kindness of the Lesvos community we came across and in particular the hospitality in Molyvos. A special thank-you to Vagelis Vagelakis, Sophie Sakki and Marianthi Spanou for sharing their stories.

I am also very grateful for the help and encouragement from the following friends who shared their input, stories and expertise: Jake Simkin, Susan Dabbous and her father Omar Dabbous, Clarissa Ward, Holly Dagres, Alexia Loughman, Seema Jilani, Dion Nissenbaum, Irene Nasser, Dana Karni, Susan and Omar Dabbous, Feras Hanoush, Elif Ensari and Emily Walker.

I want to share my admiration and gratitude to all the librarians, educators and booksellers who have been kind enough to let me into their amazing world. And I send so much love to all the readers; you give me the courage to keep writing.

My dream of writing and sharing stories would not at all be possible if it wasn't for my loving and encouraging family. My mother and father, Mahnaz and Wahid, flew halfway across the world to take care of my baby to give me the space to research and write. My baby boy, Arian, sacrificed time with "Mama!" But I knew he was in good hands, thanks to Mercy Morales.

And finally, and most importantly, my amazing Conor. Absolutely none of this would ever be possible without your continued belief in me, even when I stop believing in myself. Love you, *azizam.*

Author's Note:
Two Years Later

I wrote *A Land of Permanent Goodbyes* to try to humanize the refugee crisis.

I was first motivated to write this story in 2015. That summer, I was in California visiting my parents when my father opened up a folder and found my birth certificate and some old medical papers. Among the documents were our refugee papers, alien identity cards, and old passports—identification materials I had been too young to even remember receiving.

A few weeks later, my eyes, along with those of many others around the world, were glued to the television screen as we witnessed hundreds of thousands of people escaping the Syrian war. Individuals and families alike were risking their lives on boats, trekking along the sides of Europe's busy highways, and pushing strollers and wheelchairs through muddy fields. They were a group of people who, only a few years prior, had lived normal lives in their comfortable homes surrounded by the love and stability of family. They were people who had belonged to a nation they loved, despite its imperfections (which all countries have). Watching these people on my TV screen, I realized just how similar they were to my parents.

My parents had their own terrifying and harrowing escape. When they fled from Afghanistan because of the Soviet war, my mother was eight months pregnant with me, and my brother was only two years old. They arrived in West Germany, where I was born a refugee. A year later we were welcomed as refugees to the United States of America. Life continued to have its challenges, but to this day I count my blessings for the decisions my parents made and the risks they took to save our family. I have often wondered what would have happened if they had not left, and each scenario sends chills down my spine.

So while watching the Syrian crisis unfold, as a former refugee myself, I saw a familiarity that I couldn't shake. The stories almost seemed parallel: Though my parents' story took place at a different time and started in a different country, they too had lived comfortably until their lives were turned upside down at the onset of a war. Facing threats, imprisonment, and even murder, they could no longer stay in their homes. To protect their children, my parents finally fled.

I felt a pained connection to the Syrian refugees, especially to the children among them. And when I saw the vitriol they faced, my heart broke. They were human beings whose lives had been ravaged and torn apart. They did not want to leave their country; they were forced to because of circumstances that were out of their control. They weren't looking for a better *life*, they were looking for a chance to *live*.

I saw all that was happening, and I knew I had to write about it.

I wanted to do more than just write about current events, though. I wanted to dive deep, to show the human side of this massive geopolitical struggle. I wanted readers to look beyond the headlines and news clips and see the actual people. Although this book is a work of fiction, it is very much real. It is a compilation of stories I heard from those who lived the terrible consequences of war. I traveled to both Greece and Turkey to speak to the refugees firsthand, and I used phones and computers to talk with several people still in Syria as well as others who made it out.

I'll never forget, and hope never to forget, the heartache I felt day after day while researching this book—speaking with refugees, witnessing what was happening in the Middle East and Europe, standing in Greece in Lesbos's life jacket graveyard among thousands upon thousands of life vests, each representing a person who took the risk to live. One day in Lesbos, I picked up a small girl's shoe that was left abandoned on one of the boulders by the sea. As I picked it up, I wondered what this poor child and her family had gone through. It made me think of my own baby and what I would do to ensure his safety, and what my parents chose to make certain of mine. I brought it back home with me, and it continues to sit in my office. I often stare at it, especially as I write, and wonder where that little girl is now.

It has been two years since I finished writing *A Land of Permanent Goodbyes*, and although some of the pictures in the news have changed, so much of the situation still remains the same. We are seeing far fewer rubber dinghies making their way toward Greece from Turkey, and no longer do we see the strollers being pushed by parents on the sides of European highways. But while those images have faded from our TV screens, the refugee crisis is still very much alive.

Some of the previous conflicts that drove the refugee crisis have abated. But others have continued to fester, and new ones have developed. While ISIS's reign of terror has weakened in Syria, it has gained momentum in Afghanistan. European countries are sending Afghans back to war-torn Afghanistan. And many Syrians and others are still stuck in camps throughout Greece. European coast guards are now stopping ships departing from Libya outside of international waters to keep refugees from claiming asylum in the European Union. Though these refugees still face countless hardships, they have not been deterred from looking for a better existence.

In her poem "Home," Warsan Shire wrote: "No one leaves home unless/home is the mouth of a shark . . ." My hope is that this book allows you, the reader, to comprehend the shark's mouth, to understand what the refugee experience is like, even if you haven't seen it firsthand. I hope this novel can give you a better understanding of those who have lived and continue to live this crisis. But I also hope it shows that the Syrian crisis is not the only one we are witnessing: similar atrocities are happening on every continent, across the entire world. The people living through this violence and strife are more than just characters in a book. They are real people, with real lives, real hopes, real dreams. I hope that you will be inspired to learn more about those facing difficulties in the world around them and do what you can to help.

Courtesy of Conor Powell

ATIA ABAWI is a foreign news correspondent and an award-winning author who lived in the Middle East and Asia for a decade. Born a refugee in West Germany to Afghan parents who fled a brutal war, Atia was raised in the United States. Her first book for teens was the critically acclaimed and award-winning *The Secret Sky*, set in contemporary Afghanistan. She currently lives in Los Angeles with her husband, Conor Powell, and their family.

YOU CAN VISIT ATIA ABAWI AT
atiaabawi.com
and follow her on Twitter
@AtiaAbawi

AN EYE-OPENING, HEART-RENDING TALE
OF LOVE, HONOR AND BETRAYAL FROM
VETERAN FOREIGN NEWS CORRESPODENT
ATIA ABAWI

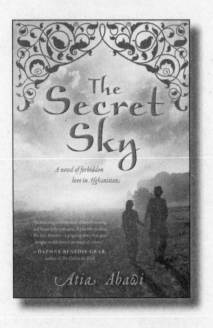

Fatima is a Hazara girl, raised to be obedient and dutiful.
Samiullah is a Pashtun boy raised to defend the tradi-
tions of his tribe. They were not meant to fall in love.
But they do. And the story that follows shows both the
beauty and the violence in current-day Afghanistan as
Fatima and Samiullah fight their families, their cultures
and the Taliban to stay together. Based on the people
Atia Abawi met and the events she covered during her
nearly five years in Afghanistan, this stunning novel is
a must-read for anyone who has lived during America's
War in Afghanistan.

"I sometimes envy th dead"

" goodbye syria. forgive us"

"we are not swimming, we are dreaming"